NEBULOUS ENEMIES

REA KEECH

Baltimore, Maryland

ISBN 979-8-9856670-0-4 Hardback
ISBN 979-8-9856670-1-1 Paperback
ISBN 979-8-9856670-2-8 Ebook

Library of Congress Control Number:
2022932120

Published by

Real
Nice Books
11 Dutton Court, Suite 606
Baltimore, Maryland 21228
www.realnicebooks.com

Publisher's note: This is a work of fiction. Names, characters, places, institutions, and incidents are entirely the product of the author's imagination or are used fictitiously, and any resemblance to actual persons, living or dead, or to events, incidents, institutions, or places is entirely coincidental.

Cover:
Abul Fazl shrine, Ahmet Erkan Yigitsozlu, iStock.
Interior sketches:
Saint Michael: Sketch of Guido Reni's 1630 painting of the altarpiece for the first chapel in Santa Maria della Concezione dei Cappuccini.
Women in burqas, magpie on adobe wall: created from iStock photos.
Set in Minion Pro.

Nebulous Enemies

—another novel of foreign love and intrigue
by the prize-winning author of *A Hundred Veils*.

ALSO BY REA KEECH:

Uncertain Luck

First World Problems
  (Shady Park Chronicles, Book 1)

Shady Park Panic
  (Shady Park Chronicles, Book 2)

Shady Park Secrets
  (Shady Park Chronicles, Book 3)

A Hundred Veils

Kabul

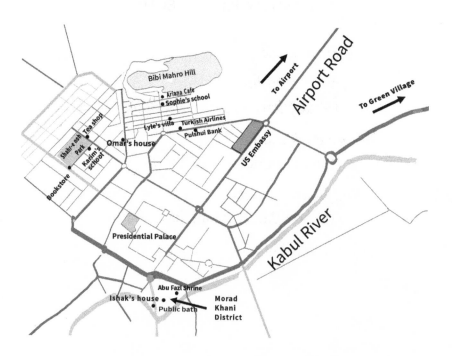

List of Chapters

I

1

A solid citizen

"Disease, insanity, and early death."

Father Joy's warning to his class sounded through the wall into the math class Roger was teaching, setting off hoots, cackles, foot-stamping.

"Masturbaaation!" Brett bleated, eyes rolled up into his head, mouth gaping, floppy-wristed arms waving. "It drove me insane."

It was 2019, and the *Baltimore Catechism* hadn't been used at St. Michael's High School for fifty years, but old Father Joy knew it by heart. Every year he browbeat students with its description of the effects of that detestable mortal sin the boys struggled in vain to avoid.

"I'm dying." Josh grasped his throat, tongue hanging out.

"My pee-pee." Dirk gaped at his crotch. "It's rotted off. Oh, why didn't I listen?"

Roger held back a smile. In this case, at least, the religious indoctrination wasn't working. He settled them down by passing back their trig tests just before the bell rang.

As the other students left for their next class, Kirk slammed down his fist. "You've got to be kidding. Oh, no. This grade has to be changed. All my answers are correct."

"The answers are correct, Kirk, but you needed to show how you got them. Besides, some of the 'correct answers' are applied to the wrong problems. How do you explain that?"

"Explain my ass," Kirk shouted. "This fuckin' grade is unfair. You're going to change it, asshole."

Roger was about to send him to the Prefect of Discipline when Father Joy puffed into the room. The priest took hold of Kirk's red necktie and yanked. "That kind of language offends the ears of the Virgin Mary, young man. Three days jug."

After-school detention never bothered Kirk. His friends were often in jug, too. Father Joy's eyes were too weak to notice them passing around and copying the homework they'd bullied the class beadle into giving them.

Roger sat down next to Inez in the walnut paneled teacher's lounge. She took off her rimless glasses and pushed her gray hair to the side. "Know what Kirk asked me in my Spanish class? 'How do you say *Go back where you came from?*'"

"Damn." Roger was tired of Kirk insulting Inez. "I'm going to talk to that guy."

"Don't, Roger. Let it go." Inez's eyes brightened. "I'm going to retire at the end of the semester."

"Good for you."

"How about you? You'll have your M.A. soon, right? You could teach somewhere else."

"I've been thinking about it." Roger had been getting more uncomfortable at Saint Michael's. Father Joy constantly urged him to join the Soldiers of Christ, which the priest said was a way to fight against "ungodly foes in our society." But the males-only Soldiers spent huge sums of money lobbying against "socialism" in general and family planning services in particular, which were declared sinful but which Roger saw no harm in. Without a master's degree, though, he hadn't been able to find a job in public education. Up to now, he'd decided to keep the job and "let it go," as Inez said. It was a phrase he himself used too often, according to his older brother.

When school was over, Roger walked to the parking lot. In the sharp spring sunlight, the school loomed like an unassailable gothic castle with its light gray stone walls and pointed arches above narrow windows trimmed in white limestone. When he'd applied to teach here, Father Joy had said Saint Michael's was a place to build character as much as educate. The imposing campus seemed designed to reinforce that claim—assuming that "character" meant adhering to various medieval beliefs.

Kirk was heading for jug in the administrative building. Roger stopped him. "Hold on a minute, Kirk. As far as I'm concerned, you can forget about offending the ears of the Virgin Mary. You need to stop offending your Spanish teacher."

"These foreigners pouring over the border—they're going to be taking over the whole country before long."

Timid, gentle, sixty-five-year-old Inez was not going to be taking over the country any time soon. "Listen, Kirk," Roger snapped. "Mrs. Gonzalez is as American as you are. She learned Spanish from her Puerto Rican parents, but she was born in Memorial Hospital, just a few miles from this school."

"Whatever. Don't forget what I said. I'm going to make sure you change my grade. You'll see."

At the top of the granite stairs leading down to the parking lot, Roger passed Father Joy reading his breviary in the shadow of the ponderous statue of Saint Michael, the Archangel. The angel's sword was held aloft, his foot trampling to the ground the head of a half-clothed man. Roger had once asked Father Joy who that nebulous enemy was whose head Saint Michael was about to chop off. "A non-believer," the priest had said. "An enemy of God."

When he saw Roger, Father Joy ceased silently mouthing one of the seven canonical offices of the day. He closed the book on a finger. "I was hoping to see you." The priest rested a thin-skinned hand on Roger's shoulder. "About Kirk. I know he's a bad sort. But you need to know something. His father is a Supreme Knight in the Soldiers of Christ and a generous donor to our school. He's currently running a campaign to become a representative in the state legislature." The priest gave Roger's shoulder a feeble squeeze. "So we have to be patient. I'm sure you understand."

Before going home, Roger stopped at the Bamian grocery shop for some fresh Afghan mantoo dumplings that his wife liked. He wasn't scared of his wife, no matter how much his brother teased. He'd simply found things went more smoothly if he gave Jill free rein.

A year ago, just before the start of classes at Saint Michael's, the two brothers had met at the E-Lite Tavern on York Road to celebrate Dan's admission to the Maryland bar. "The big curly-haired blonde at that table is looking you over," Dan said, pointing with his square chin.

With her intense green eyes, prominent breasts, and full lips, she was impressive, if a little overwhelming. And she was eyeing Roger—as hard as that was for him to believe.

"Go get her." Dan's grin was a dig on Roger's past inability to hold a woman's interest longer than one or two dates.

Roger had downed a couple of beers, enough for fraternal rivalry to kick in. He ordered a gin and tonic, slid off the bar stool, and set the drink on the blonde's table next to the one she'd just finished.

She swept some papers into a large portfolio hanging from her shoulder and nodded her thanks. Her eyebrows arched as if she found him amusing. "You look like a teacher or something."

He shrugged and started back towards the bar. But she grasped his arm. "Hold on. I like the solid citizen type."

He was sure she was toying with him but sat down, shooting a victorious glance at his brother. Jill's lips widened in a grin. It was as if he'd wandered onto a movie set and was mistaken by the leading lady for some prominent actor.

He felt her eyes appraising him. He tried to read her, waiting for disappointment to cross her face. It was strange, though. Her gaze wasn't critical or mocking. The only word that came to mind was "intense."

"Seems like you were waiting to meet somebody," Roger ventured.

"Doesn't matter. I like your sandy hair and big brown eyes. You look kind of young, though."

"I'm twenty-nine."

"Wouldn't have thought it. Well, that works out. So am I." She finished her drink. "Let's get out of here."

Nothing in Roger's life had prepared him for that night. The minute he closed his front door, Jill pulled him towards her. This was something that happened to people in the movies, not to him.

Afterwards, Jill didn't get up to leave as Roger expected. She sat naked on the couch. "So, Roger, you're actually a teacher? Where? Have you ever been arrested? Any complaints filed against you? Driver's license ever been suspended?"

Roger rubbed his arm where she'd squeezed him a little hard, then pulled his shirt over his lap. Jill continued her interview naked. "Money problems? Debts?"

It felt like an interrogation for a security clearance, but Roger went along. Maybe this was Jill's way of determining if he was really a "solid citizen." She seemed pleased with the answers.

"Anything to eat in the fridge?" She climbed into her panties and padded into the kitchen—a room that Roger's mother told him he had to get the landlord to "do something about." The old green walls were spattered with grease above the stove, the window curtains were yellowed, and the cracked linoleum floor was slippery. Jill didn't seem to care.

"Mind if I …?" She pulled a bowl of leftover chili from the whirring vintage refrigerator. "How about we split this?"

Roger was too excited to eat. He stared speechless at her half-naked body as she wolfed down the whole bowlful.

"So," she concluded, "how about if I move in?"

When Roger was startled, his mouth tended to open. The students sometimes imitated this quirk.

"Don't look so surprised. You've seen what we can be like together."

It was true. Jill had offered Roger the Nerd, as his students and brother thought of him, an experience that might lift him decisively out of that category. "But," he objected, "I don't know anything about you except—"

"Want to hear my résumé? Contractor with the U.S. Armed

Forces. Military training. Previous experience in Afghanistan. Currently attached to the contractor's headquarters in Washington. And I love doing it with a guy who responds like you do."

Forcing his mouth shut, Roger cleared his throat. "You say 'contractor.' Is that Grayrock? I didn't think they hired women."

"Well, they hired me. They don't deserve the negative press they sometimes get. It's an indispensable agency helping to defeat the enemies of our country."

That wasn't what Roger believed, but he was hung up on "I love doing it with a guy who ...." Maybe he could let the Grayrock thing go. After all, she was the first girl who'd ever seemed to want a long-term relationship with him.

Jill went on. "Guys find me sexy, just saying. I have a college degree in physical education. Good income, on track to make a whole lot more in the near future." She reached under the chipped porcelain table to put her hand on his thigh. "Come on. I'll show you one more time what you can have whenever you want it."

Jill slept with Roger that night. And the next day she moved in, bringing an army duffel bag with a Grayrock logo that held all she immediately needed. Other women he'd dated had made a quick excuse to leave as soon as they saw his empty, creaky house, but it didn't faze Jill. Maybe the dilapidated place felt more comfortable than an army barracks or a Kabul container hooch.

Anyway, she kept hinting her financial prospects were improving. She might even be able to buy a house in the well-to-do neighborhood off North Charles Street soon, and then they could move in there together. In the meantime, Jill seemed content to do the paperwork she took from her portfolio with her leg tossed over the arm of a torn, overstuffed chair in one of the empty rooms. She made her phone calls outside.

Two weeks went by, with Jill gradually bringing more boxes into the house from a storage cube on York Road. She said her lease on a furnished apartment had been canceled a few days before she met Roger. Then one evening she looked up from her papers. "Babe, why don't we get married?"

Roger was speechless. All he knew about Jill was that she was born in Baltimore, her father had died young in an army helicopter crash, and her mother also died young. "With no other relatives and not a penny to my name," she told him, "I enlisted in the army the day I turned eighteen."

"How did your mother die?"

"Drugs."

He couldn't deny that wasn't much to recommend her. But for some reason she had picked him out. "Shouldn't we get to know each other better first?" he suggested.

"Babe, you're right. But I'm at a point in my life where I need a stable life partner. I want it to be you."

"I don't understand what the hurry is."

"I've found what I'm looking for. I'll be sad if you don't want me, but if you don't, I'm going to be forced to start looking somewhere else."

Roger had always chuckled to hear Father Joy quoting the *Catechism* to the boys on an important purpose of marriage—"a remedy for concupiscence." Jill would definitely be that. On the edge of a cliff, seeing the dreary past of a lonely, single mathematics teacher behind him and a totally unknown but definitely intriguing future ahead of him, he took the leap.

The marriage license was downloaded the next morning, and they drove together in Jill's company Land Rover to the drop box at the courthouse on Calvert Street. Three weeks later, with Roger's parents in the Florida Keys, unable to come, and Jill's parents dead, they were married in the same courthouse. His brother Dan was their witness. He'd tried to get Roger to take some time to "let his head clear," but Roger dismissed him as obviously jealous.

In the year since then, he'd begun to change his mind. Jill was a handful. Talk about her job was off limits. She was in and out of the house at unexpected times whenever her partner Lyle in Washington demanded. When she came home, she tossed her

15

empty cups and chip wrappers on the grass, left her dirty clothes on the floor for him to pick up and wash, and kept heavy metal music blaring so loud they had to shout to each other across the huge, echoing rooms of the old house. But Roger still felt a flutter in his chest when she came through the door. She'd kept that one promise she'd made him.

Roger heated oil in the wok to cook the Afghan dumplings. Jill liked them fried. When they were done, he scooped them onto plates and started to boil some broccoli.

The front door slammed open against the wall. "Roger! Where are you?"

"Out here in the kitchen, making your favorite—"

"I found this note on our door." Jill burst into the kitchen holding a piece of paper.

"What is it? Let me see."

She scrunched it into a ball. "Never mind. I take it you didn't see who left it? Didn't read it?"

"No. It wasn't there when I came home. I've been back here in the kitchen—"

"Give me the keys to your car. The Rover's on empty."

In a moment she was gone, leaving the front door open.

2

Missing person

Jill often went on "missions" she didn't explain to Roger, but she had never run out with such urgency. Now and then she went to her "stateside operations center" in North Carolina to train new recruits. But she'd never left without even saying a word. Roger stayed awake as late as he could, waiting for her, his confusion turning to anger until he finally fell asleep on the couch. When he awoke the next morning in a sweat, she hadn't returned.

He searched from room to room for some hint of where she'd gone. The FAX machine she'd brought with her was still on a table next to the chair she worked in. No papers. She kept them all in her portfolio. Her closet was mostly empty. But that was normal. The floor was scattered with the clothes she'd worn over the past week. The few pieces of jewelry she wore on weekends still lay on top of the dresser. She hadn't been planning to leave. That was clear.

It had to be the note.

Roger dressed for school, hoping there was enough gas in the Land Rover to get him to the Exxon station. It was a Grayrock car, and he wasn't supposed to drive it, but Jill had left him no choice. Then he realized there was another thing she hadn't left him. The keys. Of course. She kept them in that leather portfolio always hanging from her shoulder. She'd rushed out without ever taking it off.

"You're already here?" Inez frowned as she sat down beside him in the teachers' lounge. "I didn't see your car in the lot when I parked."

"I came in an Uber. Out of gas."

"You OK? You seem a little ... I don't know."

Roger cleared his throat. "I'm fine."

All day a picture of Lyle, Jill's partner, kept forcing its way into Roger's mind. About once a month Lyle drove from Washington to meet them for drinks at the E-Lite or dinner at an Afghan restaurant in Baltimore where Lyle knew the manager. Lyle had known Jill much longer than Roger had. They talked in army lingo Roger didn't understand. Sometimes it was as if Roger wasn't there.

The pupils of Lyle's eyes were disconcertingly large, and he had an annoying habit—annoying to Roger, at least—of winking. He winked at the E-Lite bartender, at the Afghan restaurant manager and the hejab-clad waitress who brought them their Kabuli pulao. Even at Roger. But mostly at Jill. It was as if there was some secret all of them were in on. Driving home one night, Roger asked Jill why Lyle was always winking at her. "You're not attracted to that little guy, are you?" Her answer was to reach over and touch him in a way that made him lose his train of thought.

After school, Inez gave him a ride home. He pointed out his brown-shingle house on Shadow Cove Avenue shaded by towering walnut trees. His black Civic wasn't there.

Inez had a way of pushing out her lips to show she was puzzled about something. Roger knew what it was. "Jill borrowed my car. It's her Rover that's out of gas."

"We could get you some gas in a lawnmower can."

"She has the only key."

"Is something wrong, Roger? I know it's not my business."

Her motherly tone encouraged him to open up. "Last night Jill found a note on our door and left in a hurry. I'm worried about her."

"She didn't say where she was going?"

"No. That's Jill. I mean her job involves some secret stuff, so …."

"If you need a ride anywhere, you can give me a call. I'll be home with my dog, grading papers."

Roger's phone rang. Dan. He wanted to meet Roger and Jill at the E-Lite that night to introduce his latest girlfriend.

"Jill's away now."

"Come by yourself. I think this lady's the one."

"That's what you said the last time."

Roger took an Uber and got there first. The bartender looked disappointed. "Here alone? That awesome wife of yours too good for the humble E-Lite any more?" Without asking, he poured Roger a draft of National Bohemian beer. "She was in here a couple days ago with that friend of yours, the guy with his head shaved all around the sides. The guy who's always winking."

"Right. She told me." She hadn't.

Dan came in alone. "Yeah, that didn't work out."

"Back to square one?"

"Uh-huh. You and Jill—I don't know how you've stayed together a whole year. You're like ice and fire."

Roger told him Jill had disappeared.

"If she's not back tomorrow, maybe file a missing person report."

"I guess I should. Of course, she's a person who'd be hard to find if she didn't want to be found."

"So, what? Just *let it go*?" Dan chuckled.

Roger told him about Jill finding a note on the door.

"Ah-ha." Dan toyed with his glass of beer. "Maybe I'm jaded by my own experience with women, but what can you tell me about that partner of hers? The two of them are tight. Anybody can see that."

"I guess."

Dan gave him a pat on the back. "Don't mean to get you worked up over nothing. But I can see why you hesitate to report this to the police. They'd be sure to ask some embarrassing questions about anybody she might have ...." He looked up. "Couple more beers here."

When Roger got home, the house was still empty. He dropped a batch of trig tests on the kitchen table, but it was hard to concentrate. Jill had some kind of encrypted phone, and he wasn't supposed to call it, didn't have the number. He didn't remember her asking him for his number either. It had worked out all right. Roger wasn't the kind who needed to be in constant touch with his wife. He laughed at couples who were forever texting each other. Still, it made him angry that he couldn't call Jill now. Or call her friends or relatives. Because she didn't have any relatives, as far as anybody knew. And Lyle was the closest thing she had to a friend. He couldn't call him either.

3

An invitation

Roger had trouble concentrating on the math lesson the next day. When the Uber stopped at his house after school, his car still wasn't there. "Hold on," he told the driver. He found a nearby locksmith on Google and showed the driver the address.

It was a dusty, cluttered shop, its shelves filled with old locks, keys, some boxes of new electronic locks, and a jumbled display of security cameras. The pictures on the boxes showed that you could be notified on your phone if somebody broke into your house or even your car. It was a sign of the times, Roger thought. People on social media fed each other's fears that someone would break in and shoot them. Gun sales were soaring as people thought they needed them for personal protection. In fact, there actually were plenty of shootings in houses every month, but it was almost always one spouse killing another or somebody killing his lover's husband or ….

Roger shook the thought out of his head and said he'd lost his car keys. The locksmith ran his fingers through a shock of black hair and smiled. "I guess you've come to the right place." He asked what year the car was.

"It's brand new."

"Then it's complicated. I'll have to get a signal from the car, change it, and make a new key. It takes a couple of hours. And it's expensive."

"That's all right."

The locksmith reached for a leather pouch and asked where the car was. "I'll just need to see the registration."

"I don't have that. It's my wife's car. Her company car, actually."

The locksmith peered into Roger's eyes. "Ah."

"Will that be a problem?"

"Is your wife home?"

"No."

"Then it's a problem. There are legal restrictions." He put his pouch back under the counter. "I'm sure you're honest, but you wouldn't believe the vehicle theft, divorce battles, and revenge vendettas a locksmith can get caught up in. How about coming back later with your wife? Then I'll be able to help you."

Another Uber to a nearby Toyota dealer and Roger had leased a car. He was now thinking he should report Jill missing just to have it on record.

The Baltimore Central Police District building was in an infamous part of the city called the Block. In the first half of the last century, there had been several city blocks of burlesque houses. These gradually became strip clubs, sex shops, and bars. The several blocks of these seedy establishments eventually shrank to one or two blocks that stopped just at the Central Police Station. Roger's brother said the police liked the arrangement because they could keep an eye on what was going on. Of course, that meant *letting* it go on, but at least the area was confined.

Roger squeezed the car into a space on a brick side street and walked past Harem Nights, Girls Galore, the Adult Movies Club, the We Have It All Sex Toys, and into the Central Police Station. He walked down the stale-smelling hallway towards the intake desk.

The heavyset officer behind the high counter handed Roger a form on a clipboard. "Fill this out over there."

Roger took it to a narrow shelf against the wall. A middle-aged man stood there filling out a form while a man in a shiny suit holding a worn briefcase sidled up to him. Roger heard the briefcase man say, "Sure, file a missing person report, if you think that'll help. It almost never does. Here's my card in case you need it."

A plain clothes officer came, took Roger's clipboard in his yellowed fingers, and led him into a small room with a desk and three chairs. "Missing person. Wife. Hmm." He tapped his pen on the clipboard, looked Roger in the eye, waited.

"There was a note on our door. My wife read it and ran out. She hasn't come back."

"What did the note say?"

"I don't know."

"Anybody who might have wanted to harm her? Any problems between the two of you before she disappeared? Anybody you know she might have had a romantic relationship with?"

"She worked with a man named Lyle White. I don't know."

"Office colleague?"

"She doesn't work in an office. She mainly works from home. Now and then she has to go and meet Lyle."

"How can I get in touch with Lyle White?"

"He and my wife work for Grayrock, the army contractors in Afghanistan. The headquarters is in Washington."

"Have you tried to contact him yourself?"

"I can't. Grayrock is kind of hush-hush."

"What was the relationship between your wife and Lyle White?"

"All I know is they worked together on projects they couldn't talk about. When he called, she'd go to meet him."

"We'll try to contact this Lyle White. Meanwhile, if you think of anything else that might help, let us know." He wrote down the plate number Roger gave him for his missing Civic. "But I should warn you. If she's run off with Lyle White, or with anybody else, even if we find her, there's nothing we can do about it. We're limited to looking for any criminal activity, you realize?"

Roger sat at the kitchen table. If Jill thought she could insult him like this, she was mistaken. He googled Grayrock Security, LLC. There was an 800 number. He called, waited on hold, got disconnected, called again, waited, finally got a recording that directed him back to the Grayrock website before abruptly disconnecting. By now Roger was furious. He remembered Lyle and Jill talking about

Grayrock's head lobbyist, Ignazio Corelli. He got that number after an exhausting internet search. A secretary answered, offered to give Mr. Corelli a message.

"This is Roger Williams. I'm calling about Lyle White. I have some information that concerns his safety. This is important."

In minutes, "Iggy" Corelli called him back. "Are you on a secure line?"

"Yes." These guys deserved to be lied to, Roger thought.

"What code are you using?"

Roger used his anger to summon up courage. "Come on, Iggy. You want to hear what I have to tell you or not?"

"Go ahead."

"My wife Jill works with Lyle White. I think you know her."

Iggy said nothing.

Roger was too embarrassed to say he was looking for his wife. He said, "She's with Lyle. I have some crucial information for him. I need you to put me in touch with him right away."

"That's not possible. He's on assignment. You can use Grayrock's secure server to transmit your message. Otherwise, I can't help you. I don't get into things at this level. I'm going to hang up now."

"Wait. On assignment where?"

Iggy clicked off.

Roger paced around the house wishing he'd never heard of Grayrock, much less been so foolish as to marry someone who worked for them. His hands were shaky, and he realized he was hungry. He'd eaten all the leftover dumplings. What was there in the fridge? Nothing.

The Khyber restaurant wasn't far. Roger had become friends with Omar, the manager, through Lyle. He'd gone to Omar's house several times to help his cousin's son with math. The last time Roger met him, Omar had showed him a picture of his new granddaughter born in Kabul and talked about going back to see her soon. He said he hoped to bring his daughter and her family back with him when he returned.

Roger asked the waitress to tell Omar he was here. In a few seconds Omar appeared. "Mr. Roger, you have come without your wife? And I know your friend Mr. Lyle is in Kabul. I talked to him just yesterday. I'm going back at the end of the month to see my new granddaughter. Mr. Lyle promised to visit me there."

"In Kabul?" Roger saw it all now. Jill had run off to Afghanistan to be with Lyle. She probably assumed Roger would eventually file for divorce on the grounds of abandonment when he got tired of looking for her. No arguments, no explanations, and for Jill not even any paperwork.

"You say you talked to Lyle, Omar? You can talk to him from the States?"

"If you have WhatsApp on your phone. It's best with an unlimited data plan. But talking to Lyle is one-way only. He can call you, but you can't call him."

That sounded familiar. Roger must have looked distraught because Omar sat down at his table. "Did Mr. Lyle ever tell you how we became friends?"

The fact was Lyle had never said more than a few words to Roger.

"Two years ago he saved my grandson's life. Since then he and his friends are welcome any time in my daughter's house in Kabul. She and her family love to entertain Americans." Omar grinned. "A chance to practice their English."

Saving a boy's life didn't fit the picture Roger had of Lyle. "You say Lyle—"

"Your face tells me it's important to talk to Mr. Lyle." Omar stroked the stubble on his chin. "He never calls while he's on assignment. But he promised to get in touch with me when I go to visit my daughter." Omar looked into Roger's eyes, then slapped his hand on the table. "How about this. You have a summer holiday soon, yes? Come to Kabul with me. It's Ramadan, but my family is loose in observing the fast, especially if we have guests. You can bring your wife. Mr. Lyle will come to see us. We'll have a good time. And my daughter and her family can practice talking to native speakers before I bring them here." Omar grinned. "Maybe you can even give my grandson a little help with his math."

Roger caught himself with his mouth open. "Can Americans go to Afghanistan?"

"I'm American. I go there twice a year. You have to get a visa. Let me see …." Omar looked at his phone calendar. "Yes, there's enough time. Mr. Lyle would be very surprised to see you."

"I'm sure he would."

"I really hope you'll come," Omar urged. "My grandson, the whole family would love to meet you. Call me and let me know what you decide."

When he got home, Roger couldn't believe he'd even given a thought to going to Afghanistan. He pounded his head with both hands to shake the idea out and dropped his forehead onto the table trying to figure out how all this had happened.

When he first met Jill at the E-Lite, it had to be Lyle she'd been waiting for. He was her partner, yes. But their meetings seemed to be mostly social. And then there was her erratic work schedule. She was home for days at a time, until Lyle called and she rushed off to D.C. to meet him. In her job—he'd always assumed it was her job—she was at Lyle's beck and call. And then there was the note. The most likely explanation: it was Lyle summoning her.

And Lyle was in Afghanistan.

Not long after they were married, Jill had told Roger she might have to go to Afghanistan "if something important ever comes up." She'd laughed at his reaction. "Your face is so white. Well, I guess I know where I could go if I ever wanted to get away from you. Don't be such a wuss, Roger."

At St. Michael's after school, Father Joy trundled into the teachers' lounge wearing his three-peaked biretta. That meant he was there on business. He held out a contract to teach an extra May-June crash course for seniors who needed to pass math so they could graduate. "Going to help the math-challenged again this year, Roger?"

"Not this year, I'm afraid, Father." Roger said he had other plans.

"Other plans? Ah, I realize it's no fun teaching Kirk and his underachiever friends, but I urge you to consider—"

"As a matter of fact, I'm going to Afghanistan."

The old priest's white eyebrows rose. "I hope this is a joke."

"I'm serious."

"You can't do that, Roger. You're liable to be killed." Father Joy's hands were trembling. "Islamic extremists. You saw what ISIS did to the Yazidis. Conversion by the sword."

"Don't worry, Father. I'm not going to be converted by the sword. To any religion."

4

A mission of his own

Roger had known for some time that his marriage was probably a mistake. At the beginning, he'd found it exciting that the worldly, experienced Jill would take any interest in him, and he refused to worry about why. After two or three months, the excitement began to wear away into something more like exasperation at her puzzling, quirky behavior. Now this.

He should probably just let her go, accept his status as an abandoned husband. Be the Roger she counted on him being. But he wasn't going to do that. He felt driven to find out why she left, why she married him in the first place if she liked Lyle better. Besides, there was Jill's assumption that he would be too much of a "wuss" to track her down in Afghanistan. It galled him.

If she wanted to be with Lyle rather than him, so be it. It wouldn't surprise him that she preferred a man who could save a boy's life, as Omar said Lyle had done. But Roger needed to know. As crazy as it seemed, flying to Kabul with Omar and simply waiting for Lyle to come visit would probably be easier than trying to track the two of them down when they came back to Washington and were ensconced in the Grayrock labyrinth of secrecy there. Plus he'd get to prove to himself he wasn't a wuss.

Roger started reading news reports about Afghanistan. The U.S. and the Taliban had begun a new round of peace negotiations in Qatar at the beginning of the month. That was encouraging. But just over a week previously, an Afghan journalist and member of parliament was assassinated in Kabul. Then, on the same day that Roger gave his final exam, a girls' high school in Farah Province was burned to the ground by Taliban insurgents. That was not encouraging.

In any case, he'd found out that, yes, Americans could get an Afghan visa and fly there. Yes, they could travel within Afghanistan. Credit cards were even accepted. The cellular network in Kabul was rated excellent.

There were a few precautions in the State Department travel advisory he found online. Make a will before going. Give power of attorney to a trusted family member. Establish life insurance beneficiaries and obtain medical evacuation insurance. Discuss funeral provisions with loved ones.

The will and power of attorney his brother Dan took care of. He got an online term life policy benefitting his mother without her knowing. He'd only be away for a short time. He'd tell her about the trip when he got back. Medical evacuation insurance? None available for Afghanistan. The funeral arrangement thing? He skipped that. No sense being pessimistic.

Roger wondered what he'd say to Jill when he found her. Most women would be mortified to be caught with their lover. He pictured Jill more amused than mortified. What would she say?

His phone rang. Dan. "Roger, did you see the evening news? Soldier killed at Fort Davis, right over in Anne Arundel County. No information whether it was a man or woman. I called because Jill is missing and I hoped—"

"You mean ... oh. Oh, no."

"You haven't been notified? If it was her, I'm sure you would have been."

"I haven't." Roger took a breath. "And besides, Jill's no longer a 'soldier.' She's a Security Contractor."

"Mm. Well, I just wanted to let you know."

As soon as Roger hung up, he got another call. "Roger, it's Inez." She sounded out of breath and paused, as if waiting for him to say something. Finally, she began, "I saw a news report that scared me."

"The soldier who was murdered at Fort Davis?"

"I think you told me your wife was a soldier."

"Used to be. Now she's a military contractor. So—"

"It's just, my heart jumped when I heard it."

"No investigator has called me, so I assume it wasn't her."

"I didn't mean to upset you. I'm sorry."

"No. I appreciate it, Inez." He was glad his mother down in the Florida Keys probably hadn't heard the Maryland news.

That night Roger turned on the late local news. After reports of some local shootings and an exhaustive discussion of how no end was in sight for the dry spell the city was experiencing, the murder of the soldier was finally mentioned. But investigators hadn't given out the name yet. Roger didn't know what kind of identification Jill carried in that leather portfolio always hanging from her shoulder. It was possible she had some ID from her previous career in the army and had been misidentified as a soldier. That didn't seem likely, though.

Dan drove him to Dulles airport. "Mom called me. I told her where you're going. She asked me to try to change your mind."

"I won't be there long. Tell her not to worry. Omar will take care of me." Roger added, "It's dangerous in Baltimore, too. Just last month seven people were shot at a drive-by shooting at a barbecue not that far from where we live. No known motive. We're on track to end the year with the city's highest-ever murder rate." Roger glanced at Dan. "No need to mention that to Mom, either."

Roger had packed his things into a duffel bag—the bag Jill had left behind. It was a long, irksome drive through traffic to the airport. Roger found Omar in the Turkish Airlines waiting area. They were flying overnight to Istanbul, where there was a nine-hour layover. They'd have the afternoon and evening in Turkey before taking another overnight flight to Kabul. "I've always wanted to see Istanbul," Roger mused. "But I wish ...."

"Your wife was with you?" Omar finished for him. "I'm sorry she couldn't come. But don't worry. Mr. Lyle told me she's seen Istanbul lots of times."

"Right." Actually, Roger had only meant to say he wished it was a direct flight. He needed to focus on his mission. That's what Jill would have called it. A mission.

The pretty, plump flight attendants brought grapes and apples rather than peanuts and crackers. Some of the passengers spat their seeds on the floor. Omar had brought tissues, offered Roger one. Roger was still puzzled by something. "How was it Lyle saved your grandson, Omar?"

"It was two years ago. Little Karim, twelve years old, and I were walking along Sher Ali Khan Road. Karim saw a shaved ice vendor near a grocery shop and ran ahead. Before I knew it, a Humvee sped by and screeched to a stop beside Karim. An American in a black T-shirt jumped out, threw him to the ground. They'd had a tip there was a bomb. Karim running looked suspicious. The bomb went off in the shop entryway before the other Americans even got out of the truck."

Roger knew his mouth was gaping.

"The grocery shop wasn't open. Nobody was hurt. The shop was destroyed, but we rebuild fast in Afghanistan. You'll see the new shop. It's more modern now." Omar chuckled. "There's a lot of this kind of modernization going on in Afghanistan."

Omar fell asleep as soon as the cabin lights went out. Not Roger. His mind was racing. He was never going to save a child from a bomb. That was for sure. If that's the kind of man Jill wanted, she could have stayed with Lyle. She was already "tight" with him, as Dan put it. Then why did she marry Roger?

He fell into a fitful sleep until an announcement came that the plane was about to land. The Black Sea appeared below, dotted with tiny white boats. Roger snapped some pictures from his phone.

Three thirty p.m. Istanbul time. The plane to Kabul didn't leave until after midnight. Guides rushed the travelers. "See Hagia Sophia. Topkapi Palace."

Omar glanced at Roger. "You must want to see these places. We have time. I've seen them often, but I'll go with you."

"Thanks, but I'm too tired now to enjoy them." And he had too much on his mind.

Another night flight. At sunrise, a treeless landscape streaked with bare, sharp-edged mountains glowed golden below them. In only a few moments, the bright glow changed to a matte tan. Some mountain tops still wore caps of snow, and as the plane descended, narrow strips of green appeared in some of the valleys. The plane got lower and lower before Roger could make out some signs of human habitation—flat-roofed buildings the color of the desert. A bigger cluster with some tall modern buildings meant they were approaching Kabul.

"Sher Ali Khan Street," Omar told the taxi driver. He explained to Roger, "My house, I should say my daughter's house now, is one of the few remaining old ones on the edge of the Shirpur district. Just inside the Green Zone."

"That's good, right? Safer?"

"Yes and no. In the Green Zone, people are, as you say in English, 'on edge.' Especially the police, the militias, the American and U.N. troops, and the hired armies like Mr. Lyle's Grayrock. There's more chance of being harmed by them than by the Taliban." Omar gave Roger a pat on the knee. "So being blown up by a terrorist—less likely in the Green Zone. Being arrested or shot on suspicion of *being* a terrorist—more likely in the Green Zone." Omar rubbed his chin. "For example, I saw you taking pictures from the plane. You can take pictures in the real Kabul, but I wouldn't take any in the Green Zone."

"It would look suspicious?"

"Anything could."

5

Euclid in translation

The taxi stopped at the Shirpur gate post. The guard examined their passports and waved them in. Omar grinned. "If you live in Afghanistan, nothing makes life easier than having an American passport."

Everybody still called it Omar's house, but it now belonged to Omar's son-in-law, Hekmat, who owned the Quick Mart nearby. "Outside the Green Zone wall," Omar explained, "it's Kabob-e-Hafez or Furushgāh Sa'adi. Inside the wall, it's Speedy Burger, Donut Shoppe, and Number One Supermarket."

Omar's front door opened onto a wide room with no furnishing except a huge tribal carpet covering the whole floor, surrounded by cushions to sit on. Omar put his arms around his grandson Karim, now fourteen, kissing him on both cheeks. His daughter Amal stood by with her baby. She had Omar's light brown eyes and seemed about Roger's age. When she saw Roger, she pulled a scarf over her hair. Omar introduced him as "a very good friend of Mr. Lyle." The whole family seemed to understand at least a little bit of English.

Amal introduced Musa, an eight-year-old boy with a shaved head who stood shyly eyeing Roger from an open passage at the end of which Roger caught a glimpse of a garden. The boy ran and knocked on the door of a room off that passage, and Sima, a seven-year-old girl, appeared. In minutes, Amal's husband Hekmat arrived sporting a bag marked with his Quick Mart logo in English and Dari. "Pepsi," he beamed. Roger soon learned that some Afghans assumed it was the main thing Americans drank.

Omar's grandson took down a paper taped to the pale stucco wall—his primary school diploma. Omar gave the boy a bear hug, breathing out, "Bah-bah. *Barik-e-allah.* Good job." He turned to Roger. "Only a small percentage of students make it to high school."

"Mr. Roger is a high school teacher," Omar told Karim. The boy's face turned serious, and he gave Roger a bow.

It was early morning, but the family had a huge breakfast waiting for them. Sima, in a black headscarf, helped Omar's grandson spread a cloth they called a sofré over the carpet, and everybody sat around it on embroidered red cushions. Musa brought soft-boiled eggs, flat bread, feta cheese, and tea. Omar told Roger that Musa and Sima were orphans, the only survivors of a bombing a year ago that destroyed both of their houses. "Hekmat found them begging in front of his store. They've adopted them. Amal is teaching them to read and write. We've applied for visas to bring the whole family to America."

Roger finished everything they kept putting in front of him, then got sleepy. Omar actually drifted off, leaning back against the wall.

The dishes cleared, the sofré removed, Omar's son-in-law went back to his store, and his grandson came to sit next to Roger. Eyes averted, he took a breath. "I learn the English."

Roger saw he was holding a cell phone opened to Google Translate. Roger took out his phone. The conversation went better than he'd imagined.

"Which subject do you teach?" Karim read from his phone.

"*Riāziāt,*" Roger read from his.

Karim gave an unexpected sigh. "My *riāziāt* teacher, he died." It seemed that there was no math teacher for the ninth-grade now.

Karim brought his math notebook and showed what he'd been learning before the teacher died. Beginning geometry. Roger had taught it at Saint Michael's the semester before. He showed Karim a few quick and easy proofs that had impressed his students.

Karim's mother stood watching from the passage to the garden, still holding her baby, Laila. "Karim," she said in English, "you've greeted Grandpa. You must go back to school now."

"Come see my school, Mr. Roger?"

"I was hoping to talk to Mr. Lyle ...." Roger glanced at Omar, now stretched out on the carpet, snoring lightly.

Amal understood. "I will send Musa to see if Mr. Lyle is back from his assignment yet. You can go to school with Karim for now."

Unlike coming in through the Shirpur gate post, leaving wasn't a concern. Sleepy uniformed guards slouched there and at the entrance to a hospital on Peace Road, as Roger's phone translated it, which they followed towards the Shahr-e-Naow Park. Japanese-made cars and trucks of all sizes clogged the street, horns honking. Huge red, pink, and yellow umbrellas lined the thronging sidewalk on the sunny side of the street, each one shading a box-shaped portable stand with a merchant seated behind it. From some of the umbrellas hung goldfish tied in plastic bags of water. Roger saw crocheted dolls, costume jewelry, shishlik kabobs, fruit drinks, prayer beads, cigarettes, DVDs.

Afghan men and older boys seemed to dress in layers. An outer layer of Western clothing appeared like a façade over a base layer of indispensable Afghan garb. Traditional baggy tunic and baggy trousers were covered by a Western jacket or suit coat. Roger brushed against a gray bearded man in a flowing white robe covered by a formal waistcoat, then a suit coat, and finally a black leather jacket shorter than the suit coat. His figure was set off by a wide floppy hat with its rolled-up lower brim. "*Bebakhshid*," the man murmured to Roger, which Karim told him meant "Excuse me."

Some of the men wore floppy hats like this, but most left their dark hair exposed. Older men sometimes wore brimless flat-topped prayer caps, mostly white. Like Karim, the younger boys dressed just like any American boys, except that a few as young as about five wore little Western suits. Roger had to tell himself not to stare at people, especially at the women.

He was startled by the ghost-like blue figures draped in full body burqas with a mesh face screen that they could apparently see through. No information about the women in these coverings was available, not age or body shape or relative beauty—or their thoughts as they flitted by, sometimes turning their faceless figures momentarily towards the light haired Roger.

Most women wore only head scarves or hejabs, although some wore body-length chadors draped over their heads and held closed with their hands—or with their teeth when they were buying something. Roger and Karim maneuvered past a group of chadored women admiring a rack of traditional Afghan dresses, red and black, with intricate gold and silver needlework. It was a mistake, Roger realized, to assume from their drab public coverings that these women didn't want to wear beautiful clothes. Maybe the idea was that feminine beauty was enhanced by reserving it for the most private occasions.

The Mamtāzi High School was in a row of monolithic Soviet-style buildings across the street from the park. "Who are those men lying on the grass in the shade?" Roger asked. "They look sick."

Karim's answer was laconic. "Morphine. Heroin."

In the school corridor, they passed by a wordless poster depicting a plain wood coffin with a hypodermic needle pointing towards it. "Government warning," Karim explained. The classroom door was open. In a bare white room, behind scuffed wooden benches, forty dark-haired boys sat shoulder to shoulder. Karim introduced Roger to his English teacher, who had just finished his lesson.

"A math teacher? This is wonderful. You are from UNESCO?"

"Oh, sorry. No. I'm just visiting." Roger saw the teacher's face drop. The boys shifted their eyes back and forth between him and Roger. He'd never experienced such rapt attention from a class. Karim tugged at Roger's sleeve, tapped on his math notebook.

Roger understood. "You say their math lesson is scheduled for now? Maybe I could teach one geometry theorem. But could they understand it in English?"

"I can help translate. But look at this." With a proud glimmer, the teacher showed him the English compositions they'd turned in. On the top one, the student had written something in Arabic.

"Davoud," the teacher scolded, "you know we don't write this on papers in my class." He explained to Roger, "A religious phrase. You must think we're backward people."

"What does it mean?"

"In the name of God, the merciful, the compassionate."

"That's interesting. Where I teach, they write A. M. D. G. on their papers. *Ad majorem dei gloriam.* To the greater glory of God."

"In America? This surprises me."

"You're not afraid of getting into trouble? I mean for forbidding religious dedications?"

"It's a chance I'm willing to take."

The portable blackboard was so white with chalk Roger had to press hard to make his lines visible. He created a problem in which land between a river and a mountain range had to be divided equally between Ali's family and Hamid's family. He had students come to the board to give suggestions—apparently something never done in Afghanistan—until they had chalked in separate but identical parallelograms that avoided the trees and pond he'd drawn in. "Congratulations," he told them. "You've just proved Euclid's Proposition 36."

"Is this really the American way to divide land?" one of the boys asked. "It wouldn't work in Afghanistan."

Roger took the bait. "Why not?"

"Here we would have to call a village council and discuss the matter until everyone agreed."

"It would take twenty years," another student called out.

When they walked back to Omar's house, the street was even more jammed with cars, buses, and trucks moving slowly and honking. A jeep sped by half on the sidewalk, forcing the crowd up against a building.

"Was your math teacher old, Karim?"

"No. Same as you."

"That's too bad. How did he die?"

"Hit by a car."

6

Deep blue eyes

Back at the house, Roger told Omar he was anxious to see Lyle.

"He's still away. Musa says there's only a foreign woman in the house now. She didn't know when Mr. Lyle would be back. But never mind. This just means you can be our guest longer."

The woman had to be Jill. Busted!

Roger tried to sound casual. "I'd like to go ask her myself. You say it's not far from here?"

"I'll take you if you really want—"

"Thanks, but I'd rather go by myself."

Lyle's house was about five blocks away in the exclusive Wazir Akbar Khan district. Omar said it was safe to walk there as long as he got back before curfew at dark. Roger found the house on what the Americans named First Street near the former Belgian Embassy. Although Omar had told him some American Embassy staff and Foreign Service personnel lived in converted metal shipping containers on the embassy compound, Lyle was employed by Grayrock. He lived in an Italianate villa.

Roger knocked. A latch clanked and a narrow metal panel in the door slid open. Two deep blue eyes peered out. Not Jill's.

"Um, I have a message for Lyle. From the D.C. office."

The door slowly opened to let Roger in. The blue eyes belonged to a pretty young woman in a loose white blouse and black slacks. She spoke with an accent Roger couldn't place. "Lyle is in Kabul, but he's on assignment now. I do not know when he will be back." She stood waiting for Roger to say more.

"My wife works for Lyle. Maybe you know her. Jill Williams? I could give the message to her."

"I'm sorry. I don't know your wife."

"She's American, about our age, dirty blond curls, green eyes, your height, taller than Lyle."

"Lyle has never mentioned her. I have lived here more than a year, and I've never seen her."

Roger frowned. The young woman introduced herself. "Sophie Martens. I work with Femmes en Crise, a Belgian NGO, a non-governmental aid organization."

He shook the hand she offered. "You say Lyle's 'on assignment.' Did he go alone? No one from Grayrock with him?"

Sophie's eyes paused on Roger's before she spoke. "Again, I'm sorry. Lyle tells me nothing. Only that he is protecting American personnel from enemies." Her cheeks turned pink and she gestured towards a maroon leather couch, over which hung a US Army ceremonial sabre. "Lyle doesn't want me to have visitors, but …."

When she sat next to him, he asked what she did at the aid organization.

"Education of women. I guess you know the Taliban want to restrict girls to religious education. Everything women need to know is in the Koran, they say. They claim we're enemies of God." She took a breath. "But that hasn't stopped us. We have set up a teacher-training school in Kabul. With a full curriculum."

"That's impressive." Roger was having a hard time seeing Sophie as Lyle's type.

She bit her lip. "The Taliban oppose our work. They burned down a girls' high school in Farah Province recently. And the Islamic State, they are worse."

Roger said he'd read about the school burning. "But have you had any success?"

Sophie pushed her long dark hair aside and smiled. "A little. That's what keeps me going."

Since his geometry lesson that morning, Roger had in the back of his mind the notion of spending a summer volunteering to teach in Afghanistan. Listening to Sophie made him think this might be possible.

Sophie folded her arms. "I know. You probably think we're wasting our time. 'Simpler to just wipe the Taliban out.' That's what Lyle says."

"Not at all. I admire you. You're doing something important."

The flush in her cheeks deepened.

"Besides," he said, "wipe the Taliban out? What would that even mean?"

She held trembling fingers to her chest. "Please don't misunderstand. I would never complain about Lyle. Please don't tell him I said that."

"No. Of course not." Roger resisted the instinct to put a reassuring hand on her shoulder. He found Sophie puzzling. She was devoted to helping Afghan women improve their lives. Yet she was living with Lyle, a man who saw violence as the only way of fixing things. "So you and Lyle—"

Sophie glanced away. "My friend Lexi came to Kabul to work for Femmes en Crise, so I wanted to join, too. But there was no room in their Green Village housing."

"Green Village?"

"It's different from the Green Zone. It's a guarded compound southeast of the airport where international companies and aid organizations stay."

"But you came anyway? Even though there was no room in the Femmes en Crise housing?"

"Yes. Our director met Lyle. He needed somebody to keep his house in order." Sophie pursed her lips. "He doesn't trust 'hajis,' as he calls them."

"That's Lyle. But I wonder how your director met him?"

"It was after the USAID robbery last year. He and a U.S. army colonel invited Femmes en Crise to the Grayrock headquarters to explain that a big shipment of grant money for our program had been stolen. It was terrible. USAID delivered the money to Lyle and a Belgian guard at the Bagram Airport. When they were transporting it to our Ministry of Foreign Affairs in Green Village, four men ambushed them. Lyle said the Belgian guard was killed. The ambushers got away with the cash. All in U.S. dollars."

"I never read about that."

"I'm told the U.S. likes to keep incidents like this quiet." She gripped her hands together. "We were planning to build a second school in Kandahar. Now we're not sure we can afford to."

"I'm sorry. And you say you've lived here for more than a year?"

Sophie frowned. "Yes. Six months after I got here, there was an attack right outside the Green Village walls. The United Nations staff left. Femmes en Crise stayed, but most of our women quit and went home. There are only three of us now. So when the director moved into a room of her own, I wanted to move in with Lexi." Sophie bit her lip. "But Lyle said no."

"He wouldn't let you?"

Sophie's cheeks reddened. "He has a strong personality. Is that the way you put it?"

Roger would have put it another way, but he only nodded.

Sophie blinked away a tear, and Roger was moved by her dark eyelashes. Her deep blue eyes met his. "You're a friend of Lyle's. I should offer you something." She lifted a little brass bell from a mahogany table next to the couch, rang, and called out in Dari to someone in another room.

Roger noticed an envelope on the table from the "Pulshui Bank" addressed to Lyle in English. He'd walked past that bank on the way here. The building seemed to be nothing more than a door with a sign over it wedged between a shoe store and a casket maker.

Sophie saw him eyeing the unopened envelope. "Lyle tells me nothing about his business. I've learned not to ask."

A handsome Afghan boy about twelve years old in a black prayer cap came in and placed a glass of wine and a can of Budweiser on the table. One of the boy's arms was in a cast.

"It looks like he hurt his arm," Roger commented when the boy left the room.

Sophie toyed with her wine glass. "Oh, it's nothing. A simple fracture."

"I was just wondering. You know, because of all the bombings, attacks on civilians—"

"It was nothing like that. Lyle caught Ishak loitering near a Grayrock truck and grabbed him, thinking he might be a terrorist. Lyle's a powerful man. The arm was broken. Of course, Lyle was sorry when he found out the boy was not one of the enemy, just a boy on the street. He brought him here to be his house boy." Sophie sipped her wine, leaving a faint trace of pink lipstick on the edge of the glass. "Lyle is very enamored of Ishak. I don't know if enamored is the right word."

"Well …." Roger snapped open the can of Budweiser.

Sophie smiled. "I thought you'd like that beer. It's Lyle's favorite."

How could this woman speak affably about a man who considered her work a waste of time? Who broke a boy's arm?

"I know what you must be thinking," Sophie murmured. "Lyle can be violent. But I've learned how to 'stay out of his way.' That's what Lyle tells me."

Sophie took another slow sip, gazing at Roger over her glass. Now Roger felt his own cheeks warming. "You should be proud," he told her. "You're helping people. I wish I could do the same."

"Why can't you?"

"Maybe I could for a little while." He told Sophie about the lesson he'd taught in Karim's high school.

"*Formidable!* You could get a position like mine to help train Afghan teachers. Check with USAID." She smiled. "You'd be perfect."

Roger sipped some beer.

"The pay isn't bad," Sophie went on. "Not anything like Grayrock pay, of course."

"I don't know. I don't think I could do that for more than a few months. Not a whole year like you."

"We get thirty days' leave every six months. R and R, Lyle calls it. In fact, my leave is coming up soon. I was thinking of visiting my aunt in America. She has a bakery in New York." Sophie paused. "Is it dangerous in the U.S., though? I read that a family planning center was bombed. They said it was the second time that the same place was bombed." She touched her heart. "And two men who worked there were murdered before that."

"That was about twenty-five years ago."

"So things are better now? Yet I read about a Molotov cocktail bombing of a family planning center just last winter."

Roger took the last sip of his beer. He wished he could guarantee Sophie she wouldn't find strains of Taliban-like thinking in America. But the thought of Father Joy still preaching his catechism to the boys at Saint Michael's silenced him. People like Karim's English teacher and Sophie risked their lives sticking to their principles. All Roger risked if he let his objections to the Saint Michael's indoctrination be known was losing his job.

Sophie checked the time on her phone. "Almost curfew. You should probably be going. You're welcome to come back tomorrow." Her face reddened as she added that.

Roger realized he'd completely forgotten why he came here. "Will you give Lyle my phone number, ask him to call me when he gets back?"

"He doesn't have it?"

"Uh, just in case." He turned on his phone.

"All right. May I?" She put her hand under his and texted herself from his phone to get his number.

When she stood at the door, Sophie said, "I hope nothing I've said made you think I'm critical of Lyle."

"I'd hate to think you're afraid of him, Sophie."

Without responding, she took his hand. Her blue eyes met his. "I'm pleased to have met you. I hope you find your wife soon."

43

7

An emergency stop

Friday, a holiday. Amal and Hekmat came in from their bedroom along the walkway to the garden. The thick sleeping mats they called toshak that Roger, Omar, and Karim slept on in the main room had to be folded away so breakfast could be laid out on the sofré that was spread over the huge red Turkoman carpet.

"How about coming with us to the Al-Taqwa mosque?" Omar suggested. "A prominent imam is preaching. He supports families of Afghan soldiers who died, condemns Taliban suicide bombings, speaks out for women's rights, and favors cooperation between Coalition forces and the Afghan government."

"Sure," Roger agreed. "Not that I'll understand anything."

Omar's daughter stayed home with baby Laila and the adopted children. The rest crammed into a taxi and headed for the mosque about seven miles away. On the road, Roger felt a bout of traveler's diarrhea coming on. "I hate to ask," he gasped, "but I need to use a toilet. Can we stop somewhere?"

There was a silence. "We'll be late," Omar's grandson Karim objected in English. But Omar asked the driver to stop at a tea house.

Roger made his way past men in long robes sitting cross-legged, sipping tea, and puffing on hookahs. The toilet in the back had a smell that almost caused him to faint, and he made it back to the taxi very quickly.

Karim was squirming, checking the time on his phone. "The service started fifteen minutes ago." He flashed the phone towards Roger to show him the time, but all Roger could make out was the date, May 24.

"Be polite," Omar chided his grandson. "Mr. Roger is our guest.

He had an emergency. There's nothing wrong with arriving a little late."

The taxi crossed a river, turned towards a small neighborhood of streets, and Roger could see the blue dome of the mosque. Just at that moment a terrific explosion jolted the taxi.

The driver jerked to a stop. At first there was silence. Then screams resounded from the mosque. As some people rushed towards it, others began carrying wounded people out. Their sirens blaring, police cars and an ambulance sped past the taxi.

Omar, his son-in-law Hekmat, his grandson, and the taxi driver all began calling out to Allah. They got out of the taxi and started towards the mosque, but the driver stopped them. "He says sometimes there's a second strike after a crowd gathers," Omar explained.

Neighborhood women shrieked and men beat their breasts when a body in a bloodied white robe and gray vest was carried out on a stretcher. "It's Samiullah Rayhan himself," Omar gasped.

"We could have been in there," Karim said, holding both hands to his cheeks.

The way back to the house was jammed with police and emergency vans racing towards the mosque, sometimes using both sides of the road. When the taxi pulled up to the house, Omar's daughter rushed out in tears and pulled each one of them into her arms, even Roger. She'd already seen the report on TV.

The explosive device had been put in the microphone that the imam was using. He'd been the target, but at least nine other people were also killed and more than a dozen were wounded. The police assumed it was the work of the Taliban, but the Taliban denied it.

No one spoke much that afternoon. Hekmat fingered his prayer beads, moving his lips in some kind of silent prayer. Amal rocked back and forth, baby Laila tight in her arms. Roger felt he was witnessing the despair of a whole country.

Until he wasn't. Karim was the first to jump up. He took a soccer ball out into the street. Roger could hear other boys yelling with him.

Amal laid the sleeping baby on a blanket and went to the kitchen to make Roger some tea. Omar's son-in-law turned the TV back on to a soccer game. When Roger had dutifully finished two glasses of tea, he checked his phone. It was still morning in Baltimore. Amal assumed he wanted to call his wife. "Texts work inside. The phone reception is better outside."

Roger walked out into the adobe-walled garden behind the house and dialed his brother.

"Ah, Roger! You OK? I've been watching BBC news since you left. I saw there was an explosion in Kabul. I didn't know how far it was from where you're staying."

"Yeah, it was pretty far away."

"So you're not hurt? How about any of the people you're staying with?"

"We're all fine."

"Have you found Jill?"

"No. Lyle's still away somewhere on assignment. I haven't seen him or Jill yet."

"How long are you going to keep looking?"

"If I can't find her or talk to Lyle by the end of next week, I'm coming home."

"You are? So I won't have time to use my Power of Attorney to scarf up all your possessions after all?"

"Tell me, Dan. Have they identified that soldier who was killed at Fort Davis?"

"No, they say the investigation is ongoing."

"If the city police turn up anything on Jill, I gave them your name as a contact."

"Right. I went by your house this morning. Your car's still not there."

"If you drive by again, I wonder if you could pick up my mail. I'm expecting my M.A. diploma."

"Sure. Keep in touch."

There was a slightly raised pond in the yard with a single goldfish.

Roger sat on a warm stone at the edge, watching the fish swim aimlessly back and forth. It seemed to be searching for something. But there was nothing else in the pond.

Yellow flowers with tall, tough stems were planted along the high adobe walls. At the back of the yard was an old wooden outhouse. The main toilet and shower were rooms that opened onto the exposed walkway, but Omar had pointed out the outhouse in the yard. "You see? We have a two-bathroom house." Maybe it took a good sense of humor to survive in an environment plagued by violence.

A large black and white bird with a long tail settled on the edge of the garden wall. It might have been the fish it was appraising, but it seemed to be peering at Roger. He shifted, but the bird kept its focus on him. Roger waved his arm. The bird gave a high-pitched *ak-ak-ak* before it flew away.

Roger began to see his trip to Afghanistan as ludicrous. Coming all this way to find a wife who'd left him without a word? Still, he wanted to confront her. He'd give it a little more time. He'd go back to Lyle's villa again tomorrow. Even if Lyle wasn't there, he'd have a chance to talk to Sophie again, ask her more about the program for training teachers.

Although Omar had said his family weren't strict in observing the Ramadan fast, they still ended the days with a huge meal after sundown. "It's the part of Ramadan we observe religiously," Omar joked.

Roger had been accepted immediately as part of the family. When he said he might go back home earlier than planned, everybody objected. "I was expecting you'd stay the whole time I'm here," Omar complained.

Amal agreed. Karim said something in Dari, and an animated discussion broke out. Finally, Omar turned to Roger. "We hope the incident at the mosque didn't change your mind. Believe me, these disturbances are rare. You shouldn't be afraid. As they say in English, life goes on."

"Of course, he's not afraid," Amal put in. "I know what it is. He misses his wife."

Omar and Hekmat studied Roger, gravely nodding. "Yes, yes," Omar agreed. "This must be true." The matter was settled.

That night as Roger tossed on the mat trying to fall asleep, his mind ran through conflicting pictures of what might have happened to Jill. She was in an army morgue at Fort Davis awaiting positive identification. She was off with Lyle somewhere—neither of them with the least concern about being unfaithful, not Jill to Roger or Lyle to Sophie. That is, if Sophie and Lyle were really a couple. She'd said she took care of his house when he was away. But Lyle was in Kabul now, and she was staying there. He didn't know what to think. The vision of Sophie's long eyelashes, deep blue eyes, and delicate pink lips lingered in his mind as he fell asleep.

8

Plan B

By the next morning, there was still no call from Lyle. Roger told Omar about Sophie encouraging him to apply for a job training teachers.

Omar's eyes widened. "This would be wonderful. Let me see. Saturday. Foreigners usually don't work on Saturdays. You could go talk to her and get more information."

Roger needed no more encouragement.

A massive tan camouflaged truck was parked in front of the villa. There was a driver by the truck. As Roger paused, the house door opened. A short man with the sides of his head shaved came out—Lyle. He winked at Roger and pointed to the truck. "I was just about to come for you. Get in."

Lyle told his driver to wait there. He'd drive the truck himself. The engine growled to a start, and Lyle headed out in the direction of the airport.

"Where are we going? We could've talked at your house."

Lyle turned his head and winked. "Safer out here. Damned hajis can't be trusted. Could be bugs anywhere." He pulled off the road, and the truck slammed across a dry ditch and stopped on a bare, dusty field. "I assume Jill sent you here. I hope you're going to tell me why she hasn't been returning my calls."

Roger was totally caught off-guard. It seemed best to say nothing.

"I guess she told you a witness turned up in the States. That's why you're here?"

"Witness?"

"Informant. Whatever. The guy who says he saw us with the bags. Guy who told Jill he wants to be cut in." Lyle's mouth twisted into a grin. "Of course, she told him to shove it."

Roger swallowed, managed a tentative nod.

"Jill found out the guy could be dangerous. Special Forces type." Lyle cocked his head. "You mean to say this isn't what you came here to talk about?"

"She doesn't tell me anything. Now she's disappeared."

"Disappeared? Shit. Just what I was afraid of." Lyle lit a cigarette, squinted at Roger. "If Jill's gone, I'm going to need your help to access the money. The LLC paperwork was filed in your name." He snapped his Zippo shut. "You seriously mean she's kept you in the dark about everything?"

"Well—"

"The bank transfers? Beverage Supplies, the shell company you're the nominal administrator of? No? When was she going to get around to telling you?" Lyle stuck a thumb in his belt. "If that Special Forces witness killed Jill, it's you and me, Mr. Clean. Jill guaranteed me she found a guy with a spotless record who can fly under the radar when we use him to make the withdrawals."

Roger's flesh crept. "I guess she didn't think it was time to fill me in yet."

"Uh-huh." Lyle gave a squinty-eyed wink. "Well, I guess now's the time." He looked around—as if there could possibly be anyone listening in the barren field they stood in. "Jill was assigned to the USAID guys who delivered a lot of money to me and a Belgian guard. The guard and I were assigned to transport it to a Belgian NGO. She never told you that?"

Roger shook his head.

"Unbelievable. So anyway Jill tells the AID guys she'll stay and ride along with me and the guard when we take the money to the Belgians." The pupils of Lyle's eyes widened. "I could see the wheels turning in that curly head of hers. When the AID guys drove away, I gave Jill a wink. All we had to do was say the money was stolen. I offered to let the Belgian guard in on the heist. He acted up, tried to stop us. I took care of him." Lyle chuckled. "You wondering why

I didn't take Jill out, too? Simple. I needed somebody Stateside to handle that end of the business."

Roger's head was spinning.

Lyle stamped out his cigarette. "I'll be in the country a while longer. Working with a guy at the Pulshui Bank. I assume you brought the key?"

"Key?"

"The other key to the Grayrock vault at Camp Rectitude where we're holding the money."

"I don't know anything about a key."

Lyle squinted so deeply his huge pupils seemed to disappear. "Don't lie to me. Jill had one key. I had the other—the only way we could trust each other. You're not going to give me any trouble about this, are you? That wouldn't be smart."

"But I don't have it."

"Then you need to go back and get that key right away. It touches nobody else's hands but yours. If you don't bring it to me toot-sweet, I'm coming after you. Talk to Iggy in the D.C. office about transportation."

"But—"

"And hold on to the paperwork."

"Paperwork?"

"All the papers you signed."

"I didn't sign anything."

Lyle smirked. "The hell you didn't."

"I don't know what—"

Lyle gripped Roger's shirt. "And no one knows anything about this. You-Tell-No one. If anybody starts asking questions, I'll take care of them, and I'll know who they got their information from. You'll wish you'd never been born. Understand?"

Roger closed his mouth and gave a single nod.

"All right. I'll let Iggy in the D.C. office know he can trust you." Lyle pointed to the truck. "Get in. I'll drop you off by my house. I can't visit Omar right now. I have an appointment with a senator who flew in from the States." Lyle started up the truck. "Too bad about Jill."

Roger gaped through the truck's rattling windshield. Clearly, in Lyle's mind, Jill was already dead and gone, killed by the "Special Forces type" witness. Lyle had dismissed her as easily as stamping out his cigarette: All right, then—plan B.

True enough, Jill wasn't the kind of person who inspired people's concern. She gave the impression of being able to take care of herself. Roger's time with her had been a year of sporadic, reckless excitement marred by a persistent undercurrent of sad humiliation. But it seemed she wasn't having an affair with Lyle, after all. Roger no longer wanted to be married to a woman who'd stolen money from a humanitarian program and was complicit in "taking care of" a man. But he couldn't help hoping she hadn't been murdered.

He wouldn't tell Sophie anything. She was safer from Lyle knowing nothing, at least for now. But if he could do so without Lyle finding out, he would go to the USAID office and report everything—the murder of the guard, the theft of the funds designated for Sophie's teacher-training program, the apparent plans to launder the money.

He wondered if there actually was a USAID office in Kabul, considering the current U.S. President's reported ignorance of and lack of interest in foreign aid. But recently the President had discovered he could use foreign aid punitively, so maybe there was an office here, probably somewhere in the huge U.S. Embassy compound.

When the truck stopped in front of the villa, Lyle grabbed Roger's shoulder. "You get back to the States, you keep your head down. That Special Forces guy, I'm sure he's capable of anything. If he threatens you, you tell him nothing."

A white and green Afghan police car cruised by. Roger started towards the U.S. Embassy, a twenty-minutes' walk according to Google Maps.

"Hey!" Lyle called. "You're going the wrong way, Mr. Clean. Omar's house is that direction."

The police car drove slowly by again as Roger reversed course and walked towards Omar's house. Now he was thinking maybe it wasn't a good idea to report Lyle to USAID right away. Lyle might assume it was Sophie who discovered his crimes and informed on him. Roger stood on the street thinking. He'd only just met Sophie, but her sincere manner stirred something like a protective instinct in him. She wasn't safe living with Lyle. Nobody was.

Behind him Roger heard the growl of Lyle's truck starting up and driving away. Now would be a chance to go in and talk to Sophie. He'd try to convince her to move out of the villa without telling her why. But what if the houseboy later told Lyle he had been there again? It was too risky. He decided to phone her instead.

It rang quite a few times before he heard her faint "Hello."

"Sophie, it's Roger Williams. I'm worried about you. Lyle's dangerous."

"A little, maybe. But I'm used to him."

Roger wished he could talk to her in person. She might take his warning more seriously. "Can we meet somewhere other than Lyle's house?"

"Yes." The word came out like a whisper. She named the school where she worked. "Take a taxi. There's a tea house next to the school. The Ariana Café. They're used to foreigners there." She texted directions.

The police car drifted by again, then stopped.

"Sophie, I have to hang up. I'll meet you there."

Two police in blue uniforms got out. One pulled Roger's arms behind his back, shouting something in Dari. The other spoke English. "You are walking up and down on this street. Let me see this." He pulled down a visor on his helmet and gingerly took the phone Roger still held in his hand as if it might be a trigger device for a bomb. "Cellphone? Why are you calling on the street?"

Roger was now handcuffed. The first cop patted him down.

"Answer, please. Why are you walking in front of these houses? You are searching for something?"

"No. I mean … uh …." Roger suddenly had an idea. "Yes."

"What? What are you searching for?"

"I'm looking for Pepsi."

The cop flipped up his visor. "Pepsi?"

The other cop said something in Dari that included the word "Pepsi."

"Passport," the helmeted cop demanded. He took it from Roger's pocket, studied the picture, studied Roger's face, showed it to the other cop. "Yes," he said. "You are American. You want Pepsi."

The handcuffs were taken off.

"With your permission." The cop tapped on Roger's phone, entered something. "Here. Here is Pepsi." He'd brought up the Google Maps directions to the Quick Mart owned by Hekmat, Omar's son-in-law. "Go with God. Drink it in health." Both cops shook his hand before they drove away.

Before catching a taxi for the Ariana Café, Roger stopped at an ATM outside a grocery store on Wazir Akbar Khan street. He was shocked that the only withdrawals since Jill disappeared were made by him. He remembered what the Baltimore police sergeant had told him. "As long as she's taking out cash, she's alive. If she makes no withdrawals after some time, we worry."

9

An evil jinn

Thick smoke circled below the darkened ceiling of the little café. Roger tried to identify the smell. "Welcome," an old waiter in a white apron said in English.

Roger looked down the long, narrow room. Near the door, foreign men in suits went over papers spread on a table. A man in a rolled up hat and a woman wearing a hejab sat at another table sipping tea from little glasses and talking in low voices. A group of young foreign contractors called for a hookah and passed the hose from one to another, and Roger now recognized the smell of hashish. There was a woman in a delicate light blue hejab sitting alone. She signaled him with a finger and smiled. Sophie.

"You can relax," she told him. The owners know foreign men and women sometimes meet and talk here. About work or business, I mean." She pulled back the hejab to expose more of her hair. "I wear this in public. No need to offend their sense of etiquette."

"It's beautiful."

The waiter set down another glass and filled it from the huge cracked and patched teapot on the table. "Yes," the old man repeated. "Beautiful." He was looking at Sophie's eyes, not the hejab.

"I asked Lyle about your wife," Sophie said. "He told me he hasn't seen her, doesn't know where she is. I'm sorry."

"Yeah, it doesn't look good."

Sophie put her hand on his. "Don't worry. You'll find her." Then she quickly pulled her hand away.

"Lyle thinks she's dead. He's sure of it."

Sophie gasped. "No, he didn't tell me that. Oh, Roger—"

"I think … I'm afraid he's right. She hasn't made a single

withdrawal from our joint account since she disappeared."

"You really think … ? Roger, I'm so sorry."

"Sophie, you probably realize Grayrock employees like Jill and Lyle do some questionable things."

Sophie stared down at her tea. "I know Lyle does."

"Some criminal things." Roger decided to say no more than this. The last thing he wanted was Lyle to think Sophie knew about the theft and murder.

She pursed her lips without raising her eyes. "I don't know what to do. Just today Lyle told me he's going to need me to help him with something important. I have to stay in the villa with him until then."

Roger lowered his voice. "Do you really want to keep living with a man like Lyle? He's dangerous, Sophie."

She nodded and dabbed her eyes with a corner of her hejab. "You're not the first person to tell me this. My colleagues Lexi and Nora want me to come back permanently to the aid workers housing in Green Village." She clenched her hands.

"Would you leave if we could safely get you away from him?"

"I don't know." She swallowed and looked back into his eyes. "Yes."

Omar was waiting for Roger when he got back. "You found Mr. Lyle? I'm surprised he didn't come by to see us."

"Lyle's busy with some banking business, and he went to meet with a U.S. senator." Roger was uneasy letting Omar think Lyle was some kind of hero. "He told me things I didn't like. He's not as honest as people think."

Omar fixed his eyes on Roger, waiting for more. But Roger thought he'd gone far enough for now.

"Yes," Omar admitted. "I know Grayrock men sometimes have to kill the enemy."

Roger supposed that in Lyle's eyes the guard he'd killed for trying to prevent him from stealing USAID money was the enemy.

Omar shrugged, switched his frown to a smile. "Anyway, come

have some tea." It was the Afghan anodyne for any problem.

Amal put a dish of pistachios next to Roger's glass of tea. When Omar left the room, she said, "I heard you talking about Mr. Lyle. I think my father is wrong about him."

"What do you mean?"

"Have you noticed his eyes?"

"The large pupils, you mean?"

"They're not human. My father laughs at me, but I know he's a *jinn*."

Roger smiled.

"Believe me, a jinn appears in different forms. As a human, an animal, often as a scorpion. A jinn can be good or bad, but I can tell from those eyes. Mr. Lyle is an evil jinn." Amal sighed. "But all my father sees is the man who saved his grandson."

"I know."

"If that's what you can call it. Mr. Lyle wasn't meaning to save him. It was just an accident. I don't know if my father told you the story."

"He did."

Amal grinned. "I guess I could say you saved Karim, too."

"What do you mean?"

"Your diarrhea. Karim, everybody would have been in the mosque when the bomb exploded if you hadn't made them stop." Her chest heaved in a deep throated chuckle.

The mats were rolled out and everybody was going to bed when Roger's phone rang.

"Ah-ha." Amal raised her eyebrows at Roger. "I saw that magpie land on the garden wall when you were out there before. It's a sign you were going to get an important message."

"He doesn't believe in those superstitions," Omar groused.

Roger took the phone outside. "Dan, I've met Lyle. He's—"

"Listen, Roger. I found something."

He heard Dan taking a breath. "I went to pick up your mail.

Squirrels were chasing each other across your porch. One was burying a nut in your front yard. I watched him and noticed some trash scattered in the dead grass, so I went to pick it up. There was a balled-up piece of paper there along with potato chip wrappers and paper napkins. I unwrinkled it, spread it open. I couldn't believe it. It said in all caps and no apostrophes, YOU WONT GET AWAY WITH THIS. YOUR GOING DOWN."

Roger gasped. It was the note Jill had found on the door. It was all clear now. Jill had run for her life.

"You there?"

"Yeah. Dan, here's what I found out from Lyle. Some 'Special Forces type' had threatened Jill. When I told Lyle she disappeared, he was certain that guy killed her. He must be the guy who wrote that note."

"So maybe the soldier murdered at Fort Davis really was Jill? I'm sorry, Roger. I don't know what to say. But come on back right now, OK?"

"I will soon. I'll call you with the flight time and number."

Roger tossed on the mat again that night. He realized he might have been hoping Lyle was lying about what Jill had done. But now it seemed she was killed by an actual witness to her crimes. The memory of Lyle's enormous, intense pupils as he warned Roger to beware of that same witness gave him a chill. It was as if Roger had been unwillingly drawn into the scheme.

He was determined to report Lyle to USAID before he went back to the States. Then he'd fly home immediately. But as he started making plans to do this, the thought of Sophie's sincere blue eyes stopped him. He didn't want to leave Afghanistan until he found a way to help her safely move out of Lyle's grasp. Sophie would be safer if she went back to the aid workers' housing in Green Village. The problem was that Lyle would know something was up if he saw her leaving with baggage.

10

Earned leave

Lyle came to the door in silky blue pajamas, blinking in the bright daylight, rubbing the shaved sides of his head. "What the hell?"

"Lyle, something important came up. I need to talk to you."

Lyle opened the door wider. Roger saw Sophie come down a circular stairway already dressed. He caught her eye. "No," he told Lyle loud enough for Sophie to hear. "I won't come in. I need to talk to you somewhere in private." As Lyle turned to go get dressed, Roger gave Sophie a slight nod.

Lyle left his driver posted by the villa door. When the truck pulled off the road onto the same barren spot as before, he growled, "This better be real important. You were supposed to be on a plane back by now."

"That's what I needed to talk to you about. I'm going to stay here another week. Omar insists."

Lyle's whole head turned red. "The hell you are. You're going to take the next plane out of here and bring that key to me."

Roger needed to keep Lyle away from the house as long as possible. "You expect me to get you the key when you've never told me what's going on. What's this bank business you keep talking about?"

Lyle squinted. "I don't know whether you're playing dumb or you are dumb. Jill must have explained this. Right now the money's in a vault at Grayrock's Camp Rectitude personal asset storage facility. We needed to make sure the Pulshui Bank president could be trusted before we moved all that cash into an account in his bank. Had to be sure he wouldn't take it all for himself or give it away to friends and politicians like the Kabul Bank CEOs who got caught doing that back in Karzai's regime. But this guy, Daghal, checked out. He's strictly a money launderer for depositors. He's been at it a long time. He gets ten percent of each transfer to Germany." Lyle winked. "There's somebody else who gets a cut, too, but Daghal doesn't know about that yet. I'll tell him when we deposit the money."

"But Jill never—"

"Forget about Jill. She's out of this now. My job is to deposit the money in the Pulshui Bank account of a fake company we set up that supposedly makes and sells soft drinks here. Your job is to send Daghal monthly invoices from a phony beverage supply company we set up in Baltimore, which he'll pay by transferring money to its account in a German bank that keeps its customers' accounts private. I'll let you know when to start. As the money comes in, transfer it from the German bank into the Bank of Baltimore account that Jill opened."

"This is all new to me. I'm not sure I can—"

Lyle twisted Roger's wrist. "You don't understand. Your time is running out. I need Jill's key to get the process started."

"Doesn't Jill herself have to be in possession of the key? I don't know how these things work, but—"

"Don't worry about that. Nobody knows what Jill looks like. There's another woman I can use to stand in for her."

Roger needed to keep Lyle talking. "But what if I can't find the key. I mean I already looked everywhere for a spare key to Jill's Land Rover and didn't find one. I guess I can look again. She never told you where she kept it, did she? Because—"

Lyle's phone rang. Roger heard the driver's voice. "Miss Sophie, she left with two suits case."

"Huh? You mean suitcases? And you didn't you stop her?"

Roger didn't hear the guard's reply. Lyle shoved his phone into his pocket. "Get back in the truck."

They stopped in front of the Turkish Airlines office. "Listen," Lyle told him. "We're on the same side. Don't you see that? You're going to be rich. I don't want to hurt you. Go into that office and book the next flight home. Grayrock will reimburse you after you bring me the key." He gave Roger a pat on the back and winked.

As soon as Lyle drove away, Roger called Sophie.

"Roger," she said, "I'm at the Femmes en Crise aid workers' housing at Green Village. I had just enough time to get out. Thank you. I wish I could thank you in person."

"So you'll be OK there?"

Sophie sniffled. "Remember when you said you hoped I wasn't afraid of Lyle? Well, the truth is I am."

"Would Lyle go to your room in the aid workers housing?"

"He might, but Lexi's with me and Nora's in a room nearby."

"What do you plan to do?"

"I don't know. I've made him angry now. He knows where our Femmes in Crise school is. I'm afraid he'll go there looking for me."

It pained Roger to think of Sophie disappearing from his life. But the best thing for her was to go back to Belgium. "I think now is a good time to take the thirty days' leave you've earned and go home, Sophie."

"That's what Lexi thinks. She wants me to leave tonight. There's an 8:30 flight."

"I'll miss you. We were just getting to know each other. But I think that's best."

"I wonder. If I do, would it be possible for you to come to the airport to see me off? Lexi and Nora can't come, and I don't want to go alone."

"I'll take you there. Pick you up at the Femmes in Crise housing in Green Village, right?"

"Yes. The taxi driver might assume you're going to Camp Rectitude. That's Grayrock's headquarters. It's in Green Village, too." She gave a nervous laugh. "Make sure he doesn't take you there."

The taxi finally broke through the jammed traffic circle on Wazir Akbar Khan Street and sped down a wide four-lane highway. Roger kept checking the time on his phone with sweaty hands. He caught his breath as the driver eventually made a sharp left turn narrowly missing an oncoming military transport truck. "Russia Road," the sign said in Roman letters. The taxi stopped at a gated entrance with a guard tower in a concrete wall topped with coils of razor concertina wire. Roger's American passport did the trick, and the taxi was waved inside.

They drove past acres of new cars and trucks lined up next to each other like the new cars at Baltimore's Dundalk shipping terminal. The taxi stopped at a dusty expanse of rooms on two levels that looked to Roger like a cheap 1950s motel. Sophie stood waiting outside one of the units with her friend Lexi and director Nora. The driver loaded her baggage into the taxi while the women hugged Sophie. "*Promettez que tu reviendras.*"

Dusk darkened the view along the tree-lined highway that led to the airport. Sophie sat close to Roger. She was sniffling. "They made me promise to come back. I want to. But I don't know. I'm afraid of Lyle. He's going to hate me for leaving when he told me not to."

Roger reached for her hand but stopped himself. He tried to think of something comforting. "You've been here a year. You've already done a lot of good. Maybe it's time to quit."

Traffic on the airport road was slowed behind a flatbed truck carrying a plain wooden coffin. The taxi driver cursed and passed two cars and the truck at once, pulling back into the right lane just in time to avoid being hit head-on by a bus. They stopped at an airport guard post where Sophie and Roger showed their passports, then pulled up in front of the baby blue buttresses of the new terminal.

The airport was swarming with passengers and their families seeing them off. Most were men, and most wore baggy white robes with vests or suit coats over them. Armed guards in camouflage uniforms stood everywhere, some holding automatic rifles. Everything seemed more menacing than when Roger had arrived with Omar as his guide.

He stood beside Sophie as she joined the long line at the Turkish Airlines check-in counter. In the pushing and shoving, a rancid smell of nervous sweat filled the air. Announcements in Dari,

Pashto, and English warned passengers to report any abandoned packages. The fair, blue-eyed Sophie attracted a stream of hustlers and aggressive porters as well as men who were simply curious, wanting a closer look. It was clear she'd learned long ago how to fend them off. "*Boro*," she said. Roger took it to mean *Go away.*

When her baggage was finally checked, Sophie needed to go through security inspection. Roger planned to stand in line with her as long as he could. He'd have to say good-bye when she reached the check point. She shook his hand. "I wish you were coming with me." Her face reddened. "You've just lost your wife. I shouldn't have said that."

"Maybe I shouldn't say this either, but I don't want to lose you."

Roger felt a push against his back and turned around. *Bebakhshid*, the man behind him apologized. Then Roger saw someone back by the baggage check-in with his head lifted, trying to see over the crowd. The sides of his head were shaved close.

"Lyle's here," Roger whispered. "I think he's coming this way."

Sophie pulled a black full-body chador from her backpack and threw it on. She put on sunglasses. "You have to go," she whispered. "You're too easy to recognize." She gave his hand a squeeze.

"Call me when you get home?"

Sophie swallowed, nodded.

Roger took another look and didn't see Lyle. So he went to a newsstand where he could watch the line for security inspection. Sophie had neared the front of the line, but an argument broke out at the desk. The line stopped moving. There was some shouting. Bystanders came to see what was going on. Roger saw Lyle approaching with them.

Lyle was scanning the line of passengers. Roger got ready to … do what? Anything to make sure Sophie got on that plane. He edged forward, gripping his fists, holding his breath.

Lyle was pressing as close to the passengers as the crowd allowed. On tip-toes he looked closely at the three or four foreign women, then studied the figure in the black chador. She was hunched over now like an old woman. The pack under the chador gave her the appearance of a hunchback. Roger took another step forward, but Lyle turned and shoved his way out of the crowd, heading for the airport exit.

Roger followed him at a distance until he saw him leave, then hurried back to the departure area. But Sophie had already boarded the plane.

He stood by the window and watched it take off.

He'd report Lyle to USAID the next day. After that, there was no longer a reason to stay in Afghanistan. He'd already told Omar and Amal he was probably going home the next evening. He bought his ticket before leaving the airport.

11

R & R

Early the next morning, Roger found Omar in the garden. "You told me you wanted to bring your whole family to the States, Omar. I hope we'll all stay close friends when you get there."

"Yes. But this is the problem, Mr. Roger. You have heard of the Muslim ban? It's now Muslim ban, attempt number three, and this one has been approved by the Supreme Court."

Roger hadn't thought of that. It was laughable to think of Omar's family as enemies of the United States. "My brother knows some American Civil Liberties lawyers. When I get back, I'll ask if there's anything we can do."

His hand on his heart, Omar thanked him. When Roger said he needed to go inside to pack, Omar stopped him. "Before you leave, I'd like to know something. This friend of Mr. Lyle you saw off at the airport last night, she is truly his friend?"

Roger didn't know how to answer.

"Because yesterday our little Musa took Mr. Lyle's houseboy some sweets Amal had made, and the lady wasn't there. The boy said he heard Mr. Lyle cursing her."

"Lyle gets angry easily."

Omar rubbed his stubbled chin. "Yes, I have seen this. My daughter Amal tells me he is not such a good man. I'm beginning to believe it."

Roger couldn't tell Omar what he knew about Lyle. Anybody who knew Lyle's secrets was sure to be "taken care of." He'd tell Omar everything after Lyle was arrested. Roger had to make sure that happened. "Before I leave," he said, "I need to go to the USAID office."

He'd found out the USAID office was in the embassy compound, a city of giant concrete blocks within a city. The number
of blockades around the compound was almost comical. The taxi
driver drove him as far as he was allowed. From the main gate at
Massoud Circle, Roger had to walk, be searched, show his passport,
and explain what he wanted at station after station until he found
himself in what he assumed was the USAID office, shivering in the
windowless air conditioned room on a cold metal chair in front of
a Marine sergeant who looked extremely annoyed. Roger told her
everything he knew about what Lyle had done and was planning.

The sergeant listened but wrote nothing down. After maybe half
an hour, when he had finished, she made a call to somebody else,
then informed Roger, "This is a matter for USAID. They're in the
Café Compound across the road."

And so Roger explained it all over again to a clean-shaven
young staff member in his twenties whose trembling hands gave the
impression he was new at the job. He did take notes. "This seems
serious," he said in what Roger considered an understatement. "But
you can rest assured your report will go directly to the U.S. senator
who oversees the Grayrock mission."

The farewell meal went on and on. One dish after another was
set on the sofré cloth, and Amal heaped more and more food on
Roger's plate until he begged her to stop. He had never drunk so
much Pepsi in his life.

He called his brother and arranged to be picked up in D.C.
Omar's whole family was coming with him to see him off at the airport. Roger walked out of Omar's house in front of the others, and,
when he did, Omar threw some water on the ground behind him.

Roger turned in surprise.

"For good luck on your trip," Omar explained. "Not that I'm
superstitious."

At the airport boarding ramp, Roger got more hugs than he'd
ever had in his life.

After he said goodbye and started onto the boarding ramp, his phone rang. Sophie.

"Roger my connecting flight in Istanbul was canceled. I'm stuck here for another day."

"I'm headed there right now." The phone connection was weak. He heard Sophie say "overnight." Roger backed up against the ramp enclosure to let the passengers pass by him. "Sophie," he nearly shouted, "where are you staying?"

"The hotel at the airport. Do you think we can meet?"

"Yes. I'll be there in six hours."

Roger leaned his head against the cool plastic curtain over the plane window. His heart was pounding. He and Sophie were about to meet in a neutral country where nobody knew them, nobody could find them. He realized he'd wanted this for some time but hadn't admitted it to himself.

When he got off the plane, she was waving to him at the debarkation ramp. He dropped his duffel bag beside her and reached to take her hand. Sophie moved as if to give him a hug, then checked herself. They stood looking in each other's eyes for a moment until Roger threw his arms around her. Her arms held him, too, and she murmured against his chest, "Oh. This is …. Look at us."

The tour guides had already spotted them. "Topkapi. Hagia Sophia. The Blue Mosque."

"How much time do you have?" Sophie asked.

"How about you?"

"Until this time tomorrow."

"I'll change my flight, call my brother."

"I was hoping you would. I didn't go to any of the sights. We could go together."

They went to Hagia Sophia first—"my namesake," Sophie said. The tour guide assumed they were married. It felt like they were. The guide offered to take their picture. "Don't worry," Sophie told her. "I'll never forget we were here."

They stood looking at the church, turned mosque, turned museum. "*Formidable*," exclaimed Sophie. "But it looks somehow squat and industrial compared to a real mosque like the ones in Afghanistan. They're more beautiful."

"You sound like an Afghan. But I know what you mean."

When they got back to the tour bus, Sophie rubbed her eyes. "The Blue Mosque is next. But I'm tired. I didn't sleep much last night."

"Neither did I."

They left the tour and took a taxi back to the Airport Hotel. In her room, Roger kicked off his shoes. "All right if I just lie here on the bed a minute?"

The next thing he knew, a pink setting sun was framed in the tenth-floor window. Sophie was lying next to him, asleep. With her long black lashes, her eyes were beautiful even when closed. He touched her cheek. It was even softer than he'd imagined. She didn't wake up. He edged closer, put his arm around her, and felt her breath on his neck.

The roar of a plane outside the window made her stir. She opened her eyes. "Oh. Roger."

"Looks like we both fell asleep."

She sat up, blinking. Pulled her hair aside.

Roger sat beside her. "We're in Istanbul, in case you forgot."

"I did, for a second." Sophie lifted her face towards his, searched his eyes, and then closed hers. Roger leaned towards her and felt her soft lips on his. She slid her arms around him. "What if we stayed here forever?" she said. "Started our life over again in a country where nobody knows either of us?"

They went to the window and looked down on the sprawling metropolis. Roger imagined all his problems floating away as he stood behind her, arms around her waist.

"Are you hungry?" Roger asked. "I could call room service."

"Later. I want to take a quick shower."

She came back out in a white bathrobe.

Roger showered, too, and when he came out, Sophie was standing by the window in an ornate Afghan dress. "Surprise!" She turned her back towards him. "I need some help."

She stood motionless while he fastened the long line of buttons, allowing his fingers to slide along her back. She stood there, her hand over her mouth, as he took his time. "There," Roger finally said. He bent to kiss her neck.

She spun around, her flowing dark hair accenting the silver embroidery on the red silk cloth. "What do you think?"

"I think you're beautiful."

She twirled again, sending the long skirt flying. "I wondered if I'd ever have a chance to wear it. You know when I first imagined putting it on?"

"When?"

"That day I met you."

He pulled her close and the touch of her lips stirred a warmth in his chest he'd never felt before. Her gentle kiss responded to his.

"I'm not hungry any more," Roger said.

"Neither am I."

"I don't want to wrinkle your dress."

"Well, at least you saw me in it for a few minutes. Maybe I should—"

He reached around and began to unbutton it. "Oh," Sophie gasped. "Guess what I have on underneath."

"What?"

"Nothing."

Roger's heart was pounding as his fingers continued down the line of buttons.

They lay together, and she clung to him, closing her eyes, taking sharp little breaths when he touched her. Roger sensed he was holding the person he was truly meant to be with.

It was a long night of gentle, intimate love, and in the morning

Roger didn't want to go home. "Maybe we could stay here longer," he ventured. "I could call my brother—"

"I will if you want." Sophie sounded tentative. "My mother told everybody I'd be home this evening."

"So you should be there." Roger bit his lip.

"Come to Belgium with me."

"I'd like to. I can't, though. There are some things I have to take care of when I get home."

"Maybe I could come to America."

"Sophie, I have to tell you. You're safer in Belgium right now. I know of crimes Lyle has committed and I've reported him to USAID. It won't be long before he finds that out."

"What are you talking about?"

"I'll tell you if you promise to stay in Belgium until I know you're safe from Lyle. The money that was supposed to go to your teacher-training program? Lyle and Jill stole it."

Sophie's eyes slowly teared up. She dropped her face into her hands. "I'm so stupid."

"No. No. Lyle has everybody fooled. For a long time, Omar considered him a great hero."

"But Lyle's in Afghanistan, Roger. Wouldn't we be safe in America?"

"Lyle killed the Belgian who was guarding the money. He won't hesitate to track down and kill any 'enemy' informer."

Sophie was sobbing. "Like you? You mean he might go after you in America?"

"And you, too, if he thinks you reported him. I want you to come to America, Sophie. I really do. But not until Lyle is arrested. I need to follow up on that report I made to USAID in Kabul to make sure they get him."

Sophie's eyes met his. "Are we ever going to see each other again?"

"I'll find a way."

"*Enshallah*? Is that what you mean?" She collapsed onto the bed, her face in the pillow.

Roger put his hand on her shoulder, stroked her hair. "I'll make sure of it, Sophie. I promise."

Sophie's flight took off first. Roger stood with her in the security inspection line. When she passed through and turned to throw him a kiss, he stepped out of line, took a bottle of water he'd bought, and poured some on the tile floor behind her. Sophie grinned, gave him a thumbs up.

A guard rushed forward and seized Roger, taking the water bottle. Roger was sure he was headed for an infamous Turkish prison. But the guard's grip on his arms loosened as he eyed the puddle on the floor. He looked at Roger, then at Sophie, and slowly broke into a broad smile. Roger allowed himself to take a breath. It seemed that the farewell custom was understood in Turkey as well as in Afghanistan.

12

Butter on the wrapper

Dan waved to Roger at the Dulles arrival gate. He shouldered Roger's duffel bag. "You look terrible, Buddy. Losing your wife, that must be heartbreaking."

"Yeah. There's a lot I have to tell you."

On the ride home, Roger told his brother everything he'd found out about Lyle and Jill.

"Shit. So you're saying Jill was in on it?"

"And somehow I'm all tangled up in it, too. But you have to keep all this to yourself, Dan. I've already reported Lyle to USAID. He's dangerous. He threatened to come after me and anybody I told."

As they stopped in front of Roger's dark house under the spreading trees, the headlights automatically turned off. Roger sat staring in silence at the vacant house. He thought of Lyle's warning about the witness who killed Jill: "Keep your head down."

"Want to sleep on my couch tonight, Buddy?"

"Thanks, Dan. But I just want to collapse in my own bed." And dream of Sophie.

Roger unlocked the door and gave Dan a thumbs-up as he drove away. Before going into the house, he walked off the porch and looked around. No sign of any "Special Forces type" lurking under the trees. Or behind the Land Rover. He pulled a handful of mail from the box. It was mostly junk mail, but when he sifted through it, he found his M.A. diploma. It meant less to him now than he had expected.

The house had a musty smell that he only noticed when he'd been away for some time. Before he could reach the light, he tripped against something. It was a laundry basket where he'd left it after gathering up Jill's clothes from the bedroom floor. He turned on a lamp and searched through one room after another, then stopped beside the table holding Jill's FAX machine. A skimpy blouse lay where it was tossed over the arm of the tattered chair Jill used for "business." He had a vision of her pulling it off, flinging it aside. Jill had never been shy about flaunting her body. But she'd been hiding everything else.

He now understood why she often said a windfall of money was coming her way, that she would buy a house in an exclusive North Charles Street neighborhood. The talk of a dreamer—that's what Roger had thought. He had never recognized it for the bluster of a criminal.

Roger's phone app showed Belgium was six hours ahead of East Coast time. So not a good time to call. He began a text to Sophie when the phone rang. Sophie.

"Roger, it's me. I thought you might be back."

"Isn't it almost three in the morning there?"

"Yes. I couldn't sleep. Guess what. I went to the Ministry of Foreign Affairs in Brussels and reported everything you told me about Lyle. I talked to the Deputy Minister himself."

"What did he say?"

"He asked if there were any witnesses."

"I'll talk to him if he wants."

"OK, but you aren't actually a witness."

Roger didn't want to tell Sophie about the one actual witness— the man who might be lurking around his house. "You're right," he said. "But here's what the Belgian officials could do. Keep an eye on Lyle's villa. And have somebody watch the Pulshui Bank, where Lyle's planning to bring the money to be laundered." He worried about getting Sophie involved in this. "But, Sophie, Lyle can never know you reported him. You can't go back to Afghanistan as long as he's there."

"I wish you could come here. My mother wouldn't stop asking

questions about you. I told her your wife left you. I didn't mention you were pretty sure she was dead. I couldn't tell Mom how old you were, where you were born, where you went to school, how sad you were to lose your wife ... and if she was pretty."

"Twenty-nine. Maryland. Towson University. Getting over it. Not nearly as pretty as you."

"Oh. OK. Actually, the last item was my own question."

"I suspected that."

"She also asked about your plans for the future."

"Did she? Tell her I'm open to suggestion."

"Well maybe I can come up with something."

Roger asked Sophie the same questions. She was an only child. He'd assumed as much since she'd never mentioned a brother or sister. Her mother ran a daycare center. Her father smoked a pipe, took care of their small farm, and talked about politics. She'd studied biology in college. Her friend Lexi had introduced her to Femmes en Crise. Her father thought going to help out in Afghanistan was a great idea. She wanted to go to graduate school when she finished her service in Afghanistan.

"Boyfriends?" Roger asked.

"I liked one guy in high school. He ended up with somebody else."

"After that?"

"Same thing in college."

"You mean—"

"Same exact thing."

"*Belzhik yā Afghānestān, kodām behtar ast?*" They'd both been asked the question by Afghans so many times about their own countries he'd memorized it. "Belgium or Afghanistan, which is better?"

Sophie chuckled. "I still haven't come up with a good answer to that."

The USAID official in Kabul had told Roger he'd send his report to the chairman of the Senate Foreign Aid committee. For several days Roger tried to reach the committee by phone. Finally he gave up and drove directly to Senator Steinherz's D.C. office instead.

"I've come from Afghanistan with a report on Grayrock for Senator Steinherz," he told a guard, then a secretary, then a staff member until he was searched and let in to a walnut paneled room to wait. Another young staff member in an expensive suit and haircut came in with a clipboard. "Mr. Williams, yes? The senator is occupied at the present and asked me to see if I could help you."

"I made a report to USAID in Kabul. Did you get it?"

The staffer rolled his eyes. "We get reports every day. Maybe you can tell me—"

"A robbery and murder by a Grayrock employee."

The young man flushed and tapped some papers on his clipboard. "I don't get every report myself. Can you excuse me a minute?"

Senator Steinherz came in, buttoning his suit coat and smoothing down his bleached hair. He gave Roger a long, sweaty handshake. "I understand you've returned recently from Kabul. So have I." He smiled as he studied Roger with shifting eyes. "Have a seat, young man. Can I get you anything? Coffee? Glass of the South's finest bourbon?"

"I'm here to talk about a robbery and murder."

The senator sat beside him on the couch, unbuttoning his coat, inclining his full-cheeked head towards Roger. "A mix-up. I understand. Pardon me if I don't seem alarmed. A certain amount of funds are always going missing in this business. Our AID office takes that into account. If they tried to track down every dollar that went to Afghanistan—"

"And murder? You take a certain number of murders into account?"

The senator stiffened. "Murder? Of course not. But I have to tell you. In a violent country like Afghanistan, we have to expect some fatalities." He coughed. "Don't get me wrong. I've read this report of yours. We'll look into it. I promise you. I've asked our Grayrock liaison Mr. Ignacio Corelli to make a thorough investigation."

It was like asking the fox to investigate a hen house murder,

Roger thought. "Not your own committee? They're not going to investigate?"

"You should go and talk to Mr. Corelli. I'm sure you'll find him a very competent overseer." The senator rose and gripped Roger's hand. "My office will call Iggy, tell him to expect you."

The Grayrock "government liaison offices" in the Watergate complex overlooked the murky Potomac River. When Roger was ushered into the office, a man with light, short-cropped hair looked up from an expansive desk. As Roger stepped across the thick gray carpet, he noticed a book on the desk entitled *Triumphs of the East India Company: A Strategy for Success.*

"Curious about that book, are you?" Iggy sniggered. "The Grayrock president lent it to me. He plans for Grayrock in Afghanistan to evolve into a version of Britain's East India Company, running the whole show."

Iggy didn't stand but leaned forward in his padded leather chair to take Roger's fingertips. He jerked up his eyebrows to dismiss the woman who'd brought Roger in. "Senator Steinherz told me to expect you. I have it from Lyle White that you can be trusted."

"The senator said he was going to ask you to investigate—"

"Don't worry about that. Sit down, please. We need to talk. First of all, I must offer you my sympathy on the death of you wife. A terrible mishap. Lyle gave me the disturbing news."

"I'm not here to talk about Jill."

Iggy ignored this. "Lyle warned her there was somebody causing trouble. Grayrock has its enemies. You need to watch your own back. There's always a blackmailer or somebody who wants his cut. Lyle insists this Special Forces guy will *not* be cut in."

"Don't you realize I gave a report to the USAID office in Kabul detailing Lyle's armed robbery and murder?"

"And that report was forwarded to the senator. Again, Roger, put all of that out of your mind. I'm sure the senator told you the government expects some money to be diverted. They factor it in. It's like the butter left on the wrapper after you take it off. There's not going to be any investigation. The senator thought I could straighten a few things out for you."

"What are you talking about? You mean the senator—"

"Is a friend of Grayrock. We have nothing to fear from him."

"You're talking about bribery?"

"Well, Grayrock makes generous campaign contributions." Iggy gave an amused snort. "But with some people, other things count even more than money. There might be personal activities the senator doesn't want to become public."

With a start, Roger realized that Lyle would never be charged and arrested. All he could do now was keep himself safe from him.

"Cheer up," Iggy said. "You need to understand you haven't lost everything. The portion of the assets you and your wife were to share will now revert solely to you." Iggy forced a thin smile. "Everything's in place. Just take Lyle the key."

"I'm not sure if I—"

"Lyle needs that vault key. Grayrock has a charter transport plane leaving from Baltimore-Washington International Airport in five days. I've already notified the crew you'll be on it. If you're not, Lyle's going to come looking for you in search-and-destroy mode."

13

The Straw Man

If neither USAID nor the senator's Foreign Aid Committee nor Grayrock were going to pursue Lyle, it was up to Roger. He had to find that key. He'd take it to Lyle, hoping to find a way to trap him when he went to take money from the vault in Kabul.

He searched the house room by room until the humid air had him dripping with sweat. Exhausted, with nowhere else to look, he went out to sit on the porch and cool off. He had five days to keep Lyle from coming for him in "search-and-destroy mode." That is, if the Special Forces guy who killed Jill didn't get to him first.

He cast his eyes around the yard alert for movement, shadows—a habit he'd gotten into since he'd been back. Nothing. The Land Rover, covered with green and yellow pollen, sat planted in his driveway like a permanent affront. It was the only place he hadn't looked for the vault key. Couldn't look.

In a combination of desperation, fear, and despair, Roger gritted his teeth, walked to the edge of an overgrown flower garden, wedged up a concrete block, held it over his head, and smashed it through the Land Rover window. A high-pitched alarm blared out.

Roger reached through the window, opened the door, popped the hood, and twisted off one of the battery wires. The alarm stopped, and Roger looked around. The houses on Shadow Cove Avenue were old and separated by tree-filled lots. If anybody did hear the alarm, nobody came out to check. False alarm—that's what people usually assumed.

Roger swept the little chunks of safety glass from the car seat onto the floor. The glove compartment was locked. He got a screwdriver and pried it open. There was nothing inside.

Where would you hide something in a car? He opened the rear hatch. There was a compartment in the floor. He lifted the cover, exposing a jack and lug wrench. No sign of a key. But the carpeting on the hatch seemed loose. It was slit. He slid his fingers inside and pulled out a sealed manila envelope. He tore it open. It held legal papers of some kind.

And a key.

He called his brother but could hardly hear over the blaring music and raucous chatter. "Where are you, Dan?"

"Ocean City. An office retreat. That's what we're calling it. Spouses and friends, all invited."

"When are you getting back to Baltimore?"

"We're here for a week. Lots of feminine pulchritude on the beach. Come on down. There's an extra bed in my room."

Roger couldn't wait a week for Dan to get back home. "If you're sure it's OK."

Cars were backed up over the Chesapeake Bay Bridge, and it took over three hours to get to the condominium Dan's office colleagues had rented. "Just in time," Dan grinned. "We invited some ladies on the next floor to join us at the Irish Pub for happy hour."

Roger ignored that. "Dan, I need to discuss something important." He showed him the documents.

"Nothing in a manila envelope is more important than ladies waiting for us in a pub. Perfect chance for a newly single guy to get back in the mix."

"All right, I'll go with you. I didn't mention this before, but I guess you could say I'm already 'back in the mix.'"

Dan put down his beer, stared at Roger for an explanation.

"I've met a girl."

"What, in Afghanistan? You've got to be kidding."

"I'm serious. She's Belgian."

"When were you going to tell me?"

"I was embarrassed. I wanted to wait for proof that Jill's dead.

They still haven't identified the soldier killed at Fort Davis, right?"

"Not yet." Dan picked up his can of beer and drained it. "I'm worried about you, Roger. You let Jill come on like an ambulance chaser and sign you up for life. How did that turn out? And now you tell me—"

"She's nothing like Jill. She's a teacher. She works for the aid group that Lyle and Jill robbed."

"Uh-huh. Uh-huh. And you've known her how long? Oh, no. This time you'll need to get approval from all of us before you—"

"I'll go along with that."

"Shake on it. There will be a formal interview process, you understand? Mom and Dad, with me presiding."

Roger knew he deserved Dan's razzing. "See? That's why I didn't tell you as soon as you picked me up at the airport."

Dan pulled two cans of National Bohemian from the mini-fridge. "Here. Loosen up. The ladies are waiting. Never hurts to expand your options."

Irish melodies rang out onto the boardwalk. Inside the pub, the customers sang along with a long-haired mandolin player. Dan's colleagues called him to a group of tables pulled together. A few young women sat with them, but it was too noisy to talk or do anything but drink pitchers of beer and sing. Roger, in fact, began to loosen up. He started to sing along with the others, faking the words he didn't know.

"Your brother says you were in Afghanistan," a reddish-haired woman nearly shouted in his ear.

He nodded.

"On business?"

"Sort of," he shouted back.

"My husband and I aren't with Dan's outfit. We work with the ACLU."

Roger put his hand to his ear.

"The American Civil Liberties Union," she shouted. Her husband reached across her to shake his hand. "John. My wife Chrissy."

"What's it like it over there?" Chrissy asked. "We're working with people applying for visas from that part of the world."

Over the beer drinkers roaring out a chorus, all Roger could say was "It's different from here."

"More beer, you say?" John poured some into his glass until it overflowed onto the table.

Chrissy emptied her glass. "I love coming down the ocean. You?"

Roger nodded. "Me too."

Chrissy and John got up to leave. "See you at the beach tomorrow?" John suggested.

Across the table, Dan and a woman with freckled cheeks faced each other singing. When the song ended, he signaled for another pitcher. Roger went out for a walk on the beach.

The moon hung low over the ocean. He slipped off the sandals he'd brought from Kabul and waded at the silvery edge of the surf. Sophie would be asleep now. He wondered if she liked swimming in the ocean. Maybe she'd never done it. Or if she would like going to Irish pubs and singing along. He wondered if life in America, or at least his life in America, would seem as strange to her as life in Afghanistan at first seemed to him.

He walked along the beach and back to the condo. Maybe it was the beer, the beach, the singing, the thought of swimming tomorrow, but he dropped onto his bed feeling more relaxed than he'd felt for a long time.

The next thing he knew it was morning and Dan was waking him up. "You going to sleep all day? Come on. The women are waiting on the beach."

"Women?"

"My Freckle Face and the others. Don't remember their names."

Roger glanced at the manila envelope on the dresser, then looked through the window down at the beach. Dan was right. Business could wait a little while.

The ocean washing over his body brought back the thrill he remembered from when his mother and father used to bring them here when they were kids. He swam far out, floating easily in the salty water, and caught wave after wave, body-surfing them back to shore.

"Hey." It was Chrissy. "Nice ride. You caught a good one."

Her husband John offered him a chair under their umbrella. "Dan says you have friends in Afghanistan?"

"Yeah. In fact they're trying to get a visa for the whole family to come here. They thought they were approved, but then some glitch turned up."

"Maybe we can help," John suggested. "We've had a little luck recently despite the Muslim ban. The way the application is filled out is crucial sometimes."

"Let us know if there's something we can do," Chrissy added. "Seriously."

Roger asked if they used WhatsApp.

"Chrissy nodded, dug her phone out of a basket, and took Roger's number.

"How many in your friend's family?" John asked.

"Mother, father, four children. Two of them adopted."

"Officially adopted? Papers to prove it?"

"Yes, I'm pretty sure."

"Who's bringing them here?"

"The woman's father. Omar. He's a U.S. citizen."

John nodded. Chrissy said they'd need "the names, birth dates, lots of other information."

"I'll get you that information," Roger said.

Even under the umbrella the sun was hot. The three of them ran into the ocean to cool off. They swam far out, staying until they were exhausted. When they came back, Dan joined them under the umbrella—sans Freckle Face.

Later they all ate hot dogs and French fries and walked along the boardwalk. The day was over before Roger knew it. "Glad you came," Dan told him. "Tomorrow maybe we try crabbing in the bay."

"Dan, I can't. I have to go home tomorrow."

"What's the hurry?"

"It's a long story. I have to go back to Kabul." He told Dan about the flight he had to be on to bring Lyle the vault key. "You'll understand better if you look through these documents."

Dan spread the legal-sized papers out on the table in their room, frowning. "What the hell are you up to?"

"Jill must have forged my signature. I never saw any of these before."

"You're the 'Nominee Director' of a company. That's a straw man that the real owners hide behind so nobody will know who they are."

"So I'm the Straw Man. The one without a brain."

Dan wasn't listening. "Everything's in your name. Jill and Lyle aren't mentioned anywhere." Then he chuckled. "This is hilarious. *Beverage Supplies*, located at a post office box near your house, pretends to be a vendor of vats, funnels, syrup, bottles—everything for making soft drinks. The plan is for them to send bills to another shell company in Kabul called *Bebsi LLC* that pretends to make and sell the drinks."

Roger saw that the Bebsi address was the same as the Pulshui Bank.

Dan fanned out another stack of papers. "Look at all these invoices. They have to add up to a fortune. All signed by you. No dates on them yet. They're ready to be sent out little by little."

"Lyle told me to hold on to them and he'll let me know when to start billing that Kabul company."

"Bebsi, you mean. The invoices go to *Bebsi*." Dan was enjoying this.

"Then I'm to transfer the payments I get from a bank in Germany to the Bank of Baltimore."

Dan kept reading through the papers. "Look here. You've already signed an undated resignation letter. I've heard of this before. It's so they can get rid of you if you ever start wanting to act like a real director and do anything other than let them keep using your name."

"I'm not sure what to do."

Dan grinned. "Well, you could just *let it go.*"

"Huh?"

"You could just do what Lyle says. As soon as he gives the go-ahead, start sending out the invoices—and get rich. The receiving account here in Baltimore is in your name as Nominee Director."

"Until Lyle decides to get rid of me once the money transfers start. He could set up a new unsuspecting straw director and keep all the money for himself."

"That seems likely. Anyway, I was kidding. Of course, you have to take these papers to the FBI."

"I know. But my name's all over them. Do they put me in any legal trouble?"

"I don't think so. Big companies do this all the time to hide their money. Believe it or not, the laws allow setting up fake corporations and straw directors. One difference here, though. The money comes from a robbery and murder."

14

As if nothing has changed

The front door of his house was open when Roger got back from Ocean City the next day. He was sure he'd closed and locked it. Carefully, he stepped inside. The couch cushions were pulled up and all the kitchen drawers had been emptied onto the floor. "Anybody here?" He peeped into the bedroom. The dresser drawers were pulled out. Roger checked the rest of the house. Somebody had been searching for something. It had to be the witness who killed Jill, probably looking for Jill's key to the vault.

He called the Baltimore Police and was connected to the officer who'd taken his missing persons complaint. "You say nothing valuable is missing? Sounds like the wife returned to pick up a few things. You didn't have a restraining order on her, did you? All right. I'll send some guys out to try to get prints, but there's not much else we can do."

In half an hour, two policewomen arrived, took Roger's fingerprints, and went through the rest of the house in a painfully slow process of trying to lift prints from knobs, cabinets, and drawers. "Can't say we found much that's going to be useful," one of them said as they left.

Roger was sitting at the kitchen table with his head in his hands when Sophie called. "Me again."

"Ugh, not again!"

Sophie chuckled, but her voice quickly turned serious. "I told the Deputy Minister of Foreign Affairs what you said. He now says that before charging an American coalition partner with a crime he needs proof."

"I might have found some proof." Roger told her about the papers he'd found. "But I don't want to take them to USAID."

"Why not?"

"They'd certainly be turned over to Senator Steinherz, just like my report was. And Steinherz would do nothing. I found out he's is in Grayrock's pocket."

"Pardon? Oh, I think I see what you mean." She seemed to be thinking. "Well, the Belgian Deputy Minister of Foreign Affairs isn't in anybody's pocket. If he got the papers, that would be the proof they need. Do you think you could bring them here to Belgium?"

Roger's heart quickened at the thought, but it was impossible if he was going to bring Lyle the key on the flight Iggy had arranged for him. "As much as I want to, I can't right now. But hold on." He searched Google. "FedEx International Next Flight. I'll send them."

She sounded disappointed. "OK. Send them to me in care of the Deputy Minister at the Belgian Ministry of Foreign Affairs. I'll text you the address."

"I love you, Sophie."

"*Moi aussi. Je t'aime.*"

FedEx sent the papers off on the flight to Brussels that evening. It was definitely too late to call Sophie again. But in Kabul it was already six the next morning. He texted Omar, asking if he'd heard from Lyle. Just before Roger went to bed he got an answer. *Still hasn't come to visit. Houseboy says he is on a mission.*

Before going to bed, Roger turned on the late news: two people shot and killed that day in Baltimore; a third in "serious condition." Police had no suspects or motive. But the serious faces of the newscasters shifted immediately to giddy delight as they reported that rain was finally on the way.

The next morning Roger awoke to a tremendous downpour. No need to rush and close the windows. With the Special Forces man who killed Jill on the loose, even though Roger had no air conditioning, he was keeping all the windows closed and locked. He went out onto the covered porch, which was streaming water from leaks in two places. The rain battered on the tin roof and on the cars in the driveway. Roger noticed it pouring through the broken window of Jill's Rover. With a feeling of great satisfaction, he sat in a porch chair to watch.

He didn't know how long he'd been sitting there when Sophie called.

"I thought you'd be up by now. I went to the Foreign Ministry early this morning. They got the papers. The Deputy Minister was shocked. He's flying to Kabul. He's going to contact the Afghan Major Crimes Task Force. They work with the FBI."

"Sophie, one thing I haven't mentioned yet. Lyle needs a second key to get into the Grayrock vault. I found it along with the papers I sent you. Can you suggest the Belgian minister hold off until Lyle gets it? Then it should be possible to trap him taking the money to the Pulshui bank."

"You'll send the key to Lyle?"

"Yeah, or whatever." The transport plane to Kabul that Roger needed to be on left the next day. But he didn't want Sophie to worry. He'd tell her after he delivered the key and Lyle was arrested.

"OK." Sophie seemed distracted. "I told the minister—his name's DeWoot—that Lyle was texting me, insisting I come back. So, um …."

"What?"

"DeWoot thinks I could help if I go back."

"No! What do you mean?"

"I could go back to Lyle's villa. Keep the Afghan Major Crimes office aware of where he goes so they can follow him, catch him trying to access the money."

Roger remembered Lyle saying he'd get a stand-in woman for Jill to come to the vault with him with the second key. He must have meant Sophie. "No, Sophie. You can't do that."

"They'll protect me."

"No. Please don't go."

"Roger, if Lyle finds out people are looking for him, he'll assume the information came from you and I'm afraid he'll find you and hurt you. If I can help catch him, I have to go."

Roger tried everything he could think of to convince her to stay in Belgium, but it was no use. DeWoot had already scheduled a Foreign Ministry flight back to Kabul the next morning, and Sophie had agreed to be on it. "Don't worry," she assured him. "I'll tell Lyle I had to rush home to Belgium because my mother was sick, but she's better now so I came back. I'll act like I don't know anything. I'll move back in with him as if nothing has changed."

The rain was still pouring down. But Roger's elation at watching the Rover fill up had vanished. He called Dan to let him know he was leaving the next day for Kabul.

II

15

Back in the I R of A

The limo driver who picked Roger up had a heavy Russian accent. "You go to Afghanistan? Heh-heh. America is there so long. Russia learned fast. Can do nothing."

If Grayrock and its collaborators would just do nothing, Roger thought, the Islamic Republic of Afghanistan would be better off.

The National Airways transport plane had seats for five in the front. Iggy had told Roger to wear a suit and tie. The pilot and crew called him "Sir." Behind them was a closed door. Roger asked what they were carrying.

"Ice cream, Sir."

Roger closed his eyes and soon fell asleep.

Refueling in Frankfort, and on to Kabul. When he stepped onto the tarmac, Roger saw dry ice vapor streaming from the plane as the wide rear hatch dropped down. A black Cadillac pulled up next to him. The Afghan driver got out, held a hand on his chest, put Roger's bag in the trunk, and held open the car door. No passport check. No customs inspection. Superseded by the Grayrock command.

The silent, air conditioned car came to a stop in front of Lyle's villa. Sophie was also due to arrive in Kabul today. If she had already moved back in with Lyle, Roger needed somehow to make sure she was safe. He'd insist on talking to her before giving Lyle the key.

The limousine glided away. Roger shouldered his duffel bag, walked up, buzzed the intercom.

No reply. He buzzed again. Waited.

Finally a young boy's voice said something in Dari that sounded like "*Alān kesi nist.*" Roger didn't know what it meant, but it was clear the boy wasn't going to open the door.

Omar gave Roger a bear hug and a kiss on both cheeks. His daughter Amal shook his hand. His grandson Karim bowed and couldn't stop grinning. Hekmat opened bottles of Pepsi. It was like the return of a family member they hadn't seen for years.

"I knew you were coming," Amal told him. "Yesterday I found a green tea leaf floating in my tea. A sure sign that someone is coming."

Omar seemed to sense something was wrong and didn't ask why Roger had suddenly come back, where his wife was, or any questions at all. Neither did Amal or her husband, although Roger noticed a few surreptitious glances among them.

After a long drawn-out breakfast, Omar took Roger out to the garden. They sat at the edge of the pond. "You have come alone again. We are thinking you have very important business with Mr. Lyle."

In his mind, Roger heard Lyle's warning "You-Tell-No one" and his threat to "take care of" anybody who found out about his crimes. He couldn't put Omar in that position. But it wasn't fair to keep him in the dark about how dangerous Lyle was.

"It's all right, Mr. Roger. I don't mean to pry."

"Can I just tell you this? Lyle is not my friend. He's done some terrible things. He said he'd kill anybody who found out about them. So it's best you don't know."

Omar stood up. "But you know? Are you in danger?"

Roger had pulled on the thread, and the cloak of secrets was beginning to unravel. "No, Lyle won't hurt me as long as he thinks I'm on his side. But I have to tell you something else. When I first came here, I was looking for my wife. I found out she and Lyle have both committed serious crimes." He paused. "And now I've learned she's dead."

Omar gasped. He put his hands on Roger's shoulders. "I am so sorry." He called for his daughter to come out. "Mr. Roger's wife is dead."

Amal clasped her hands on her breast. "Mr. Roger, this is terrible.

I don't know what to say." She ran back inside to tell her husband.

Omar began pacing around the pond. His lips were moving, but no words came out. Finally, he stopped and said, "Mr. Roger, what you told me about Mr. Lyle doesn't surprise me as much as you imagine."

"Then I'll tell you I've come back to help get Lyle arrested."

Omar frowned. "Arrested for ... do you mean that Mr. Lyle and your wife ... that she betrayed you with him?"

Roger felt his face warming. "No. When I first came here, that's what I thought. But I found out it wasn't true. She and Lyle weren't lovers. They were partners in crime. It's best if I don't say any more."

Omar took another trip around the pond, his hands clasped behind his back. When he stopped, he said, "After you left, I wondered why Mr. Lyle didn't come to visit. I sent little Musa to ask at his villa. Mr. Lyle's houseboy Ishak told Musa something dreadful about Mr. Lyle that I'd rather not mention."

Roger wondered what dreadful thing the boy knew about Lyle that he didn't.

Omar changed the subject. "Ishak also said that you and the foreign woman looked at each other 'in a certain way.' This is not my business, of course."

Now Roger's face was on fire. The cloak was unraveling fast. "Omar, the boy is right about me and Sophie. I don't know how it happened. She's in a group trying to help Afghan women, and—"

Omar nodded. "Yes, I also know this from the boy. And so does my daughter. She wanted me to invite this Sophie to our house before she left." Omar grinned. "Without Mr. Lyle, she said."

"Actually, Sophie's coming back to Kabul today."

"Well, well. We need to tell Amal."

As they headed back to the house, Roger's phone pinged. Message from Sophie.

"Sorry," he told Omar. "I'll explain everything later. I have to go somewhere right now."

In the taxi, he texted Sophie back. *I'm in Kabul, too. Glad you're staying in your Green Village room. Coming right now to see you.*

The Afghan guard at the Green Village compound noted Roger's suit and tie and only gave a perfunctory glance at his passport. Roger walked towards a dust-colored row of aid workers' housing that showed no signs of life in the baking sun. He wasn't sure which door was Sophie's. She'd been standing in front of the housing strip when he picked her up to see her off. There was a guard in front of the complex. "Femmes en Crise? Female housing?" Roger asked, but the man just held his hand over his heart and bowed.

"Hey." The voice came from a second-floor doorway. Sophie. "Come up those stairs." She stood gripping the railing. "You shouldn't have come back. It's dangerous."

"You shouldn't have either." On the balcony, Roger turned and glanced down at the guard. He was sitting by the gate to the compound with his back to the building in a chair shaded by a blue umbrella.

Roger squinted in the sunlight reflected from the dusty road and colorless stucco buildings. "The whole compound looks vacant. I guess your roommate—"

"My roommate Lexi has gone to Kandahar for a few days. Our director, Nora, lives in the complex behind this one." Sophie took Roger's hand and led him inside.

The room was narrow, clean, and stark. Two beds were set against one beige wall and two narrow tables against the other. The tight space in between led to two closets closed off by beige curtains. At the far end of the room there was a sink, and a door at the rear was probably a bathroom. Roger chuckled. "I can see why you preferred to live in Lyle's villa. But I'm glad—"

She stopped him with a kiss. In the back of his mind was something she'd said on the phone about moving in with Lyle again if she had to "as if nothing has changed." But her lips were warm. He kissed her and decided to let it go.

"I told Deputy Minister DeWoot you were mailing the key and it wouldn't get here for a few days." Sophie's cheeks were bright pink.

"Actually, I brought the key with me."

Sophie giggled. "He doesn't know that. He said he'd use the time until it gets here to find out who to contact on the Afghan Major Crimes Task Force. He wants to make sure the person we show the money laundering papers to is honest."

Roger was excited to be holding her again. He was hardly listening, running his fingers lightly through her long hair. "Do you think … I mean it's 'female quarters,' right?"

She buried her head on his shoulder.

"Does the guard stay there all night?"

"I don't know. We keep paper taped over the window."

Roger brushed a drop of sweat from his forehead.

"I'll hang up your coat." She draped it over a hook on the wall. "We have a 'cooler.' Not as cold as air conditioning, but I can speed the fan up." She tiptoed to twist a switch, then locked the door. She peeled the paper back a little from the window. "Still there."

Roger loosened his tie and looked around. Both tables were piled with textbooks and papers. So were the two chairs.

Sophie pointed. "This bed is mine."

Roger sat on the edge. Sophie sat close beside him. "I'm going to text Omar," Roger said. "Tell him I'll be late." He met Sophie's eyes. "I guess there's no way I can stay with you tonight?"

Sophie's answer was a kiss.

"Does Lyle know you're here?"

Sophie shook her head. "I don't think so."

"I'll tell Omar I'm not coming back."

The setting sun reddened the thin white paper covering the window. The roar of a plane taking off rattled the door. Roger and Sophie lay side by side in the narrow bunk. In the distance, a muffled boom was followed by silence. Another day in Kabul.

"I was wrong," Roger said. "Lyle's villa isn't better than this. Let's hope he doesn't find us."

"*Chahār divār ensān rā āzād mikonad*," Sophie whispered. "That's what they say here. Four walls make a man free."

And inside the four walls of Sophie's narrow room they made love—freely and even a little noisily—until late into the night. Roger felt as if he and Sophie were ensconced in a secret cave, the rumble of the cooler and roar of the planes no more to them than a storm they were sheltered from.

Roger opened his eyes the next morning and found Sophie in his arms. Sophie awoke and blinked. "Oh." She kissed him and sat up. "We skipped dinner last night. I'll cook some eggs I saw in the fridge. Can you heat some water for tea? There's an electric samovar."

They ate at one of the little tables. Roger caught Sophie's eye. "All the preaching, all the Taliban diatribes depicting what Westerners are like. Here we are in their own country—"

"Proving them right?"

"In a way."

"*Fāheshé*, that's what they'd call me. A slut. I don't know what they'd call you."

Roger scoffed. "Nothing, probably."

"Right. I can't think of a word for the man who does the same as a woman does. In any language."

"Meaning that Femmes en Crise has work to do not only in Afghanistan?"

"I'm glad you see that."

"That impish look in your eyes is giving me a crisis right now."

Sophie giggled. "But the Bible says …. The Koran says …."

"Love one another. I'm sure that's in there somewhere."

"If it isn't, it should be. Hold on. Let me turn the cooler up all the way."

And it was back into their illusory cave of detachment from the storms that battered all around them. They loved one another until Sophie fell asleep again in his arms.

It was early afternoon, and Roger was drifting off, too, when

Sophie's phone rang. She sat up. It was Deputy Minister of Foreign Affairs DeWoot. She held her nightgown over her as if he might be able to see. They spoke in French.

When she hung up, she explained, "I told DeWoot you'd decided to bring the key in person. He asked if you'd been in touch with me. I lied. I said no. He doesn't want you to take the key to Lyle before he meets with you." Sophie gave her jaw a little twist. "He's worried you and Lyle will just take off with the money. I promised him he could trust you."

She showed Roger a long list of messages on her phone. "Look. All from Lyle."

You went home? Told you not to leave. I need you here.

"So I told him I went home suddenly because my mother was sick."

If she doesn't get better soon, come back anyway. And come straight to the house. Might not be home when you arrive. Escorting some big wigs. Wait there for me.

"That's the last one. Yesterday. He must still be on the escort mission."

Roger told her he'd tried to give Lyle the key yesterday. "But the houseboy wouldn't open the door."

"No, he won't when he's there alone."

"So where's DeWoot?"

"The Belgian Embassy shut down over four years ago. Our Ministry of Foreign Affairs has set up temporary headquarters and a guest house here in Green Village in the former UN compound. I told the minister I'll text him when you get to Kabul." Sophie met his eyes. "I'll do that maybe tomorrow."

Roger went to the window, peeled back a corner of the paper. "Still a guard there. I think it's a different guy now. I dread walking out of here past him. But we ate all the eggs. I guess we'll have to go out sometime."

"Not really." Sophie chuckled. "As long as you like MREs."

"Huh?"

"Meals, Ready to Eat. Lots of spaghetti and beef stew. You can heat them up without a stove."

"And we could just stay in here?"

"At least for another night."

"I'll text Omar. Tell him not to worry."

"OK. I'll heat up an MRE."

"Uh, unless you're really hungry, maybe put that off?"

"Good idea." Sophie blushed.

16

No waterboarding

The roar of the early-morning plane from Istanbul woke them up. Roger and Sophie lay unclothed on the tousled sheet, her leg draped over his. He dreamily stroked her back, soothed by the warmth of her breath on his neck.

A loud knock rattled the door. "Oh, no." Sophie sat up, groped on the floor for her clothes. Roger scooped up his clothes and ran to the bathroom. He heard Sophie struggling to get dressed. "Who's there?" she called out.

"MCTF Police."

Roger opened the bathroom door a crack to peep out. His suit coat was hanging on the wall.

Sophie tried to straighten her hair. "Just a minute. What do you want?"

"Miss Sophie Martens? Major Crimes Task Force. Open, please." He spoke English with close to an American accent.

Sophie glanced out from a corner of the paper curtain, then held her hands to her cheeks. She looked back towards the bathroom with a finger over her mouth. When she opened the door, a tall man in his late thirties held up a badge. "I have to ask you some questions." He had a trim moustache and wore a dark suit over a black turtleneck jersey. "My name is Siavash. Is there some place we can sit down?"

Sophie moved books and papers and sat him with his back to the bathroom door. She fastened a last button on her blouse.

"Sorry to come unannounced," he said without further explanation. "Deputy Minister of Foreign Affairs DeWoot contacted me, and I wanted to talk to you alone first." He slipped a little leather-covered notebook from his jacket. "Would you e-spell your name?" The pronunciation of the word, and perhaps his moustache, were the only signs that he was an Afghan. Roger had heard these agents were trained by the FBI, often in the States, and were often graduates of U.S. universities. It was a separate, elite department of the police tasked with investigating crimes like kidnapping, robbery, murder, and money laundering.

"Mr. DeWoot says you gave him some papers from a U.S. company called Beverage Supplies and an Afghan company called—he checked his notes—Bebsi. He believes these are shell companies set up to launder money sent from here to Germany and then to the States."

"Yes."

"Can you tell me how you got these papers?"

"From a friend."

"The name?"

"Roger Williams."

"The nominee director of both companies?"

"Well, his name was listed without his knowledge. When he found out, he reported the laundering plan to USAID."

"And gave the documents to you. Why is that?"

"To pass on to Minister DeWoot. He's the person you should talk to."

"Still, I'm curious why Mr. Williams gave the papers to you rather than to his embassy or the FBI. Do you know where he is now?"

"I'd rather not say any more."

Agent Siavash tapped a pen on his moustache. "I see you are upset. I'm sorry. We can suspend the interview for now." He folded his notebook and glanced around the room, stopping when his eyes fell on Roger's rumpled suit coat. "Miss Martens, this is female quarters, am I right?"

Sophie turned and saw the coat, too.

"Is anybody else here with you, Miss Martens?"

Roger was dressed now except for that coat and his shoes, which were at the foot of the bed. He opened the bathroom door and came out.

Siavash stood and showed him his badge, then shot Sophie a disappointed look.

Roger reached for the passport in his coat, and the agent seized both his arms. For the second time in Kabul, Roger found himself in handcuffs.

"I'm Roger Williams," he said. "My passport is in my coat."

Sophie was crying. Siavash directed Roger to a chair, now noticing Roger's shoes beside the bed. Siavash's face turned a purplish red. He seemed lost for words.

Roger imagined that kidnapping and money laundering investigators didn't often find themselves in situations like this. Siavash examined Roger's passport, nodded, then turned to Sophie, his practiced, professional tone faltering. "Miss Martens, I wish you had ... I wish you had told me this man was here."

She hid her face in her hands.

"You understand," Siavash told her, "I'm only here to investigate charges of money laundering, theft, murder." He turned to Roger. "Are you willing to answer questions?"

"Of course."

There was no available chair, and Siavash started to sit on the edge of Sophie's bed but caught himself and stood. "Mr. Williams, you are listed as director of two fraudulent companies. I understand you have a key to a vault at Camp Rectitude containing a large amount of stolen cash. Can you give me a reason not to arrest you?"

Siavash whisked Roger off the Green Village compound in his police truck. Beyond the airport they took a turn towards the Hindu Kush mountain range at the northern edge of the city. When the road curved, from the window Roger could see a winding trail of dust behind them.

His handcuffs were off, but Siavash held his arm as he climbed the black wrought iron stairs into a windowless metal building that looked like a huge storage facility from the outside. The expansive room he was taken into hummed with fluorescent ceiling lights and was filled with new-looking identical beechwood desks, each with a laptop on it. Siavash took Roger to a corner desk. "You understand you're not actually under arrest. You're only here for questioning."

Roger flinched.

"Don't worry. We're more humane than the Americans. We're not going to waterboard you." Siavash called to an assistant to bring Roger a glass of tea while he shuffled through some papers. "Minister DeWoot is setting up a meeting with Miss Martens. Before that I need some information from you."

Siavash took a recorder from the desk. "First tell me. I'm confused. Is Miss Martens your friend or Lyle White's friend?"

Roger started from the beginning. The more he went on, the more he realized how much it might look like he and Lyle were the money launderers.

"And where is the key?" Siavash asked.

"At my friend's house." It was actually in his pocket.

"This friend you mentioned who's also a friend of Lyle White?"

"Omar doesn't know much about Lyle."

"And does Omar know everything about you?"

When Roger didn't answer immediately, Siavash said, "Well, go on. Finish your story." It was clear that the agent didn't fully believe Roger. When Roger finished, Siavash said, "And you are staying with Miss Martens? Why didn't you give her the key?"

Roger cleared a catch in his throat. "I'm not actually staying with Sophie. And I didn't give her the key because Lyle threatened to kill me if I didn't give it directly to him. I tried to as soon as I arrived, but he wasn't home."

Siavash gave him an uncomfortably long stare before saying, "All right. Please write down the name and address of the friend you're 'actually' staying with."

Roger copied the address from his phone, saying, "But Omar and his family know nothing about this."

Siavash ignored him. "We'll set up surveillance on his home and on Lyle White's villa." He asked to see Roger's phone. "I'll put in the number for you to call the moment Lyle White gets the key. You can go now. My driver will take you to Omar's house."

A red and white cell phone tower dominated the ridge of the barren mountains, casting a strong signal to Roger's phone. Siavash's driver opened the door for Roger, but before he got in, Roger dialed Sophie. No answer. He held up his hand for the driver to wait and texted her. All he could think of to write was *Call me.* The last he'd seen her she was clinging to his arm as Siavash nudged him into his truck.

The road made use of a dried-up riverbed for part of the way as they left the range of mountains. Little villages surrounded by adobe walls appeared here and there, some with small flocks of skinny sheep or goats penned behind low mud walls, some with groves of sparse fig trees. Men in prayer caps and worn, faded vests over baggy robes and trousers worked alongside women in equally faded and baggy clothes that fanned out more from the waist. Their faces and hands were browned by the sun as they scratched in the earth with hoes, moved sheep from one pen to another, carried earthenware pots hanging from a pole across their shoulders. A few used sticks to urge on donkeys pulling carts of hay. On the outskirts of one village, Roger saw a man bending down on a piece of rug saying his noon prayers. The people within these villages, he thought, had led the same simple, peaceful lives for centuries, isolated from the political and religious strife that beleaguered other parts of the country. "Four walls make a man free."

Almost abruptly, the road entered the more densely settled outskirts of the city. The houses, most still the color of the desert, were crammed together, and except for children kicking soccer balls, most of the people Roger saw were sitting at little tables outside of shops sipping tea or playing backgammon. As soon as the tall buildings of the city could be seen, the car was slowed to a crawl by traffic. Horns blared, brakes squealed, engines roared, yet no one was moving ahead very much. Soon the traffic came to a stop. The driver got out and shouted, pointed to his license plate, showed some kind of badge, but it would have taken more than that to force his way through the tangled lines of cars, pickup trucks, buses, vans, and motorcycles filling every inch of the street and overflowing onto the sidewalks.

It was late afternoon when they arrived at Omar's house.

17

Comfort tea

Omar was standing outside. When the white Ford Ranger dropped Roger off, Omar squinted, watching it drive away. "There's a police license on that truck. Are you in trouble, Mr. Roger?"

Before he could answer, Amal rushed to the door. "Mr. Roger, come in. We were worried." She held a hand on her chest. "My father told us your warning about Mr. Lyle."

Omar led him to a cushion at the low table. "We were on edge the past two nights when you were gone. My daughter and I think you'll be safer here with us. Just a couple of days ago, for example, there was another roadside bombing. The lead truck of a U.S. convoy coming from Jalalabad was blown up just on the outskirts of Kabul."

Amal called to her son. "Karim, bring some tea, please." Roger had slighted them by keeping them in the dark about why he'd first come to Kabul. Then, after returning, he'd mentioned Lyle's crimes and Jill's death to Omar only to disappear for two nights without explanation. But there apparently was nothing that couldn't be amended by a discussion over tea.

Amal sent her son to his room to do his homework. "But Grandpa is here, and we have a guest," the boy complained in English, which he'd become more confident in using.

"You can still sleep here in the main room with Grandpa and Mr. Roger, but you need a quiet place to do your homework."

Amal's husband Hekmat came in from outside and sat next to Roger. "Glad you're back." He lowered his voice. "Anything wrong? There are two men outside. They seem to be watching the house."

Everyone turned to Roger. "Yes," he said. "Today I reported Lyle to the Major Crimes police. Lyle's away on some mission. The

Major Crimes police are watching this house and Lyle's house until he comes back. They plan to arrest him."

"Why this house?" Hekmat seemed more nervous than the others.

"To protect us. Maybe you find it hard to believe, but Lyle is a dangerous man." Roger didn't mention what was probably another reason they were watching this house—their lingering doubt about Roger himself.

Little Musa came in to refill the samovar. His eyes glittering knowingly, he glanced sideways at Roger but said nothing and left the room.

Roger took a sip of tea. "Omar probably told you I've become friends with a woman I met at Lyle's house who works for a Belgian aid organization. She's also helping the police. She's living at their quarters in Green Village now. I stayed at that compound last night and the night before." Roger knew his face was red.

Amal cleared her throat. "This young woman you mention. It's Miss Sophie, yes?"

Roger nodded, sipped more tea.

"We know about Miss Sophie from Musa, who heard about her from Ishak, Mr. Lyle's houseboy. Ishak told Musa she's very nice. He was sorry she left the villa."

Roger's phone dinged. Message from Sophie.

Back from school. DeWoot wants to talk to us tomorrow. Coming back to my room tonight?

Omar and his family held their eyes on Roger like students who'd been told he had an important announcement. "It's Sophie," he explained. "She's scared. I might have to—"

Amal burst out, "Scared? She can come here. Karim doesn't use his room when Grandpa's here. She can sleep there."

Hekmat looked worried. "We don't want to get involved with the Major Crimes police, though."

Omar chuckled. "Mr. Roger hasn't said which crimes they're tracking down, Hekmat, but I think it's something more serious than buying Pepsi on the black market."

Hekmat glanced away.

"Not that you've ever done that," Omar added.

Amal giggled, pointed to Roger's phone. "Tell her she can stay here. We want to meet her. I'll put on some more tea."

Roger spoke no Dari, but Sophie did. Omar's family were thrilled. Sophie was now the center of attention. She'd worn her blue hejab when she first came in, not simply out of respect for Afghan customs, Roger sensed, but also for the same reason Afghan women wore it, to shield herself from the curious stares of strange men. It wasn't long before she pulled it down over her shoulders.

Amal sat beside her with Laila on her lap. Sophie couldn't take her eyes off the baby, and Amal let her hold her. Mixing Dari and English, "*Nazar nakoné,*" Sophie said. "Not to give her the evil eye."

The whole family seemed surprised and impressed. Omar told Roger Sophie had used a phrase to prevent bad luck from falling on a baby when making a compliment. "My superstitious daughter is delighted with your friend."

Musa and Sima knelt out in the hallway looking on. Karim peeped in from his room, which he'd been straightening up. All the rest sat on cushions in a circle around the low table covered with tea, pistachios, and a growing number of other dishes. The conversation alternated between Dari and English, then settled into English, largely for Roger's benefit. He and the adopted children were the only monolingual people in the house.

"Another American lady who visited us," Amal said, "never spoke Dari. 'Speak English,' she always told us."

"*Quit that gibberish!*" Hekmat sang out in his imitation of Jill's voice.

Even Musa and Sima laughed.

Sophie lowered her eyes.

Omar changed the subject. "Miss Sophie, excuse me if I'm being too personal, but I have to ask. Are you afraid of Mr. Lyle?" He eyed

Musa in the doorway, his informant on Lyle's violent temper, but of course Musa hadn't understood his question.

Sophie bit her lip.

Amal spoke up. "Please stay here with us. Karim's room is ready. He likes to sleep out here with his grandfather and Mr. Roger."

Sophie glanced at Roger, then nodded.

Amal said something to Karim, who brought a red square of cloth the size of her palm with gold embroidery on it. "This will protect you," Amal told Sophie. Would you let me sew it inside of your jacket?"

Sophie seemed to know what it was, but Roger asked to see it. The embroidery was a line of writing. "What does this say?"

"Let Karim read it," Omar insisted. "It's Arabic. We'll see what he learned in school."

Karim shook his head but finally took the talisman, then smiled. "Easy," he said. *"He is with you wherever you are."*

"From the Koran," Amal explained. "Talking about God."

Sophie slipped off her light jacket. Sima brought a sewing basket. As Amal sewed the talisman inside the jacket, she uttered a few *tsk-tsk* sounds. "A different American woman laughed at me when I offered this to her. What a shame."

Once again, Omar spoke out to change the subject. "Karim, Musa, Sima. Bring the dinner, please. It's sundown. Time to eat."

After getting by on the military MREs, Roger was ready for a real meal. Sophie ate with gusto, too. The more they ate, the happier the family became. Afterwards, Hekmat took his son Karim aside to help him with his homework. Amal took Sophie for a walk around the pond in the cool of the evening.

"Girl talk," Omar commented. "Is that what you call it? I wonder if Miss Sophie really believes that talisman will protect her. Or was she just being polite?"

"Well, she is polite. But I'm sure the quote appealed to her."

Omar lowered his voice. "My daughter's probably telling her about jinns. How they can take the form of humans and scorpions and whatever. She gets all that from her mother, God rest her soul."

"Your daughter's a very caring person."

Omar breathed out a loud sigh. "Yes, yes. If she would only let me drink beer in her house."

"I heard that," Hekmat said. "And I agree."

Roger slept in the main room with Omar and Karim. He couldn't sleep with Sophie, but just having her safely here in the same house with him helped him sleep peacefully. It was like they were part of a family.

18

Stakeout

In the morning Roger awoke to women's laughter—Sophie and Sima chasing a hen out of the kitchen. Sophie stopped to answer a text in the garden.

After breakfast, she told Roger, "The Major Crimes agent told DeWoot you're here. They want us to meet to devise a plan. The best place I could think of is in my school building. Nobody's there today. It's Friday."

The taxi stopped near the Bibi Mahro Hill at a group of abandoned buildings mixed in with some that were refurbished. The school was a one-story stucco rectangle with a blue tile roof. It had been built by Femmes en Crise. A wide dirt road ran in front of the school, and on the other side was the Ariana Café, where Roger and Sophie had met before. A stream of smoke came from its tin chimney, and a few bicycles, mopeds, and small motorcycles leaned against its stained stucco walls. In central Kabul there was a constant racket of engines, horns, shouts. Here, on a Friday, everything was quiet.

Roger and Sophie stood outside the school waiting for DeWoot. In the distance a range of angular brown mountains, some with snow on their peaks, pierced a pale blue sky. Roger and Sophie stood gazing at the mountains. Soon a trail of dust rose along the road in the distance. A black car slowly came into view. Sophie shielded her eyes with her hands. "That's him."

A small, thin man in a black suit, white shirt, and bow tie got out of a Suburban SUV he'd driven there himself. He wore round horn-rimmed glasses and had a tawny moustache. When Sophie introduced him, he gave Roger a quick handshake and his Ministry of Foreign Affairs business card.

Sophie led them along a tile hallway into one of three classrooms filled with desks. Everything looked new. Sophie's name was printed in all capital letters on a newish whiteboard. She turned three desks to face each other.

"So, it's English you speak?" DeWoot asked Roger. "Very well." He frowned. "Agent Siavash of the Major Crimes Task Force was supposed to be here." DeWoot took some papers from a black attaché case. "Mr. Williams, you are the nominee director of a shell company called Beverage Supplies, LLC?"

"Yes, although I—"

DeWoot held up a bundle of papers. "And you have signed these invoices to another shell company called ... let me see, Bebsi. Is that right?"

"This was all without my knowledge, you understand?"

"And you are in possession of the key to a vault holding stolen USAID funds that were to go to the Belgian organization that operates this international assistance school?"

Now Roger just gave him a stare. DeWoot waited. Sophie finally interrupted. "Roger is here to help us get Lyle arrested and recover the money."

"I understand." He put the papers back in his briefcase. "I've suggested to USAID that they get the FBI involved, but everyone I talked to says the matter is already taken care of and Grayrock is investigating it."

"Grayrock will do nothing," Roger retorted. "They have enough leverage over Senator Steinherz, the chairman of the Senate Foreign Aid Committee, to force him to quash any investigation."

"Yes. The senator is 'in their pocket.' Is that how you put it?" DeWoot seemed intrigued by the phrase that Sophie must have repeated to him. "My talks with U.S. officials seem to support that. That's why I decided to take our charges to the Afghan Major Crimes Task Force. Agent Siavash said he would—"

Outside the school a truck door slammed. Agent Siavash rushed into the classroom and pulled up a desk. "Sorry I'm late. Traffic accident jammed things up." He looked at DeWoot. "So you and—if I may use first names—Roger have met?"

DeWoot asked Siavash if he was satisfied Roger was "not complicit in this crime."

Siavash met Roger's eyes. "For the time being, yes. The proof will be if he helps us recover all the money and arrest Lyle White."

"That's why he's here." Sophie put her hand on Roger's arm.

Siavash looked away. "Yes. Surveillance of the villa is already in place. The next step is to deliver the key to Lyle. My men say he's not back yet from some mission. I tried to get Grayrock to tell me where he went and when he's expected back, but they said that's all confidential."

DeWoot asked Sophie, "Do you think the houseboy knows where Lyle is?"

"Definitely not. Lyle would never even tell me where he was going."

Siavash said his men were also watching the bank. "If you can call it a bank. It's licensed for banking operations, but we know its only business is money laundering."

"This should be a case for the FBI," DeWoot contended.

Siavash agreed. "Our contact man for the FBI is due back from the States in a few days. In the meantime, here's what I suggest we do. Sophie should move into Lyle's villa. She'll text Roger when Lyle comes back, and he'll bring Lyle the key. Sophie will let us know when he's about to take her to the vault. We'll arrest him as he takes the money to his Pulshui Bank accomplice to launder."

"No," Roger said. "I don't want Sophie to move into Lyle's villa."

Sophie agreed. "I'll contact Lyle when he gets back. But I'll tell him Femmes en Crise insists I stay at our Green Village housing."

"So that's where you'll be?" Siavash took out his black note pad.

Sophie turned to Roger, her cheeks reddening.

"She's actually staying at my friend Omar's house." Roger tried to sound assertive. "It's safer."

Siavash frowned, "Safer? But Green Village is heavily guarded."

Roger grasped for an excuse to keep Sophie with him at Omar's house. "Yes, but ...."

Siavash raised an eyebrow and smiled. "Good enough. We already have a stakeout at Omar's house. It'll be easier for us to keep an eye on both of you if you're in the same place. We all have each other's phone numbers, correct?" He put his notebook away. "For now, I guess all we can do is wait."

The next day Roger led the boys at Karim's school in estimating how many tiles it would take to re-roof the classroom—which Karim had told him was leaking. He sent two boys to bring in a tile lying on the ground outside the building. They measured it. "We need to know the length of the building," they concluded. Roger handed them a meter stick from the chalk ledge. "You mean we can go outside?" The English teacher serving as translator seemed as surprised as they were.

"*Befarmāid*," Roger said, holding the door open. He was finding this word for *Please, You first, Help yourself*, or literally *Command me* quite useful.

After a struggle over who would hold the meter stick, they got the job done. Roger told them to assume the roof was flat, which it almost was. They rushed back inside and did their calculations on the blackboard, led by two of the brighter students. Finally, "Four hundred," they called out together.

"I already knew that," a boy with a hint of a moustache claimed. "Four pallets. My father's a roofer. I help him sometimes."

When the lesson was over, Karim's English teacher seemed impressed. "This wasn't the way we teach here. I liked it. Can you keep teaching the class until the new mathematics teacher arrives?"

With no idea how long he'd have to wait for Lyle to get back from his mission, Roger said he'd try. Karim bounced happily as they threaded their way through shoppers and honking traffic back to the house. Roger was more certain now than ever he wanted to come back to Kabul in the summers and volunteer as a teacher. Or if Sophie kept her job with the Belgian aid group, maybe he could get a job with them. Hommes en Crise?

19

Body bags and Xanax

While waiting for Lyle to return, Roger and Sophie fell into a routine. She would go to her class in the morning. He would teach at Karim's school later in the day.

Sophie wasn't back from the Femmes en Crise school when Roger and Karim got home one day. Roger checked his messages several times, laughing at himself for acting like the spouses he'd ridiculed for needing to be in constant touch with each other. He felt even sillier when he went out into the garden to check if the magpie was sitting on the wall. No. No message coming. He texted Sophie, got no reply. Omar and Amal could tell he was worried. "Come have some tea," Amal insisted.

But when Roger hadn't heard from her by the time he finished his tea, he went to the garden again to try calling her. Her phone rang and rang unanswered. He'd taken only a few steps back to the house when a guttural *ak-ak-ak* burst from the garden wall. Roger's phone rang.

"Roger Williams? Doctor Smith, Grayrock hospital in Camp Rectitude. We need you here ASAP."

"Hospital? Why?"

"You'll know when you get here." The Grayrock doctor hung up.

Omar could see something was wrong the minute Roger came back into the house. "Mr. Roger, you're shaking."

Roger repeated the message in a trembling voice. "It's Sophie, I'm sure. Maybe she went back to her room in Green Village after school to pick something up. The Grayrock guy said 'hospital.' She must be hurt."

"There's been no news of another attack on Green Village."

"Maybe Lyle came back from his mission, found that Sophie hadn't moved into his villa, and went to get her at her school."

"Do you think he would hurt her, Mr. Roger?"

"I'm going to find out."

Roger cracked open Omar's front door and peered across the dusty street. Siavash's stakeout man lay on a blanket in the narrow passageway between two houses—sound asleep. Omar wanted to go with Roger, but Roger asked him to wait at his house. He knew it would be easier for somebody who *looked* like an American to get into Grayrock's Camp Rectitude.

The suit and tie, U.S. passport, and a lie that he was a doctor got Roger escorted along a gravel road to Grayrock's hospital. It was identical to most of the Camp Rectitude buildings, a tan metal quonset hut that seemed big enough to hold an airplane. He didn't repeat the lie to the guard at the steel door. "I was told to see Doctor Smith."

The guard let him in. "Drop your phone in that crate. Morgue's down that way."

At the strong smell of formaldehyde, Roger's knees weakened. He made his way down a windowless corridor, its walls and ceiling paneled with varnished plywood reflecting a string of overhead LED lights. He reached an open door signed *Recovery and Retrieval. Doctor Smith.* The Grayrock doctor sat at an unfinished plywood desk eating a quart carton of rocky road ice-cream. "Sit down," he mumbled, "while I finish this."

"Why did you call me here?" Roger's voice was quavering.

The doctor swallowed a mouthful. "Body ID. That's all. Just a sec." He scraped the last bit from the carton.

Roger grabbed his arm. "What body, you idiot?"

The guard grabbed him around the neck from behind.

"Let him go." The pot bellied doctor got up. "Come on, follow me." At the end of the corridor, they ducked under some plastic sheathing in front of a door and stepped into a chilly steel-walled room lined with cots, some loaded with black body bags. The acrid odor of disinfectant made Roger struggle not to vomit.

"Over here." The doctor stopped by a bag that looked only half full. He zipped it open.

Roger cupped his hand over his open mouth. Two wide black pupils stared up blankly from a head placed crudely above half of a naked torso.

Roger gasped. "It's Lyle White." He pulled a handkerchief over his nose.

"Right. Damn shame, too. I'm told he was as good as they get. His tags were lost, so protocol requires an outside ID before Grayrock ships the remains to the nearest of kin in the States. Or the designated mortuary, in his case. Believe it or not, a couple times the recipient claimed we shipped them the wrong body."

The doctor zipped up the bag. "Happened three days ago. Completed his mission and was hit by an IED on the way back here, not far from Green Village. Killed him and his driver."

Roger tried to shake off the picture of Lyle's staring pupils.

"It took a while," the doctor said, "to find somebody outside the camp who knew him. Then one guy remembered he was shacked up with a Belgian broad. The guy knew where she worked."

"Sophie! You brought her here? Where is she?"

"Had to sedate her. She kept yelling she needed to call you. She said you knew Lyle. We got your number from her phone. Always good to get extra confirmation of the ID."

Roger followed the doctor into another room that wasn't as cold. Two bandaged men lay in beds watching an American film on a large screen. Sophie lay motionless on a cot next to them. Her face was colorless, her breathing shallow. Roger lifted her icy hand. "Sophie, can you hear me?" He pressed her wrist but couldn't feel a pulse. "What did you give her?"

"Just an injection of Xanax."

"An injection?"

"We don't fool around here. She'll snap out of it soon enough.

Come back to my office. Something for you to sign."

When Roger resisted, the doctor signaled a guard, who pulled him away from Sophie.

The form the doctor pushed across his desk had already been filled out and signed by Sophie. As Roger put his signature below hers, a young man in a white jacket with a gun on his belt handed him a bundle wrapped in brown paper. "Lyle White's effects, Sir. What he left behind when he moved into the villa." He turned. "Doctor, she's awake."

Roger rushed back to Sophie before anybody could stop him. She blinked and gave a weak smile but said nothing.

"Are you OK?"

Sophie whispered, "Yes."

"Can you sit up? Let's get out of here."

Another whispered "Yes."

The doctor concurred, "If she can stand, she can go."

The white jacket man called for a Grayrock car to take them back.

Sophie seemed to be in a fog. It wasn't until the car left the Green Village compound that she spoke. "Those eyes!"

"You know what Amal thinks."

Sophie shivered. "That Lyle was a jinn?"

Roger knew it must have upset her to see the corpse of the man she'd known for more than a year. "That was a terrible sight," he offered.

Sophie held her hands to her cheeks and moaned. "*Quelle horreur.* To see him taken off to jail, that would have been a relief. But this!"

"I know." He wiped a tear from her cheek and took her hand.

"Roger, stay with me. I don't know what I'd do without you."

"I will. I promise."

Sophie gripped his hand. She seemed still foggy from the tranquilizer. As they turned onto Omar's street, Roger peered through the car's tinted window to see if Siavash's man was still asleep. He was. It didn't look like he'd even moved.

Omar stood waiting at his door. When he saw Sophie sitting next to Roger in the car, he called inside. At once, Amal, Hekmat, and Karim rushed out. Musa and Sima peeped from the doorway, Sima holding baby Laila. Omar opened the car door before the driver could get out. "Bah! Bah! Miss Sophie, you are all right?"

"*Alhamdulillah!*" Amal cried out. "Praise God!" She gave Roger a nod of approval as if he'd saved Sophie from the clutches of an evil jinn.

Sophie unashamedly clung to Roger, her customary deference to Afghan social norms forgotten, a result either from the appalling sight at the Camp Rectitude morgue or from the Xanax. She sat with her shoulder pressed against Roger's as the family formed a circle on cushions. Roger eyed the others for a surprised or negative reaction to this public familiarity but there was none.

"We have shocking news," Roger announced. "Lyle White is dead. Hit by an IED."

"*Vāy, khodāye man!* Oh, my God," Amal exclaimed.

Omar breathed out a long sigh. "It's a terrible thing, of course. But we're so glad to see Miss Sophie is unhurt."

Amal patted the hem of Sophie's jacket. "You see? *He is with you wherever you are.*"

"Thanks for letting me stay here," Sophie said groggily. "I don't want to be alone."

Amal took Sophie's hand. "You must be tired. Your bed is made up."

Sophie glanced at Roger. "Tonight I don't want to sleep alone."

"Ahem-hem," Amal said. "No, of course not. You shouldn't. I'll bring my mat into the room and sleep next to you."

"Oh," Sophie said woozily. "Thanks. Good night, everybody." She bent and gave Roger a sloppy kiss on the cheek before going into Karim's room.

Sima and Musa gasped. Amal and the others stared wide-eyed.

"They gave her Xanax," Roger explained. Their widened eyes

were on him now. "Lots of it," he added.

"Ah," Omar finally said, then translated for the kids.

"Ah," they all echoed, and, Karim first, then the rest all burst into chuckles.

Omar lifted his eyes and recited something in Persian. There was loud laughter.

"What?" Roger demanded.

"It's Hafez," Omar explained. "Let me see if I can translate:

My heart is out of control. Help me, you wise men.
The story of my secret love will be told throughout the ages."

20

House inspection

Omar was already sitting up on his mat, his head in his hands, when Roger awoke. "Good morning, Mr. Roger. I've been thinking. I'm sorry about what happened to Mr. Lyle, but from what you told me, and from my daughter's intuition, and especially from something that his houseboy told Musa, I realize I was wrong to think of him as a friend."

Amal came out of Karim's room alone and took the baby from Sima. Roger found himself staring at the door she closed behind her. Amal held a finger over her mouth. "She's still sleeping."

They let Sophie sleep all through breakfast. Roger was about to ask Amal to check on her when a loud knock rattled the front door.

"Major Crimes Police." Roger recognized Siavash's voice.

In the back walkway, Roger noticed Omar's son-in-law slip from his bedroom and out the back gate of the garden. Amal drew a scarf over her head and retreated into Karim's room.

Siavash looked around. "I was hoping Miss Sophie was here. Our agent stationed at the Femmes en Crise school called me late yesterday. He'd seen one teacher leaving in a taxi, but it wasn't Sophie. I told him to search the building, but it was locked."

Roger guessed the "agent" had been napping before that when the Grayrock driver came to take Sophie to the hospital. He tried to interrupt Siavash and tell him what had happened, but Siavash was talking fast. "I called Femmes en Crise, and the teacher who works with her told me Sophie was picked up early at the school by a driver in a limousine. And then this morning our agent at the school reported she hadn't shown up. I know Sophie was afraid Lyle might hurt her, so—"

"Sophie's here," Roger interrupted. "Lyle's dead." Before he could explain, Sophie wandered in, blinking at the daylight in baggy pajamas probably borrowed from Amal. Her lips were pale, her hair tousled.

"*Alhamdulillah*," Siavash exclaimed. "Thank God. Miss Sophie, are you well? You look ...."

Sophie froze. Behind her, Amal handed her a white paisley chador, which Sophie seemed to instinctively wrap around her shoulders.

"I've been trying to locate you," Siavash said. "I even called Grayrock. They gave me a ...." Siavash seemed to be grasping for an English word.

"Runaround?" Roger suggested.

Omar spoke up. "Maybe you all need to sit down and talk."

Amal called, "Karim." It was all she needed to say for him to bring in a tray with tea. But it didn't take long before they agreed that they needed to retrieve Lyle's vault key. Then they'd have both.

Sophie, Siavash, and Roger went to search Lyle's villa. It was hot, and the underarms of Roger's suit had begun to smell of sweat, but he'd gotten into the habit of wearing it like a coat of armor.

Ishak slid open the door panel. Only his forehead was visible.

"Ishak," Sophie called out. "It's me."

The door opened. Black shadows from the bars covering the high windows stretched across the red floral carpet. Ishak stood beside a pile of clothes he was gathering on the floor. He seemed to be packing up the few things he owned. He held out a paper wrinkled with perspiration. Sophie translated for Roger. "From the *sāhib khāné*. Landlord, I guess. The man who brought it told him Lyle is dead. The lease isn't over for a while, but the landlord wants Ishak out by tomorrow."

Siavash snapped a switch for the ceiling light, but the electricity had already been shut off. He picked up a metal contraption from the top of Ishak's little pile of belongings. "What's this?" he asked

Sophie.

"It's just part of a miniature model car he's working on." She told Siavash that Ishak was interested in how things work, how they're put together.

Siavash dropped it back onto the pile and looked around. He pulled out the drawer of an end table by the sofa. Empty. "Where could he have kept his key?" he asked Sophie. "Does that hall lead to the kitchen?"

"It's not in the kitchen," she scoffed. "He never went in there."

A circular metal staircase led to a balcony that overlooked the sitting room. "What's up there?"

"The bedrooms."

Roger and Sophie clattered up the stairs behind Siavash, Ishak following. Siavash opened the first door.

"My room." Sophie led them in. "I know it's not in here."

A single frameless bed neatly made up with an Afghan quilt stood under a shuttered window. Beside it was a nightstand with nothing on it. Siavash opened a mahogany armoire. It was completely empty.

Roger forced his eyes away from the narrow bed. The whole room was more Spartan than he'd expected. A small pile of books lay on the floor beside the bed. The only other piece of furniture was a pine chest of drawers set below a mirror. Something on top of it sparkled in a stream of light coming through the shutter. Roger recognized it, a sapphire bracelet Sophie had been wearing when he first met her.

"I left in a hurry," Sophie exclaimed. "There are a few things I left behind."

Siavash picked up the broach. "This looks like it might be valuable. You kept it here on the dresser?" He glanced at Ishak waiting in the hallway.

"Yes. The boy is honest. Incapable of stealing, if that's what you mean."

The next doorway led to a larger room, obviously Lyle's master bedroom. A Persian carpet covered most of the tiled floor. Against one wall was a canopied queen-sized bed with matching nightstands at each end. But instead of a quilt or bedspread, a camouflage sleeping bag lay rolled up on the bare mattress. Two crossed swords hung on the wall over the bed.

"I've never been in here." Sophie turned away as Siavash began pulling out drawers, sifting through the pockets of clothes Lyle had left in the two armoires.

"And the third room?" Siavash opened the door. Ishak tapped a trembling palm on his chest to indicate it was his.

Two toshak mattresses lying side-by side on a frayed kilim carpet took up most of the space. On a narrow dresser below a mirror lay a washing bowl with a razor and a tube of shaving cream. A dirty towel was draped over an open drawer. Siavash shot Ishak a glance and asked him something. The boy clicked his tongue and raised his eyebrows to say *No*. He seemed to be avowing that like a devout Muslim he didn't shave.

On the knobs of the dresser hung an olive drab undershirt and shorts. A clump of dirty olive drab socks lay flung into a corner. Something silky and blue stuck out from a half-closed dresser drawer. Roger pulled it open. It was the pajamas he'd seen Lyle wearing—not something he could forget.

Sophie now had both hands over her mouth. She was obviously as surprised as Roger to realize Lyle slept in Ishak's room. "I didn't know …." Her voice was shaky.

Siavash showed Ishak his badge and asked him something in Dari.

"*Kelid*?" Ishak nodded.

By now even Roger knew the word for *key*.

Ishak drew a finger around his head and ran it down under his shirt. Lyle wore the key on a chain around his neck.

Siavash glared at Sophie. "You could have told us this. The boy says Lyle never took it off."

"I had no idea."

Siavash frowned as if to ask how that was possible. He obviously presumed she and Lyle had been sleeping together.

Roger didn't know what he presumed. He remembered Sophie telling him on the phone from Belgium that in order to help get Lyle arrested she would move back in with him "as if nothing has changed." Ever since then he found her phrase creeping back into his mind from time to time. Usually he dismissed it. But if he thought about it, it bothered him. It was like a tooth that doesn't hurt unless you touch it with your tongue.

"So you were just roommates," Siavash concluded. "I see. Sorry I misunderstood."

Sophie's face burned bright red.

Siavash cleared his throat. "Anyway, did either of you notice if Lyle had the key around his neck when you identified the body?"

Roger spoke up. "No, no key. The body was pretty much ...." He glanced at Sophie and didn't finish the description.

Clanking sounded on the staircase, then the bang of the front door. "Ishak," Siavash exclaimed. "Where do you think he's going?"

"Back to his family in the Morad Khani section of the city," Sophie figured. "It's a day's walk south of here."

Siavash kicked shut the drawer holding the blue silk pajamas. With a disgusted grimace he asked, "Did Lyle give the boy a lot of money?"

Sophie was staring at the two mats drawn together on the floor. "What? No. Ishak never had any money." Her mouth twisted as if she'd bit a piece of rotten fruit.

"Uh, well, no second key. So we all need to get together soon with Foreign Minister DeWoot and decide what to do next. Do you want help gathering up the rest of your things, Sophie?"

She answered unsteadily. "No. Thanks. I need to talk to Roger. I'll come back for them later."

When Siavash left, she led Roger to the couch they'd sat on the day they met. She fidgeted with her hands on her lap. "Roger, I have to ask you something. Did you assume the same thing about me and Lyle that Siavash did?"

The question took Roger by surprise. "I mean I wondered. That's all."

She wiped away a tear. "It's all right. I guess that's what it looked like. Even though I told you Lyle wouldn't let me leave."

"I'm sorry."

Sophie stared at the floor. "I would never sleep with somebody I wasn't in love with." She finally met his eyes. "How could you think I was ever in love with Lyle? That's what I don't understand."

"I didn't know. At first I wondered what you saw in him. Then I sensed you were afraid of him. And so I wanted to get you away from him. And finally I just plain wanted you." He kissed a tear on her cheek. "I still want you, Sophie. I always will."

She put her head on his shoulder. "I hope so."

He ran his fingers through her soft hair realizing it was fortunate that Sophie had never met Jill. She would have asked him the same questions about how he ever got hooked up with a woman like her. He didn't want to think about it.

Sophie lifted her head to give him a warm, soft, gentle kiss. "I wish we could live together."

"At least we can both stay at Omar's house."

On the sidewalk, sighing softly, Sophie turned to take a last look at the villa.

"Sad to leave?" Roger asked.

"I was happy when I first moved in. I'm a country girl, and the truth is this villa is better than our house in Belgium. I sent pictures to my mother."

Sophie put her arm through Roger's as they walked, then pulled it away. This wasn't done in Afghanistan. It had probably been taboo for unmarried couples in their own countries, as well, if you went back far enough. Roger glanced at the people in the street to see if they were watching them. They were, but doubtless just because they were foreigners.

"At first I worried about his winking," Sophie said.

Roger realized she was still thinking about her life in the villa. "Until I saw he winked at everybody." She paused. "Even at Ishak. But I never …. Sorry. I don't want to think about that."

Amal's light brown eyes gleamed when she saw Sophie had come back to stay with them again. Her husband Hekmat called out "Pepsi" to little Musa. Their son Karim spread the sofré cloth on the rug. Omar came in from the garden with a honeydew melon. The evening feast began.

After a long meal, when Musa and Sima were washing the dishes and Amal was putting baby Laila to bed and Hekmat was helping Karim with his homework under the garden light, Omar brought in another pot of tea. Roger and Sophie filled him in on what had been happening.

"He has a family?" Omar asked when they told him Ishak had gone home. "At least he has a home to go to. There are so many children here who've been forced to make their own way on the streets."

Sophie said Ishak's father had been a "digger" in a restoration project in the Morad Khani district of the city. "That's what Ishak told me. Now that the project is complete, he said his father doesn't have a regular job. I got the idea Ishak gave the money Lyle paid him to his family."

"It hurts me to say this," Omar almost whispered. "Musa told me things that made me suspicious of Mr. Lyle's relationship with that boy."

Sophie touched her cheeks. "The poor boy. If I had known what I now realize, I would have tried to get him away from Lyle." She swallowed. "Is there some way we can help him?"

"Like find him another job?" Roger suggested. "A real one."

"He likes to figure out how things work," Sophie had noticed. "He makes mechanical toys or models from scraps of metal. Lyle found him when he was 'suspiciously' looking under his truck. Ishak later told me he was just looking behind the wheel to see how it was attached. Maybe—"

Omar called in his son-in-law. "Hekmat, don't you have a friend who repairs automobiles?"

"A customer, yes. His shop is on Sulh Road, not far from my store. He's doing good business."

Omar switched into Dari to discuss his idea with Hekmat. Then he asked Sophie if she thought she could find Ishak's family in the district where they lived.

"I don't see how. All I know is his father's name, Shiazad."

Hekmat grinned. "There are a lot of Shia Muslims living in that neighborhood. You have an expression about finding a needle in a haystack?"

21

Finding the needle

Roger and Sophie set out with Omar to look for Ishak's family in the cramped, ancient haystack of mud hovels in Morad Khani. The taxi took them first through the New City past tall buildings, almost all with shops at the sidewalk level. Salang Wat, the main road leading southeast, was partly lined with trees and packed bumper to bumper with beeping cars and motorcycles. The bicycles made more progress than the cars. Open sluices lined the side streets, and people washed their cars with pails of water from these juubs, as Omar said they were called. Smoke rose from kabob stands and steam gushed from huge, shiny brass boilers tended by turbaned tea sellers. A lot of the signs were in English. Over the narrow blue door of a little shop Roger noted *Finest Supermarket*. The glass front of another shop was painted over with pictures of movie stars and the words *Hollywood Hair Styles* in letters two feet high. Next to it he saw an Apple Store.

They turned onto a narrower road that ran by a park bordered by a tall wrought iron fence. When they stopped in the traffic, Roger saw a shop with antique flintlock pistols and rifles on display that he thought must have survived from the days of British rule or before. Roger wanted to buy one for a keepsake, but Omar told him, first, there is a law against exporting antiques, although … and, second, most of them were probably copies made by skilled Afghan craftsmen.

The taxi jerked ahead and managed a turn onto the wide Ebn-e-Sina Road that led down to the Kabul River. They didn't know where to tell the driver to go, so Omar said to take them to the Abul Fazl shrine, where the road met the river at the edge of the Morad Khani district. Crawling through the traffic, they saw the turquoise blue dome of the mosque and its twin minarets against the mountains in the distance.

Omar said the shrine commemorated a Shia Muslim martyr. The cylindrical minarets were completely covered by alternating squares of dark blue and gold glass that glittered in the hot sun. The plaza was swarming with people Omar said were Shia pilgrims who'd come on the day of Ashura to pay respect to Abul Fazl, who was killed in the 680 A.D. battle of Karbala. "Afghans have a long memory," he quipped.

Around the base of a minaret, turbaned gray-bearded men squatted beside stacks of papers and books. People crouched in front of them, some getting their palms read, some watching while the turbaned men looked in their books or wrote on small pieces of paper, which they handed them. "*Falbin*," Omar explained. "Fortune tellers."

Sophie wore her blue hejab loosely tied. As soon as she got out of the taxi, Roger recognized the murmured word for "beautiful," which Sophie seemed to evoke whenever she walked among Afghans—men or women—who were in no particular hurry to go anywhere. Sophie had learned to ignore them. When she stopped to glance at an old fortune teller with hardly any teeth, the man reached up and took her hand.

Omar grinned. "He wants to tell your fortune, help you with your problems. Half-price, he says."

Sophie told the man, "I'm looking for someone."

The fortune teller gestured for her to sit. He examined her palm, then paged through a dog-eared book of palm line drawings. He asked Sophie something that made her blush.

Omar whispered to Roger, "Wants to know if it's a husband she's seeking."

Roger understood when Sophie answered that she was looking for a boy named Ishak whose father is Shiazad.

The old man gasped. The book dropped onto his lap.

"He says he knows Ishak's mother," Omar translated. "She came to him worried about her son. He gave her a verse from the Koran to recite every morning and every night. If she did, God would bring good fortune to her son."

The old fortune teller looked up into Sophie's blue eyes. "*Mashal-lah!*" he exclaimed, crossing his hands on his chest. "The work of God," Omar translated. "God has sent an angel to help this boy."

The old man called out to someone in the crowd that was beginning to gather. That man came up to Omar and Roger. "I speak English a little. You are looking for Ishak and Shiazad? I know them. I will take you."

When Sophie offered the fortune teller money, he choked up and managed only a wordless refusal.

Roger felt the onlookers' eyes on them as their guide led them into the maze of dilapidated, flat-roofed mud houses of the oldest part of the city. The narrow dirt paths were wide enough only for people or bicycles to pass. Most of the houses were vacant, uninhabitable. Some had remnants of intricately carved cedar trim on the arched doorways or windows. A few carved wooden walls remained, splintering and faded but still intact. Omar said that court officials lived here in the early nineteenth century. Now only families like Ishak's lived here, some of them descendants of the original owners.

"If I ever needed to hide away somewhere," Omar joked, "this is where I'd come."

A smell of decay from the nearby Kabul River hung in the air. Sophie pulled her hejab across her face. They weaved through crooked lanes until suddenly they came upon the carved wooden columns and Mughal arches of a two-level caravanserai completely restored to its nineteenth-century richness.

"I don't understand," Roger said.

"A British organization helped train local Afghans to rebuild it." Omar paused to take it in with narrowed eyes and a pleased tilt of his head. Roger was amazed that amid invasions, wars, and bombings it was still possible to do work like this. The future might seem bleak, but the people were still able to focus on doing their work well. The same went for the cooks, the dressmakers, the ceramic painters—everyone he'd watched busy at their trades.

It was easy enough to tell which ruins were lived in. The openings of these houses had doors or blankets covering the entrances, and some had clothes hung from the roofs to dry. The guide led them to a crumbling mud wall with a carved wooden gate still in place. Above the wall, a roof covered by a blue tarp was barely visible. Their guide banged on the gate. "Shiazad. Shiazad."

Behind the wall, the cry of a goat rang out, and soon the gate cracked open. A woman in a full black chador peeped out with one eye. Greetings, bowings, and lengthy polite phrases that Roger was by now familiar with followed as the guide introduced them and backed away, bowing again. Omar gave him some coins.

Ishak's mother seemed to recognize Sophie, possibly from her son's description. She took them into a large courtyard and through an open passage into their house. Roger and Sophie followed Omar's lead and left their shoes outside the doorway. After their walk in the harsh sun, the room seemed dark and, because of the thick walls, cool. Roger knew what was coming next. The woman put tea into a pot and filled it from a kerosene samovar. As they sat on cushions, she knelt in front of them arranging tea glasses on the sofré and called her husband and Ishak.

They came in together. Both knelt and bowed, first to Sophie, then to Omar and Roger. Ishak's cast was gone, his arm pale where it had been. His brown eyes darted nervously from one person to another as if he might be accused of something he didn't understand. Even in the dim light, his dark cheeks glowed red. His uneasiness affected his father, who began to finger his worry beads.

"Ishak," his mother said, and she must have asked him to bring in something. Roger tapped Google Translate on his phone, but soon put it away. He would have to get the details of this meeting later from Omar.

Ishak, still blushing, brought a drawing pad to his mother. She flipped through it, folded it open, and showed a sketch to the group. It was a beautiful pencil drawing of Sophie's face.

"She says God forgive him for drawing a human likeness," Omar told Roger. "She says Ishak never stopped talking about Miss Sophie. She and her husband offer condolences for Mr. Lyle's death. They say Miss Sophie must have been shocked."

Sophie changed the subject as soon as she could, turning to Omar to explain the offer to arrange a job for Ishak in an auto repair shop. Roger could see that the mother was distraught at the thought of her son leaving home again, and she tried to refuse. Ishak's father looked unhappy, too, but reluctantly agreed. Omar later told Roger that Shiazad had been one of the men hired to dig up the garbage and junk that had covered up the remains of the caravanserai and other buildings that were restored. That work had ended. Now his only income was from mending pots, sharpening scissors—whatever work he could find.

Roger looked around the nearly empty room, then out into the barren courtyard at its dried up pond and wizened pomegranate tree. In one corner he saw the vines of what looked like a small melon patch. The goat was tied to a stake and nibbling at weeds growing in the shade of the wall.

Ishak's eyes beamed. He repeated "auto repair" over and over in English. Omar gave them the address of Hekmat's Quick Mart and, Roger assumed, said that Hekmat would introduce Ishak to the repair shop owner.

His mother, according to Omar, claimed Ishak was already making some money cleaning out cages at the bird market. But before long she sighed and conceded. *"Alhamdulillah,"* she said, and Roger also heard the word *falbin*. Ishak's mother probably decided the job offer was the answer to the prayers the fortune teller had prescribed.

The father gave Ishak a talk that Roger was sure tasked him with working hard, being responsible, etc., etc.—the same talk his own father had given him when he got his first teenage job. Roger assumed the visit had come to a successful conclusion, but no. They couldn't leave without being served a meal.

Immediately there was a lot of discussion between Ishak's parents. Omar told Roger it was about what they could possibly serve their "distinguished guests." When it seemed they'd come to a conclusion, Sophie's face turned white. "They're going to kill the goat," she cried. Ishak's father went into the courtyard.

Roger stood up. "No. No. I have to go. We have to get back. Tell them. An important appointment, tell them."

Omar managed to stop Shiazad before he reached the goat. Roger had already said his *tashakor* thank you, and was standing by the gate, Sophie close behind him.

As they made their way to the river road to catch a taxi, Omar grinned. "That was an amazingly effective use of *ta'ārof*, Roger. You've definitely learned the Afghan custom of polite refusal."

22

An unqualified yes

Sophie hugged Amal and thanked Omar's family for letting her stay with them but said she had no excuse to stay any longer. She would move back into her room in Green Village. There were loud protests. Amal insisted she stay one more night.

This time Amal returned to her own bedroom with her husband and baby. Roger lay wide awake in the dark main room listening to Omar's low-pitched snore and Karim's deep breathing. The thought of Sophie sleeping alone in that other room made his pulse race. He envisioned himself creeping in there, silently holding her—something he hadn't been able to do for days—then shook the idea from his head. He picked up his phone, turned off the sound.

You awake? He heard a faint beep over in Sophie's room.

Yes.

Turn off your beep.

OK.

I can't sleep.

Me either.

We're like two prisoners sending messages from cell to cell.

Set me free!

Yeah. There's something I want to ask you but I can't yet.

I know.

You know what it is?

I think so.

There are legal things I need to figure out.

Does that heart mean …

Means we'll figure it out together.

I think I can sleep now.
Me too.
Good-night, Sophie.
Shab bekheir, *Roger.*

"You and Sophie should get married," Amal told Roger, setting soft boiled eggs in wooden cup holders in front of the two of them. Sophie stared down at her egg, suppressing a smile. Roger glanced up at Amal to see her substantial chest heaving in a silent chuckle.

"Let them eat their breakfast in peace," Omar chided. But he couldn't resist getting in on the fun. "I do know that Miss Sophie consulted a fortune teller yesterday. That's all I'll say."

Amal's eyes widened. Sophie blushed, and busied herself cracking open her egg.

"Oh, but that's right," Omar added quickly. "It was just to ask how to find Ishak. Now I remember."

"Don't tease her," Amal cried. "Miss Sophie, I hope you'll stay with us as long as you're in Kabul."

"I'd like to," Sophie replied. "But all my clothes and books are back in my room. And my roommate's coming back from Kandahar today. She'll expect me to stay with her."

When Sophie left to teach at her school, Roger kicked a soccer ball with Musa and Sima for a while, then went to teach another math lesson at Karim's school in the afternoon. On his way there, he stopped at an ATM. Already the money from his Saint Michael's salary was running out. Jill's contribution was still there. In fact, another automatic deposit had been made by Grayrock. No date. Probably before Grayrock realized she was dead. Roger hated the idea of using Grayrock money, but soon he might have to.

Just as before, teaching those boys made him feel he was doing some good—and that his effort was appreciated. One of the boys spontaneously yelled *Marhabā* when the class together solved a complex problem. Karim's English teacher echoed "Hurrah!" He still stayed to translate but that was seldom needed. Math was kind of a language in itself. Roger was gaining confidence he could do the job even without help.

Karim and his friends cornered him in the schoolyard after class, trying out their English. "Do you have wife?" "Afghanistan or America, which is better?" On the way home his phone beeped. He had a message from Inez Gonzalez, his friend at Saint Michael's.

Fr. Joy asked if you're returning in the fall. Get your M.A. yet? Summer school Spanish is gruesome. Glad to be retiring. Everything OK in Afghanistan?

Now was the time contracts for the coming year were signed at Saint Michael's. Roger didn't want to work there any more, but he needed a job. He sent Inez a reply: *Good to hear from you. Got my M.A. Can you try to stall Fr. Joy? You need to download WhatsApp to talk to me here. If you do, text me when it's a good time to call you.*

I will.

As usual, Roger went to meet Sophie at the Femmes en Crise school when her classes were over. Sophie was standing by the door with her friend Lexi when he got there. Lexi gave him a warm handshake and a broad smile. Her hair was cut short and her brown eyes seemed to be studying Roger. "I'll give you and Sophie some time alone," she offered.

Sophie hooked her arm through Lexi's. "No. It's OK. I've wanted you two to meet."

Lexi was the young woman, no older than Sophie, who'd just come back from Kandahar attempting to start up another teacher training school there. In Roger's mind, Kandahar was one of the most dangerous places in the country, the target of constant Taliban incursions and assassinations. He wasn't surprised to hear she hadn't had any success.

In the Ariana Café, the old waiter's eyes widened as he held the door to let Roger enter with two foreign young women he seemed to recognize. He brought tea to their table without asking. "We come here often after school," Sophie explained.

"To decompress." Lexi eyed Roger as if to check that the English phrase was correct.

"What a day," Sophie gushed. "This morning one of my teachers showed me a lesson she'd planned for her girls. About how viruses spread. Pictures, drawings—it was amazing. I love this job."

"Me too," Lexi agreed. "Would you believe there are only three of us left?"

Roger said he'd just come from teaching at Karim's school. "I wish I could do it full time. Today one of the boys asked me to write my name in his notebook. Then every one of them had to get my autograph."

"You're a celebrity." Sophie held her hands to her mouth as if starstruck. She held up her phone and leaned across the table. "Please. Can I take my picture with you?"

Lexi dropped a lump of sugar in her tea and stirred thoughtfully. "You know what the Belgian attaché in Kandahar did? Same thing. Took his picture with me. Probably put it on Facebook. And that was it. He told me there was no money to start a teacher training school there."

Sophie patted her hand. "Maybe if Femmes en Crise comes into some money, he'll change his mind. You never know." She shot Roger a quick look.

Lexi finished her tea and pulled her backpack onto her lap. "I see a taxi outside. You guys stay here." She glanced at Sophie. "Maybe you have things to talk about."

When Lexi left, Roger and Sophie faced each other in silence for a moment. "It's not going to be fun staying at Omar's while you stay in Green Village," Roger began.

Sophie nodded.

"I want to be with you. I'll try to find a paying job in Kabul, maybe with USAID, but I'm not hopeful. They're cutting back. There are rumors it won't be long until America pulls out of Afghanistan completely. Then what?"

"For now you can stay with me, Roger. Lexi said she wouldn't mind moving in with Nora."

"Yeah? Your salary could support both of us, me just hanging around jobless? Because I'm running out of money."

"I'm not talking about forever."

"Maybe we should talk about forever. I don't want to leave Afghanistan. But if I stay much longer I'll lose my job in America. And if I go back, I'm afraid I'll lose you."

"You won't."

"You mean …?" Roger inhaled. This was the moment. He'd come close before but never dared to ask it directly. "Will you marry me, Sophie?"

Her blue eyes danced. "Yes."

Roger paused to let her answer sink in. He didn't know what he'd expected. Something more conditional, for sure. Something along the lines of let's wait and see. He gave her a moment to qualify it. But she didn't. She was blushing happily.

"I realize," he said, "first I have to either prove Jill is dead or wait a year and file for divorce on the grounds of abandonment." Roger cringed to hear himself putting their dilemma into this cold, legalistic language. Until now he'd only spelled this out for his lawyer brother Dan. Sophie held her face in her hands and whispered through her fingers, "I know." She took a breath and looked up. *Khodā komak-e-mun.* God help us."

The waiter came over. "More tea? Anything else?"

Sophie seemed about to say no, then asked Roger, "They have good mantoo dumplings here. Want to try them?"

"Mantoo? Try them? Oh. Uh, sure."

"I bet you can't get these in America."

Roger gave a noncommittal shrug.

"I know how to make them. Guess who I learned from. Ishak." When Roger only stared at his dumplings, she went on, "Sorry. I'm chattering away. Talking about our future makes me nervous."

"Me too."

"How long can you stay here? I mean before you lose your job in America?"

"I won't leave you just to keep that job."

23

Sugar mommy

Omar's house was on the way to the Femmes en Crise housing, so Roger and Sophie shared a taxi part of the way home. When it stopped at Omar's, Hekmat rushed out. "Good news. My friend hired Ishak. He'll stay in a room over the repair shop. Miss Sophie, please come inside. Ishak sent a present for you. —Amal, they're back."

The whole family stood watching as Hekmat gave Sophie a copper bracelet embossed with tiny floral designs. "Ishak made it himself from scrap metal in the shop," Hekmat explained. Sophie slipped it on her wrist, words failing her.

"My friend says Ishak's a hard worker," Hekmat went on. "He needed help in the shop. He gave Ishak a motorcycle to use. He sends him to get new parts from a contractor at Green Village."

"Black market parts," Omar added with a glimmer in his eye.

"Well, I don't know about that," Hekmat mumbled.

Amal pulled Sophie by the arm. "At least come in for some tea. We'll send the taxi off and get you another one later if you want."

Sophie was quiet as they all sat around on cushions. She kept looking at the bracelet, turning it on her wrist. Amal brought pistachios, sunflower seeds, watermelon. Sophie ate nothing.

"You have to stay with us tonight," Amal urged. But Sophie said she was sorry. "My friend Lexi is alone. I need to go back." It was an incontrovertible imperative, Roger had already learned. In Afghanistan leaving a friend alone was unthinkable.

"Then come back to stay any time." Amal brought Sophie a package tied in brown paper, the "effects" Lyle had left at the Grayrock quarters. "You forgot these things."

Sophie started to object but then seemed to remember being given the package in the Grayrock morgue. "Oh, thanks."

As she got in the taxi, Sophie whispered, "I'll text you tonight from my bed."

Roger went out to the garden to call Dan. He hadn't talked to him since he'd come back to Kabul.

"I should have called you before, Dan. Lyle is dead. Hit by a roadside bomb."

"You're kidding? Jill and Lyle both dead? So Mr. Straw Man now takes over the Bebsi business for real."

"Actually, I'm working with an Afghan cop to get that money back to the Belgian aid group."

"Or you could just come home. Mom and Dad are worried, you know. It didn't seem to settle their nerves when I told them you're caught up in a money laundering scheme and you might get married again."

"That's something I wanted to ask you about."

"Which one?"

"Getting married. I need to know my legal status. Assuming I can't prove Jill is dead, I need to know what's involved in getting a divorce from a wife who's disappeared."

"I asked a guy in the office who handles that kind of thing. He confirmed you have to wait a year."

"That's what I was afraid of. Is there any paperwork I should start now?"

"I'll ask Bill. When are you coming back?"

"I'm not sure. My visitor's visa's good for three months."

"So I'll tell Mom and Dad … what?"

"If they would download WhatsApp, I could tell them myself. Tell them about Sophie. Tomorrow maybe I'll text you a picture of her."

Roger couldn't understand how Afghans could drift off to sleep so easily after drinking all that tea. He turned off the beep on his phone again and texted Sophie.

Great that Ishak got the job.

A reply came back immediately. *Now we need to get you one!*

Thought you were going to be my sugar mommy.

The reply to this was delayed. Sophie might have had to look up that phrase. Then *OK. I will.* And then *Problem solved.*

Send me a picture of you.

It's dark. My hair's all messed up.

Let me see anyway.

You asked for it. The text came with a picture of her face.

Beautiful. Going to send it to my family.

YOU BETTER NOT!

All right. Meet at your school tomorrow?

Yes. Unless Siavash has other plans for us. And then *I'm not sleepy yet. Wish we could be together.*

We need our own four walls. To make us free.

Roger didn't want a sugar mommy. Which meant he had to get a job either in Kabul or in the States. It was eleven thirty at night in Kabul but still two in the afternoon in Baltimore. Roger quietly rolled off his mat and tiptoed out into the yard in his bare feet. A dog barked once from outside the wall, then stopped. Roger sat on the edge of the pond and dialed Inez, who had texted that she now had downloaded WhatsApp.

"Roger, is that really you? It sounds like you're calling from next door."

"How are you, Inez?"

"Looking forward to retirement. But there's something I need to tell you. Father Joy said he's going to advertise for a new math teacher. I convinced him to wait until I talk to you."

"Inez, I don't even know if I'll be back in time for the start of the fall classes. You'd better tell him to advertise."

"Then what will you do? I can ask around and check ads for other teaching jobs, if you want."

"That would be great." It was just what he was hoping she'd say. "So, Inez, did everybody pass Spanish for Dummies?"

"Kirk didn't. He found out where I live, came here, and threatened to have his father get me fired." Inez chuckled. "He didn't know I was retiring. But Father Joy insisted I give him a D, just enough for him to graduate." Inez cleared her throat. "By the way, this is terrible. Kirk told me he threatened you, too. He said he put a note on your door saying something like *You won't get away with this.*"

Roger gasped. "What? Kirk wrote that note?"

"And he wrote *You're going down.* That's what he told me."

Roger's mind was racing.

"Well," Inez told him, "you won't have to worry about Kirk any more. He's off to Harvard in the fall, Father Joy told me."

24

Hoo-waah!

Roger trudged out to the shower stall when he woke up. He hadn't gotten much sleep the night before. The note on his door had been from Kirk. It was Kirk's bluster, trying to scare him into giving him a better grade—not a threat to Jill from some "Special Forces type guy." For hours Roger had tossed on his mat trying to figure out what that might mean.

The loud *ak-ak-ak* of the magpie on the wall made him start. It was silly, he knew, but he checked his phone. Just then a text arrived. From Siavash, asking him to call.

"Roger, DeWoot's insisting we figure out how to get the money from the Grayrock vault."

"Oh. Right."

"Any ideas?"

"Lyle told me the vault guy will open it if we have one key and a death certificate for the other key holder."

"I know. But Grayrock won't give out any information to the Afghan police. So here's what I think. You're American. Grayrock called you in to identify Lyle's body. You could go back and ask for his death certificate. Sophie should go with you. They brought her in to ID him, too."

Roger met Sophie as she was leaving her Green Village room to go to her school. "Sorry to surprise you. It's DeWoot's fault. He can't sit still until we get that money back."

"I know. He called me."

They took the taxi that had come for Sophie. Roger intended to tell her about the note on his door that he'd found out wasn't a threat on Jill's life after all, but it slipped his mind when Sophie put her arm through his and squeezed his hand. It was just a short ride to the Grayrock hospital in Camp Rectitude.

Doctor Smith wiped some drops of melted chocolate ice cream from his desk with a page from *Stars and Stripes*. "Do I look like I have time to get you a death certificate?"

Sophie's tears seemed real as they stood before his desk. Roger insisted, "She needs it for personal reasons. I hope you can understand."

Sophie folded her hands together. "Please, please, Doctor. It's so important to me."

Dealing with a pretty woman in distress had to be a new experience for this Grayrock doctor. His lips trembled slightly. "Now, now," he told her. "We've already made out a certificate. Filed away somewhere." He called out, "Manley, I need you," and the young man in a white jacket came in.

"Go through the death records in that cabinet over there. See if you can find the papers for Lyle White."

In the taxi to Siavash's headquarters, Roger complimented Sophie on her acting. "He'd never have gotten his butt off that chair if it was only me asking him."

"I was only half acting. I want all this to be over. I came over here to train women to educate the girls of the country. I knew the Taliban would oppose us, but I never imagined there would be money launderers and American contractors and even a U.S. senator working against us."

"Power corrupts."

"And money." She looked blankly through the window. "I wish I could just focus on doing the job I came here for."

"I think you should. I'll tell Siavash you've done your part and he and I can take it from here."

DeWoot was sitting in Siavash's office when Roger and Sophie were shown in. Roger dropped the death certificate on the desk. "It was Sophie who got the Grayrock guy to turn it over."

"*Barik-e-allah*," Siavash exclaimed. "Well done, Sophie."

"Yes," DeWoot echoed, "*Bien fait*. Now we have a death certificate for Lyle and we have Jill's key." He twisted his jaw. "But Jill is dead, too. So how do we—"

Siavash glanced at Sophie. "Neither the vault guy nor Daghal ever saw Jill," he pointed out. "All they know is that a foreign woman has the other key. Right, Roger? That's what Lyle told you?"

"Yes, but no," Roger answered. "You can't send Sophie to the Grayrock vault to get the money. It's too dangerous. She's done enough already."

DeWoot pulled at his moustache. Siavash twirled his pen on the desk. Neither seemed willing to look Sophie in the eye.

"It's OK," Sophie spoke up. "I'll do it."

DeWoot clapped his hand on the desk. "Fantastic. We'll need to get the guards in place. I'll call you when we're ready to go. It might take a day or so."

Roger met Sophie after her class and went with her back to her room. They'd have a couple of hours before Lexi got back from shopping. They were lying in her bed when DeWoot interrupted with a phone call to Sophie. Sophie's side of the conversation was mostly "OK ... OK ... *D'accord*."

"He's ready for us to go to the Grayrock vault and get the money." She looked at Roger and started giggling.

"Oh, yeah. The vault. We've been kind of distracted lately."

First they had to find the vault. Roger's previous interaction with Grayrock contractors didn't suggest that would be easy. U.S. security contractors like Grayrock were basically autonomous corporations with their own armed forces who were paid enormous sums and given carte blanche to help governments impose their will on a country. Roger didn't look forward to asking them where they kept their money.

"DeWoot says he can't get into Camp Rectitude but he's going to wait outside the gate with Belgian guards to transport the money to our Ministry of Foreign Affairs safe."

"Grayrock won't let in the Belgian Deputy Minister of Foreign Affairs?"

"That's what he said. He thinks an American will have a better chance of getting in."

Roger started to pace. When he passed a closet with its curtain half-drawn, he noticed a bundle wrapped in paper on the floor, still tied with string. "You never opened that? Let's see what's in it."

"Oh, I don't want to. I'm going to throw it away."

Roger tore it open. He pulled out a black T-shirt with the Grayrock eagle talon logo on the front. "Looks like little Lyle and you wear the same size," he chuckled. "I have an idea. Let's see what else is in here." He tossed out some dirty underwear, socks, khaki pants. "What's this? Looks like pouches you tie around your waist." In one of them was a wallet. "Lyle's U.S. driver's license," Roger noted. "Some U.S. money, not much. What's this?" It was Jill's expired driver's license.

Sophie wrinkled her nose. "Put that trash down. Please."

But Roger held the Grayrock T-shirt up to her. "This could be our ticket in. And the khaki pants? With the pouches and ID cards?"

"Ugh. I don't even want to touch those things."

But by the time they left her room she was fully outfitted as a Grayrock "operative" and amused in spite of herself. "As long as I can burn these and take a shower as soon as we get back."

"You look ferocious. I mean cute-ferocious, if that's a thing."

"Hoo-waah! Hand over that money!"

On a side street outside the Camp Rectitude gate, DeWoot gasped when he saw Sophie in her Grayrock outfit. "Oh, I see. Good idea." Siavash stared speechless at her for a moment, then helped Roger put on a wired device. "Record the withdrawal, get it on record that Lyle put the money there." He handed Lyle's death certificate back to Sophie.

Roger took Jill's key from his pocket, where he'd carried it ever since coming back to Kabul, and gave it to Sophie. She rolled her eyes and dropped it into a pouch at her waist.

Siavash called an armored taxi for them. "DeWoot and I will be waiting here. Good luck."

At the Camp Rectitude gate, Roger, wearing his suit, tie, and recording device, showed his U.S. passport. Sophie gave the guard a salute. "Personnel asset storage facility," Roger said, lifting into view Jill's Grayrock logo duffel bag that they had stuffed with bedsheets and blankets. "Deposit to make."

"Building A-5, Sir. Down that road and to the left."

They left the Grayrock bag in the waiting taxi and walked up to the quonset building. Another guard let them in. It took a minute for Roger's eyes to adjust to the dim light inside. A weasely man with a blotchy face sat in a room flanked by two more guards.

"Here to make a withdrawal," Roger snapped in his best Grayrock voice. "Double security vault. One depositor has her key. Hajis blew the other guy up with an IED. We have his death certificate."

In a machine-like voice, the weasel recited, "Procedures require examination of relevant documents."

Sophie unsnapped a pouch on her belt and handed him the certificate. The weasel pulled up glasses hanging around his neck and examined the document, silently mouthing the words.

Still attempting a Grayrock voice, Roger said, "You see whose vault we're talking about, right?"

The weasel put his finger on the certificate. "Lyle White. Lyle White's vault." He looked up. "We have strict procedures to follow."

On the weasel's desk sat a computer and a printer. It became clear to Roger that this man found using the computer the most difficult part of his job. "Death certificate of depositor Lyle White to account for his missing key. Possession of one key by co-owner Jill Williams." He was talking to himself as he typed in the information with two fingers.

The computer pinged. The printer whirred. The weasel dropped his glasses on their chain and looked up. "Signature of key bearing co-owner required for withdrawal." He pointed to a line for Sophie to sign on, then asked for identification. She showed him Jill's driver's license, and without looking closely at the picture, he dutifully copied down the number.

The weasel opened a cabinet under his desk and produced a key. "Personal vault number nine hundred twenty-five."

One of the guards led the way to a vault with a thick metal door. Roger watched as Sophie turned her key and the weasel turned his. The door screeched open. Side by side on a shelf were two army duffel bags stuffed full. Roger slipped his arm through the strap of one bag and was surprised how heavy it was. He asked the guard to carry the other one.

"We'll need a copy of the paperwork," Roger said.

The weasel pointed to his office. "Bring the items." He sat and began plunking out another form. "Two large duffel bags removed with unspecified contents. Witness ...." He typed his own name without stating it." The printer whirred. The weasel signed two copies of the form and slid them across his desk for Sophie to sign and keep a copy. A guard helped carry the bags to the waiting taxi.

Siavash, DeWoot, and two Belgian soldiers met them outside the gate. They loaded the bags into DeWoot's black SUV, Roger dismissed the taxi, and they drove to the temporary headquarters of the Belgian Ministry of Foreign Affairs, where Lexi and Nora burst out laughing at the sight of Sophie in her Grayrock outfit.

As soon as they brought the bags inside, DeWoot unzipped them. They were stuffed full of new bills bound into packs by mustard-colored paper straps.

"Mustard color means hundreds," DeWoot informed them. "A hundred hundreds in each pack, so ten thousand dollars per pack."

They stacked the packs into piles on the floor and counted them.

"Two hundred thirty packs," DeWoot said. "That's the whole two million three hundred thousand dollars USAID was delivering to the Belgian ministry for Femmes en Crise."

They stuffed the money back into the bags and crammed them into the Belgian safe. DeWoot asked the soldiers to return in two days to load the money onto a plane he'd arranged. "I won't rest until we get it safely into the ministry's account in the Bank of Brussels."

Roger gave Siavash the wired device. "I got it all recorded." Sophie gave him the document the weasel had produced."

"And now …." DeWoot took a bottle of Belgian jenever gin from a shelf and poured them all shot glasses full. He gave Sophie a hug and a brush of his moustache on each cheek, then did the same for Roger. "Our embassy has shut down, the German Embassy is operating out of a shipping container after being bombed, the U.S. President is calling for a drastic cutback in troops here, but Femmes en Crise will carry on—now with money even to expand."

Roger followed the Belgians' lead in bending down to sip first before lifting the glass to down it at once. A refrain of celebratory gasps followed.

"Hurrah!" Siavash shouted, heading for the door. "The money's returned. The perps are dead. For now we can celebrate. I'll be contacting you soon about some loose ends we need to tie up."

Roger noticed that Siavash left without touching his gin.

25

Coming or not coming

Deputy Minister of Foreign Affairs DeWoot was the last to arrive at the Major Crimes Task Force headquarters in the foothills of the mountains. Before coming, he'd stopped at the Pulshui Bank to check it out. DeWoot seemed insulted. "The bank president assumed I wanted to hide away some Belgian government funds. He swore the names of his depositors were confidential."

"Uh-huh." Siavash nodded. "His name's Daghal. As the Americans say, he's 'already on our radar.' We haven't been able to ...." Siavash hesitated.

"Pin anything on him?" Roger couldn't help offering.

"Not yet. We have somebody watching the bank, but we can't figure out how Daghal ships the money overseas. Money goes in, but we never see it go out." Siavash tapped a folder on his desk. "But now we have documents for fake corporations and have recovered the stolen money. I'm going to ask a judge for a warrant to record Daghal. To trap him we won't actually have to deposit any of the money in his bank. All we should need is to get him on tape agreeing to take the money and launder it. If we get that, I hope we'll be able to shut him and his bank down."

Sophie spoke up. "I'm not really clear on what you mean by 'launder' the money?"

"It's laundering," Siavash explained, "if Daghal accepts a large amount of money without asking where it came from, puts it into the account of a fake company, then starts transferring it little by little to another bank as if the fake company was earning it. The dirty, stolen money now looks like clean, earned money."

"Aren't there regulators to watch over banks?" Roger wondered.

"Under the new Afghan president, banks are getting a little more oversight than they did in the days of the great Kabul Bank scandal eight years ago. But Daghal is cleverer than those Kabul Bank criminals. He doesn't steal money or give it away to cronies like they did. He has paperwork to make the transfers look legitimate and just takes a percentage."

"You mean he does this for others besides Lyle?"

"Quite a few others. U.S. dollars pour into Afghanistan, and they pour out. If we record Daghal doing this, we're pretty sure we'll catch his other clients." Siavash took a breath. "Then we move on to the other Daghals."

"Besides Daghal," Roger said, "there's somebody else I'd like to expose." He told them about Senator Steinherz taking bribes to keep Lyle and other contractors from being investigated. "Something Lyle said makes me think the senator expected to get a cut of this money."

Siavash snickered. "So corruption isn't a problem exclusive to the Afghan government? Tell that to our critics in Washington."

"I intend to. Here's what I'm thinking. What if we recorded Daghal making a deal with the senator? We could trap them both at once."

"You mean get the senator to come here asking for a bribe? What are the chances you could do that?"

"If I could, though?"

DeWoot squirmed in his chair. "Dealing with a U.S. senator makes me nervous. Isn't he a problem for the Americans to handle by themselves?"

Roger spoke up. "Well, I'm an American. I want him exposed."

Siavash held out a hand for calm. "My FBI contact will be back in Kabul soon. If a U.S. senator's involved, I'm sure he'll want to give Roger's idea a try. Let's give Roger a little time to work on it."

It was the last day of the lease on Lyle's villa. DeWoot drove Sophie and Roger there from Siavash's office so Sophie could finally gather up the rest of her things. As the car wound down the side of the barren hillside, nobody talked. DeWoot blew the horn at a flock of sheep trundling across the road while a turbaned shepherd in baggy trousers and patched vest stood stiff and expressionless watching the shiny black Suburban pass by. Roger tried to imagine what the shepherd was thinking. He looked old enough to remember seeing Russians honking at his sheep. Before that the British had tried to put their stamp on the people's lives. Now it was the Americans. To Roger the shepherd watching the car seemed to be patiently waiting for the Americans to pass out of his life as well.

Roger helped Sophie gather up a few clothes, books, blankets, and cooking utensils she'd left at Lyle's house. When Sophie said she wanted to stay in the neighborhood and do some shopping, DeWoot offered to drop her things off with her roommate when he went back to Green Village.

"Shopping?" Roger asked as they watched DeWoot drive away.

"Well, no. I just didn't want to ride back with him yet."

"Good. Want to take a walk to the Shahr-e-Naow Park near Karim's school?"

She took Roger's hand. "We have the house for the rest of the day. Let's go back inside and pretend it's ours."

Roger closed the door behind them. "We could never afford the rent on a villa like this."

"That's for sure. Nobody except your Uncle Sam can afford this rent. America doesn't care how much it pays. No other country in NATO could afford it."

"But it's rented till tomorrow. I could text Omar and we could stay here tonight. We could sleep in your narrow bed. No electricity, no cooler, but we—"

The door burst open. Three men in army boots and baggy khaki pants stomped in wearing T-shirts stamped with Grayrock's menacing eagle talon logo. Their belts were weighed down with all kinds of radios, scopes, and other gadgets that Roger didn't recognize. "What the hell?" one shouted. "Nobody's supposed to be here."

Once again Roger was glad he'd worn his suit and tie. He stood up and gave his name. "And this is Sophie. She has the lease on this place until tomorrow."

"Sorry, Sir. But we were ordered to clear out everything in the house, take it back to Camp Rectitude."

Two of the men were bulky, to use a kind word. The third, a trimmer man, stepped forward. "What did you say your name was, Sir? Roger Williams? Then my chief has been trying to get in touch with you." He un-holstered a device as big as a Roger's mother's old portable telephone with an antenna. "I'll dial him, Sir, and you can see what he wants."

The "chief" had a surprisingly thin voice. "Roger Williams? I have a message from the D.C. headquarters for you to call Ignacio Corelli on a secure line ASAP. Hold on. It's seventeen hundred hours now. O eight thirty in D.C. Should be a good time to call. Hand me back to Chopstick. He'll put you through."

Chopstick punched in a code and a number. Roger put the phone to his ear.

"You might want to take that outside, Sir. Secure lines are for confidential calls."

Roger stepped onto the sidewalk, leaving the door open so he could keep an eye on Sophie. The black phone covered half his face, its antenna soaring above his head. He felt like a villain in a comic strip. There were weird whirring sounds and static, then "Yeah?" He recognized Iggy's voice.

"It's Roger Williams."

"Secure line, right? Nobody can hear you? All right. So, I understand Lyle White passed away."

"I guess you could put it that way."

"I don't usually get into this sort of detail, you understand, but Senator Steinherz touched down in Kabul a while ago and talked to Lyle. It seems Lyle promised the senator's cut from one of his operations would be substantial. The senator's back here now, and he's been on my ass since he found out Lyle's dead. He says nobody seems to know what operation Lyle was talking about."

"Hmm."

"Don't play dumb, Roger. I know the key you were bringing to Lyle had something to do with it."

Roger had an idea, and there wasn't time to run it by Siavash. "Maybe I can help," he told Iggy. "The senator will have to get in touch with Lyle's money man here in Kabul."

"You want the senator to fly back to Kabul?"

"That's the only way I can see it happening. I can put him in touch with—"

"Who? Who is this money man?"

"He's a bank president."

"What's his name? What bank?"

"Lyle didn't tell me. But he told me how to get in touch with him," Roger lied. "He said the bank president knows nothing about his deal with the senator. It was safer that way. So with Lyle dead, the senator himself will have to come and convince the bank guy that he had a deal with Lyle. I'll back him up."

Iggy's voice was gravelly. "I'll give the senator the message. I can't promise he'll be willing to go back to Kabul. I'll text you *Coming* or *Not Coming* and the arrival time."

Back inside, Roger handed the phone back to Chopstick.

Sophie was confronting the Grayrock men. "A lot of these things belong to the landlord. They came with the house."

Chopstick insisted, "We were told to take everything, Ma'am."

Roger picked up the bag of Sophie's things as they left.

While they waited on the sidewalk for a taxi to take Sophie back to her room, Roger told her his plan. "So I might have found a way to get Senator Steinherz to come here. If he does, we can record him leaning on Daghal to give him his cut."

"Get them both at once, as you suggested to Siavash?"

"Right. Hold on. I should call Siavash to let him know the plan." Roger drew Sophie into an alley between two houses, not wanting a repeat of the episode when the police stopped him. Siavash liked the plan.

"So it's agreed?" Roger asked him. "We wait for the senator to get here?"

"We can wait a little longer. I'll ask the judge to include Senator Steinherz in the warrant. If he doesn't show up before the warrant expires, we'll need you to go to Daghal alone and get him to incriminate himself."

"All right."

"Now we need to find somewhere to set things up. I want him on video. We can't set it up in his bank. Anyway, let me know as soon as you get word whether the senator's coming or not."

26

The fine print

While waiting for Iggy to text whether Senator Steinherz was coming to Kabul or not, Roger continued his routine. In the morning, he would give English lessons to Sima and Musa. In the afternoon, he would teach geometry to Karim's high school class. Then he would go to meet Sophie when she finished at the Femmes en Crise school. Her friend Lexi would come with them to the Ariana Café, then go back to their room in Green Village before Sophie did, giving Roger and Sophie some time to be alone—if sitting together in a café could be called alone.

"You always look excited after class," he told Sophie.

"I love the work. Now and then I have to wonder, though. When the NATO Coalition finally leaves, will the Taliban put education right back where it was before we came?"

"It seems possible," he granted. "Still, you don't give up?"

She gave a little shrug. "We have to try."

Roger checked his phone, something he'd been doing compulsively as he waited for word that Senator Steinherz was coming to Kabul.

"If he comes," Sophie wondered, "and if you catch him asking for a bribe, will that be enough to convict him?"

"I hope so. You said it yourself. We have to try."

The old waiter took away the teapot to refill it. Sophie touched Roger's leg under the table with the tip of her toe. "Tonight," she trilled.

Roger stopped breathing.

"Lexi's going to stay with Nora. She feels sorry for us."

The guard was walking in front of the housing strip, but he never looked up from his cellphone. Roger closed Sophie's door behind him. "Do you really think this place is in danger of an attack again?"

"There are rumors. But you see the walls around this compound. I felt more afraid of Lyle than the Taliban when I thought he might come looking for me here."

"Anyway, here we are. A whole night alone." Roger pulled her close and gave her a long kiss, his body trembling with the release of desire he'd kept in check forever, it seemed. Sophie responded, breathing hard, her lips even warmer than he remembered. Their hands touched each other as if to prove this was real. They lay entwined on her bed, reluctant to let go of each other long enough to take off their clothes. "Hold me," Sophie whispered huskily. "Just hold me for a minute."

The setting sun was lighting up the paper-covered window when they finally sat up, unclothed now, and calmer. Sophie still clung to him, her warm fingers on his chest. "I wish time would stop."

Roger closed his eyes in agreement.

"My Femmes en Crise service ends in nine months," she told him. "Could you stay here that long? I mean, really, we could live on MREs."

"Stay where?"

"Here in my room. Lexi says she'll move in with Nora. She says she feels sorry for me lying in bed at night sending you texts."

"Would you really want her to do that? She's your friend, and—"

"I know. She doesn't really want to move in with Nora. Nora's devoted to her work, but kind of … serious, I guess you'd say."

"I don't want to make Lexi move in with her."

Sophie sighed. "Then after tonight you're back at Omar's?"

Roger shrugged.

"How long can you stay at his house?"

"I don't know. He's hoping to take the whole family back with him to the States if they ever get their visas."

"I wish them luck, but ...."

"I'll go to the USAID office tomorrow on the chance there's a job I could do."

Sophie pursed her lips. "Roger, I asked DeWoot about that. He said the U.S., Belgium, and all NATO countries were drastically cutting back on aid missions now that the Doha agreement for the U.S. to withdraw its troops seems almost complete."

"I'll try anyway." Roger was running out of ideas for how he and Sophie could stay together. He'd already asked his friend Inez to tell Father Joy he'd better advertise the job. He held onto Sophie's hand as if to keep her with him at least for now.

"Cheer up," she said. "I have a surprise." She pulled cotton pajamas from under her pillow, slipped into them, and opened the little refrigerator. "A present from DeWoot—U.S. Grade A sirloin steak flown in from America."

"I love you, Sophie."

The next morning, as Roger got out of the taxi at the embassy complex entrance nearest the USAID office, the ground shook.

A flash of light, then a deafening boom sent up a billow of smoke in the distance, shadowing the whole city. After a moment of absolute silence, smaller explosions roared out. Then sirens blared. Roger got back into the cab. The driver was holding his hands to his ears, praying.

"Taliban," the driver moaned. "Go back to Green Village, Mister?"

Roger gave him Omar's address instead. The driver grimaced but took off on Wazir Akbar Khan Road. The circle where they needed to turn off towards Omar's house was jammed with police cars and ambulances heading south in the direction of the Afghan Defense Ministry building, but the taxi finally made it through.

Omar's family were crowded around the television. Amal examined Roger as though looking for some injury. "This is big," Omar declared. "A Taliban car bomb attack on the Defense Ministry. The fight is still going on."

Roger watched shaky videos from by-standers' phones. One showed men firing guns into a ministry building, shattering the windows. Omar translated the news reports as they sporadically trickled in. "They're firing on rescuers, too. Lots of children in nearby schools were wounded by wreckage from the exploding van." Hekmat fingered his prayer beads while Amal muttered prayers.

Sophie called, and Roger answered in the garden. "I'm OK. Safe at Omar's house."

"I heard the blast even here. I'm watching the news on my phone. You must have been nearby."

"Yeah. I never made it to USAID."

"I thought the Taliban agreed not to attack while the Doha negotiations are going on."

"They only said they won't attack Americans. This is an attack on the Afghan government. I hope aid workers like you aren't also exempt from the no-attack agreement. Somebody should read the fine print."

Sophie gave a weak laugh. "I can't see them bombing me, Roger."

"Omar thinks it's time for you to quit and go home."

"I don't want to do that."

"So, keep up our routine? I'll keep teaching the kids and Karim's class. Then I'll meet you after your school?"

"Until we come up with something better."

27

Good news

For the next few days, Omar kept apologizing to Roger for the danger he said he'd brought him into. The attack on the Defense Ministry had gone on for ten hours. Two policemen, a security guard, and three civilians, including a child, had been killed, and over a hundred people had been injured. "You could have been one of them," Omar reasoned.

"But I like teaching the kids. I like teaching Karim's class. And mainly, Sophie's here." Roger knew Omar was hoping to get visas for his family and take them to the States, so he quickly added, "I'm planning to move into Sophie's Green Village housing when you take your family to the States."

"Please, as I told you, if I have to go back alone, Hekmat and Amal want you to stay here with them. And if they can get the visas and we all leave, you're still welcome to stay in this house as long as you want."

When Omar left to help his son-in-law with inventory at the store, Roger, as usual, began his English lessons for Sima and Musa. They sat waiting with little slates on their laps that reminded Roger of schoolroom slates he'd seen in old black and white pictures. It tickled him to think that even the wealthiest Afghans might not have a private native speaker of English for their children. Sima and Musa could imitate him with a flawless American accent.

Amal set up the low table and brought tea for all three of them. She sat on a cushion by the doorway to the kitchen with baby Laila on her lap, listening. Roger heard her repeating words in a low voice to improve her pronunciation as she followed the lesson.

When Omar and Hekmat came back from the store to take a

siesta, Roger was tired and followed suit. The next thing he knew, Amal was tapping him on the shoulder. It was time to go teach geometry at Karim's school.

This time the English teacher-translator announced, "Good news. A regular math teacher has been found." A chorus of *hoo-hoo* boos burst out. With a flushed face, the English teacher settled them down vouching first in Dari, then in English, for the new teacher's reported talent. "Armaghan Khan is a graduate of Kabul University."

"A Pashtun," one boy shouted. He bellowed out something that sounded like he had a mouthful of food. Roger assumed he was mocking the accent of a Pashtun speaking Dari. The class erupted in laughter.

The English teacher grabbed the boy by the collar and made him stand in the corner as he gave the class a long lecture in what Roger could tell by now was first in Dari, then in Pashto. They settled down soon enough, glancing ashamedly at Roger, as he began his lesson in English, the only language he knew, in this room full of people who understood three. He was glad the students were getting a permanent math teacher, but he felt adrift when he realized this was going to be his last class.

When Roger met Sophie after her classes, Lexi didn't join them at the café. Sophie trilled, "Come home with me. I want to show you something." When they were inside her room, Roger stood waiting. "What is it you want to show me?"

Sophie dropped her backpack onto the floor. "Nothing. I lied. You notice Lexi's not here? She's giving us another night."

"*Alhamdulillah*, as they say here. Hallelujah!"

They were in her bed when his phone rang.

"It's from my brother. —Hi, Dan."

"Hi. Good time to call?"

Roger sat up, looked down at the half undressed Sophie pulling a sheet back over her breast. "Sure."

Sophie slipped on a pajama top and went to the kitchen. She

held up a brown bag labeled MRE, pointing to the words "Chili and Macaroni" with questioning eyebrows. Roger nodded.

"There's something you need to know," Dan said. "The soldier killed at Fort Davis wasn't Jill. A reporter for a local Anne Arundel County paper, Anthony Mansfield, broke the story. The army confirmed his report. The guy was a Special Forces sergeant with a lot of experience in Afghanistan. Killed 'execution style,' the reporter wrote. No motive found for the murder."

Roger had to catch his breath. "Not Jill?"

"Yeah. Good news, I guess."

"Dan, thanks. I have to hang up. I need time to think this through." Roger felt dizzy and sank down on the bed.

Sophie came over, took his face in her hands. "What is it? You look like you've seen a ghost. Something your brother told you?"

"The murdered soldier we all thought was Jill? It wasn't."

"Oh my God. So she's alive?"

"At least she wasn't the person killed on the army base in Maryland. She's still missing."

"But the note on your door?"

"I should have told you. My friend at Saint Michael's High School found out it was from one of my students."

"Threatening you?"

"He's a bully. He wanted to scare me into changing his grade on a test."

"But Jill—"

"She must have thought it was a threat on her life from the person Lyle called a 'Special Forces type guy' who'd witnessed the robbery and murder."

"So Jill ran."

"Yeah. I guess she went into hiding from him."

"When you first came to the villa and asked me about her, that's not what you thought, was it?"

"No."

"You thought the note was from Lyle, didn't you, asking her to come live with him?"

Roger nodded.

"It's crazy, but somehow I knew."

Roger took her in his arms. "Even crazier? I kind of knew you knew."

They ate Meals-Ready-to-Eat chili and macaroni, talked about Roger getting a job in Kabul or Sophie getting a Master's degree in the States, and made love in her little bed. Sophie was drifting off to sleep, but Roger lay eyes wide open examining a crack in the ceiling above his head. Sophie nudged her head onto his chest. "Mm, you still awake?"

"Yeah."

"Thinking?"

"Yeah."

"I know. If Jill's alive, where is she? Right?"

"Yeah. And where does that leave us?"

28

Hard bargaining

When Roger came to meet Sophie after her classes the next afternoon, she and Lexi were standing at the school doorway, Lexi with a hand to her cheek, Sophie with hands on her hips. Siavash's white Ford Ranger was parked beside the building. He was directing men unloading equipment, carrying it into the school. One had a pale face and wore a baseball cap. Siavash introduced him to Roger. "Jackson is with the FBI. He's helping us out with the sting."

"If Steinherz comes to Kabul," Jackson told Roger, "there's no way we can record him at the U.S. Embassy or anywhere in Green Village. We're setting up audio and video equipment in Sophie's classroom." He looked Roger in the eye. "It's your job to get him and Daghal to meet with you here."

Roger wasn't sure how he'd do that. "Wouldn't they just want to meet in Daghal's office?"

"We can't bug that. You need to get them to come here."

Lexi went back to her Green Village room in the taxi that had dropped Roger off. Sophie and Roger went inside the school to see where the cameras and microphones were being hidden. Siavash had Roger and Sophie sit in classroom chairs to test the equipment.

Roger could imagine any number of things going wrong. It might be possible to get the senator to come out here to the school because he wouldn't want to be seen conferring with Daghal in the bank. But wouldn't Daghal think he was being set up?

Fortunately, he didn't have long to worry about it. Before Siavash and his men finished, Roger got a text from Iggy. *Steinherz flying in tonight. Meet at Camp Rectitude east gate 0900 local time tomorrow.*

Roger had expected to have more time to figure out how to get

Daghal to agree to a meeting. In half an hour, Siavash had dropped him off two blocks from the bank. He didn't want his police truck to arouse suspicion. "Just go in and ask for Mr. Daghal," he told Roger. "Tell Daghal you need to talk to him in private. He'll think you have a stash of money to launder."

The Pulshui Bank, between a Nike shoe store on one side and a casket maker on the other, was the only business in the row of shops without a glass window. Roger straightened his tie, buttoned his suit coat, and pulled open the heavy blue metal door. An armed guard searched him thoroughly and pointed to a basket for his cell phone. Next to a door, a marble counter stretched across the room. At a barred window above the counter a middle-aged woman in a hejab sat engrossed in something on her phone. Farther behind her, a money counting machine whirred, a bored-looking turbaned man feeding it as it stacked up piles of American currency. Roger said he had business with Mr. Daghal.

Daghal came in from the door at the rear of the bank. His round face barely rose above the counter as he studied Roger through the bars with bulging eyes, then led him to a windowless office in the back with a wall safe and another door on the side. As Roger sat in front of Daghal's desk, he noticed him quickly sweep a copy of *Hustler* magazine into a drawer. "What can I do you for?" Daghal boomed in an exaggerated American accent.

"I'm sorry to tell you that Mr. Lyle White, who discussed setting up our Bebsi business account with you, was killed by an IED."

"God damn. What a country, huh?"

"I have a certificate establishing his death, and I'm in touch with the partner who has the other key."

"One of the fair sex, if I remember correctly what he told me."

"She'd like to open that account and begin depositing funds according to the original plan."

"We aim to please."

"One other thing. I don't know if you've met U.S. Senator Steinherz?"

"I know his name in connection with other accounts but not this one."

"Well, I hope there won't be any trouble. It seems that Lyle White promised the senator a commission on the deposit we plan to put into the Bebsi account."

Daghal flipped open a pack of Marlboros and, when Roger refused, lit one himself. "This is new to me."

"It's likely Lyle died before he had a chance to tell you. But I'm working with the senator. He's determined he should get what Lyle promised him. Apparently it's a substantial amount."

Daghal seemed amused. "Yeah? How much are we talking about this time? I tell foreigners no more than could fit into a bathtub."

"The senator doesn't disclose things like that to me. I'm sure you understand."

"Doesn't matter. It's your money. And where does the senator want this substantial amount to be sent? You don't know that either?"

"No."

"Still no problem. I've sent money to various offshore accounts for Senator Steinherz. If he doesn't trust you to tell me how much and where, he can tell me himself. No phone calls, though. I'm sure you understand."

"He's coming to Kabul. I'll be meeting him tomorrow morning."

Daghal let out a thin stream of smoke through puckered lips. "My schedule's free tomorrow. Bring that bad boy in."

"Has he been in here before? I know he's sensitive about bad publicity."

"Aren't they all? No, I've never seen him. Your big wig types generally get the depositors to give me the details. Now and then they meet me in some private place. Want to do it that way?"

Roger tried to speak calmly. "I'll have to ask the senator, but tomorrow's Friday. I have a key to a school building where I teach that will be empty."

Daghal pulled out his desk drawer, sifted through an assortment of business cards, picked out one, slid it over to Roger. "Text me the time and address at this phone number."

The next morning Sophie waved, rushed down the stairs from her balcony, and got into the taxi with Roger. The driver was stopped twice at checkpoints before they reached the east gate of Camp Rectitude. Roger realized he'd been expecting Senator Steinherz to arrive in a black limousine flanked by Secret Service men in dark suits and sunglasses. Instead, he stood beside an armored truck guarded by two uniformed U.S. Marines so weighed down with flack jackets, helmets, goggles, rifles, and equipment hanging from their shirts and belts that he wondered how they could move. Roger walked towards the senator and was stopped by one of them.

"That's all right, Captain," the senator called out. "The young man is a friend of mine." He ogled Sophie. "But I don't believe I've met this beautiful young lady."

Roger didn't know if Steinherz had ever met Jill or even knew she was Lyle's accomplice. He introduced Sophie simply as "Lyle's business partner."

Steinherz took her hand and held it. "So nice to meet you. I was absolutely devastated at the news of Lyle's passing."

"Sir," Roger interrupted, looking around, "The person we're meeting is waiting in a secure location. Could we—"

"By all means." He signaled a Marine to open the truck door. "Let me help you in, young lady. You don't want to scrape your pretty legs on this god-awful machinery." Roger climbed in the other side of the truck. Steinherz patted Sophie on the knee. "You'll be safe snuggled here between the two of us. Tell the driver where to take us, young man."

The road got bumpy as soon as they left the camp. Steinherz slipped his arm around Sophie. "Hold on, dear. All the money we pour into this country, you'd think they'd build some decent roads." Sophie squirmed under his arm, but the senator pulled her close. "That's it, dear. Get comfortable. —Is this going to be a long ride, young man? I'm planning to fly back tonight."

Roger heard Sophie mumble to herself, "It's definitely going to be a long ride."

As they approached the school, Roger noted Siavash's white truck parked outside of the Ariana Café. No sign of Daghal yet.

"Here we are, Senator. You can post your men outside the door."

"Sir," the ranking Marine said, "We'll need to search the building first."

Siavash and Jackson had hidden the equipment "so they'd never detect it," but Roger still worried. Sophie opened the school door, and the Marines filed in. "Clear," the first one called out from the hallway. "Clear," the other shouted from the unlocked room where the wiretap equipment was set up.

Steinherz looked at the classroom desks. "You can't be serious. What kind of place is this to have a meeting?"

"Since this is very special bank business, I was asked to find a private location, Senator."

Car doors opened and closed outside. Shouts in Pashto and Dari were answered by shouts in English. Roger ran outside. Daghal and two of his own armed guards were faced off against Steinherz's guards. "Mr. Daghal," Roger said, "thank you for coming. They're waiting inside for our meeting." He gave a nervous chuckle. "I guess the place will be well guarded."

Roger put his hand on Daghal's back, insisting he enter the building first—and venturing a phrase he'd heard so many times when one Afghan refused to enter before the other. "*Befarmāid.* After you."

"Jesus Christ," Daghal snorted. "You've been here too long."

As they went in, they heard a little yelp, then "Please!" Sophie was scampering behind one of the desks.

"Senator Steinherz," Daghal said. "I've heard so much about you. We finally meet." He wagged his finger at the senator. "You better play nice with this young lady. I understand she's the sole possessor of the money, now that Lyle White is dead."

Steinherz's baby face paled. "You're the bank president?" There were no handshakes or further introductions.

Roger began. "We're here to give Senator Steinherz a chance to explain an agreement he had with the deceased Lyle White. It seems Lyle's partner" —he nodded towards Sophie— "who still wishes to remain anonymous, isn't aware of the agreement either."

"Well, I'm not lying," the senator groused. "There's nothing exceptional about my being offered a payment for ignoring special placement of government funds. The bank president here can attest to that."

Roger said, "By 'special placement,' Senator Steinherz, do you mean diverting funds from their intended use?"

Steinherz groaned. "Iggy told me you might be dumb. Are you the only one here who doesn't understand that?"

Sophie spoke up. "Lyle was set to deposit the money into an account at the Pulshui Bank and gradually move it to the Bank of Germany. Now that he's dead, it's up to me." She turned to the senator. "I'm willing to honor his agreement with Senator Steinherz."

Daghal turned his bulbous eyes onto the senator. "I'll need to know which of your accounts to send it to. That's all."

Steinherz gave a relieved sigh. "Not the Dubai account this time. Send it to the one in Panama."

"And how much did Lyle agree to give you?" Sophie asked.

"Two hundred thirty thousand dollars."

"You're fuckin' kidding," Daghal exclaimed. "How much was this USAID heist, anyway?"

Sophie knew. "I'll just say the senator is asking for ten percent."

"Ten percent," Daghal shouted. "That's what I get. Come on, Senator, you know your take is usually only five percent."

"Ten percent," Steinherz insisted. "That's what I was promised." He glared at Sophie. "If you're not going to honor that, I'll reveal the theft. And the murder Roger reported."

"Now, now, Senator," Daghal said. "You're as vulnerable as we are. I assume you wouldn't want your past activities to come to light. Let's talk business here."

Steinherz's lips trembled as he spoke. "Eight percent."

Sophie shocked Roger by telling the senator, "I can't believe Lyle would have agreed to even five percent."

"Well, aren't you the little bitch?" Steinherz said. There was a moment of silence. All eyes were on Steinherz. "All right," he finally said, "five percent."

"Still too much. I'll go as high as a hundred thousand if you'll agree not to report the theft or the murder of the Belgian guard," Sophie countered. This was a new Sophie that Roger was seeing. He knew she was outraged by what Lyle had done. But was something else going on here as well?

Steinherz eyed Daghal and Roger, but found no support. He gritted his teeth. "You win, Missy. Give Daghal the hundred thousand dollars to send to my account in Panama, and I'll keep quiet. Now let's get out of here. I have a plane to catch."

Siavash, DeWoot, and FBI agent Jackson were ecstatic about the video. "This should be enough to end Senator Steinherz's career," the agent said. "His treatment of the young woman alone would probably be enough."

The first minutes of the video, recorded before Roger and Daghal came in, showed the senator pawing Sophie, chasing her, and bending his bottom towards her, saying, "Spank me, Teacher. I've been naughty."

"One thing I don't understand," DeWoot asked Sophie. "Why did you insist on getting the senator to take less? We were never going to give him any money in the first place."

"I just wanted to." She gave a little shrug. "Maybe I felt like humiliating him for the way he'd treated me."

Jackson made everyone promise to tell no one about the senator for now. "The FBI will want to get a full assessment of his criminal activities so we can charge him with everything. Any leaks could put him on guard and jeopardize our investigation."

Siavash said he'd take a copy of the video to the Afghan

prosecutor. "I'm not positive it's enough to convict Daghal, though. It doesn't show him actually taking the money or shipping it out of the country. You might have heard of our government's reluctance to prosecute crimes involving Americans—considering that it's money from America that pays their salaries." Siavash sighed. "We're living in a country where only petty crimes are punished, not the big ones."

"This isn't the only country where that's true," Roger retorted.

When they loaded the cameras and microphones back into the truck, Sophie sat in the back seat, this time quickly falling asleep with her head on Roger's shoulder.

DeWoot smiled at them. "You two should get married."

Siavash eyed them in the rear view mirror. "That's what I think."

29

Fondling the money

Siavash asked Roger to meet with him and his FBI partner Jackson a few days later. "How long will it take the senator to realize no money has been transferred to his Panama account?" Roger asked.

"He should realize it already," Siavash guessed.

Jackson agreed. "The FBI has eyes on Steinherz in the States. He was seen barging furiously into Ignacio Corelli's office in D.C. once again yesterday, probably to complain that the transfer hadn't been made yet."

Jackson wanted to expand the charges against Senator Steinherz. "The senator's constantly in touch with Grayrock's chief lobbyist. Iggy, as they call him. We think Iggy knows about other bribes the senator has taken."

"I'm sure he does," Roger affirmed. "Iggy told me so himself."

"So if we can find anything on Iggy, we can offer him a plea bargain if he reveals whatever kompromat Grayrock has on the senator."

"But Iggy's in the States," Siavash objected.

"He is now. But Roger knows the man." Jackson took a bulky phone from his jacket that looked like the one the Grayrock guy had let Roger use to call Iggy. "We have Iggy's code and number. Roger, I want you to get him to come to Kabul."

Roger's hand was sweaty while it rang. Iggy answered, "Senator, I assure you we'll work it out."

"It's Roger Williams."

"Ah. Just the person I need to talk to. Our senator says he met with you, the bank president, and some woman to work out a deal. Was that woman Jill? I thought she was dead."

"It was Jill," Roger lied, hoping Iggy wouldn't have any followup questions.

"Why isn't she going through with her part of the deal? The senator doesn't like waiting for the deposit to be made. He suspects some trick."

"There's a problem," Roger improvised. "The original deal was with Lyle, who's definitely dead, not with Jill. The bank president suspects he's being set up somehow."

"So convince him."

"This is the guy who insisted on talking to the senator in person, you'll remember."

"To hell with him, then. Just give the senator his share of the money. If he doesn't get it, he swears he'll cancel all future contracts for Grayrock."

"But I thought he was—"

"In Grayrock's pocket? We have enough dirt on him to send him to jail, and he knows that. But it would just be shooting ourselves in the foot."

"How do we get the money to him? The plan was for the bank president to put it in one of the senator's overseas accounts."

"Just bring it here to me, Roger. I'll make sure he gets it."

"I can't carry a hundred thousand dollars in cash into the country. They searched my baggage even on the Grayrock charter plane."

"Jill can bring it without being searched."

"She's back in the States. Detox regime." Roger congratulated himself on that brainstorm.

"Well, God damn it. I'll come and get it myself. If the senator's cut is that big, we must be talking about quite a bit of money that Lyle appropriated. I'm going to want a personal cut for the inconvenience—the same amount the senator gets."

"Understood. Jill has already agreed to go that high."

"Where are you staying?"

"The Kabul Serena Hotel."

Jackson and Siavash were recording the conversation. Jackson tapped his watch.

"When can I expect you?" Roger asked.

"Tomorrow morning, your time."

When Roger hung up, Siavash eyed Roger, chuckling. Jackson said, "You had to pick the most expensive hotel in the country?"

"Oh, I didn't realize," Roger lied. "So, I check in tonight? You have a card I can use? I'll call Omar and tell him I won't be coming back."

The plan was for Roger to meet Iggy in the hotel lobby the next morning, bring him to his room, and give him the briefcase full of cash that Jackson would somehow come up with. Jackson and Siavash would arrest Iggy when he walked out of the room with the money.

Roger asked about recording his conversation with Iggy.

"Can't bug the room," Jackson said. "He'll be sure to sweep it with a signal detector. No time to cut into walls and test like we did at the school."

"We'll think of something," Siavash promised.

Roger stretched out on the fluffy bed in the air conditioned hotel room and called Sophie. "You'll never guess where I am. The hotel where all the big shots stay."

"Can I come, too?"

"Sorry. As I said, it's for big shots."

Sophie giggled and called him something in Dari he'd often heard on the streets. All he knew was that it involved the word "dog."

"Seriously, I wish you could come. But tomorrow morning I'm meeting a Grayrock honcho here." Roger switched to his impression of a Russian accent. "I must obtain kompromat on zis hooligan."

Sophie came back with, "Zis is good thing you do, no? I give you the permission for one night. If mission not accomplished, I come for you in your bed."

Roger took a long, hot shower, plopped down on the bed, and turned on the TV to watch an English language broadcast about a car bombing outside a police station in Kandahar in which "credit" for the bombing was claimed by the Taliban, who considered the police their enemy.

Grayrock, too, he thought, considered the police—of any country—their enemy if they stood in the way of the Grayrock program, which was to make money. Grayrock was like a country in itself, not subject to U.S. or any other nation's laws. It followed only one law. Generate income. It had gotten away with bribery, grand larceny, tax fraud, and outright murder, all the while amassing more wealth than any other war profiteer.

Roger fell asleep thankfully dreaming not of Grayrock but of Sophie coming to sleep with him in the luxurious hotel bed. He slept until the alarm clock woke him.

In the lobby, he sipped an American coffee and read the *Washington Post* until he saw a man with short, light hair in a fitted beige suit come through the door, followed by three burly men in black suits. Roger stood, and Iggy recognized him. Without offering to shake Roger's hand, Iggy said only, "You have the item?"

The bodyguards followed them up to Roger's floor. Two took posts beside his room door, and the third pulled Roger back before he opened the door. He patted him down, took his phone, and handed it to Iggy. When Roger opened the door, the bodyguard went in first, waving a wand everywhere before announcing "All clear" and leaving.

While the door was still open, a tall bellboy with a thin moustache and a red cap perched awkwardly on his head came along and wheeled a clothes dolly with a man's suit and shirts hung on it into the room. Roger gave him a tip and closed the door.

It was the first time Roger had seen Iggy standing up. He was as short as Lyle, and the horizontal creases on his forehead gave him the same intense look that Lyle's large pupils had given him. "The item," Iggy demanded.

Roger stood beside the clothes dolly. "You mean your cut of the money that Lyle stole from USAID?"

"What the hell else do you think I'm talking about? I came all the way here. You better have it."

Roger slid the briefcase from under the bed. *"Befarmāid,"* he quipped.

"What? Open it."

"It's all there. A hundred thousand dollars for Senator Steinherz and a hundred thousand dollars for you."

Iggy put both hands on the cash, fanning the edges of the ten-thousand-dollar packs. He wasn't counting the money so much as fondling it. "Jesus Christ. Lyle never told me how much he took. The total payload must be, what?"

"Two million three hundred thousand dollars."

"That son of a bitch. Our operatives are required to report anything over five hundred thousand dollars to me." Iggy stood studying the briefcase, then turned to Roger. "Lyle screwed up. I guess you understand what that means. He forfeited the whole payload. You and Jill can forget about getting a penny of it." Iggy poked Roger's chest with a finger. "Now you're going to tell me where the rest of it is."

"Here's the thing, Mr. Corelli. When Lyle was killed, Jill and I talked it over. We decided to turn our lives around. Jill's in detox, as I said. The money was from USAID, designated for a Belgian NGO, Femmes en Crise. We decided they should get it. Other than what's in this briefcase, that is."

"Wrong. It's Grayrock money now. Where is it?"

Roger saw his chance to say he'd take Iggy to it and lead him out into the hall to be arrested. He paused, though, not sure whether Siavash and Jackson would be able to overcome the three bodyguards standing there. "I'll have to clear this with Jill first. I need my phone."

Iggy pulled it from his pocket. "I'll call her myself."

"OK." Roger had to think fast. "Oh, wait. It's midnight in Baltimore. The detox home won't answer calls after six p.m."

Iggy threw the phone on the floor and shoved Roger up against the wall. "I've had enough of this. Tell me where that money is or this will be the last day of your life."

A popping sound echoed outside the door. It could have been gunshots. Iggy dropped face-down on the floor. Shouts burst out, and heavy footsteps pounded from both ends of the hallway. Roger set the door chain and peeped out. Helmeted police in armored jackets pounced on the bodyguards and held them on the ground. One of the cops pried a pistol from a bodyguard's hand. Jackson and Siavash, still in his bellboy uniform, ran to Roger's door with guns drawn. Roger released the chain and threw the door open.

Iggy had crawled under the bed, his shiny black shoes giving him away.

"Is he armed?" Jackson asked Roger.

"I don't think so."

Two cops came in, and Siavash set them to dragging Iggy out by the legs. Jackson showed his FBI badge. "I'll take custody of him."

Siavash said something to the police captain, who left to arrest the bodyguards. "He'll have plenty of things to charge them with," Siavash told Roger. "But Grayrock will have them freed in less than an hour."

"Not this guy," Jackson avowed. "He's going to Federal prison."

"And here's the evidence." Siavash pulled a pen from the outer pocket of the suit coat hanging on the clothes dolly he'd rolled into the room. He started to leave, then turned and gave Roger back his tip.

30

Done all the time

There seemed to be something on Omar's mind recently. Roger found him in the garden staring into the pool.

"Any word yet on visas for your family, Omar?"

"No. That's just what I was thinking about. The adoptions are causing complications. The people at the consulate keep asking for more information, more papers. I think I'm going to have to give up."

Roger felt his temperature rising. "Our President says Muslims are our enemies." He thought of the two youngest children playing hopscotch in the street. It was hard to picture them as enemies. "Sima and Musa—could you even call them Muslims?"

"They've been told they are. That's about it."

"I guess that goes for a lot of people in the country?"

"For most of us."

Now was the time to put Omar in touch with the lawyers he'd met back in Ocean City. Trying not to get Omar's hopes up unduly, Roger told him the ACLU lawyers John and Chrissy had experience helping people from "enemy" countries get visas. "They might be able to help you with the paperwork. I've been meaning to call them. What if we call them tonight?"

Omar grasped both of Roger's shoulders and looked him in the eye. "You would do that for me?"

That night Omar and Roger went out to the garden to call John and Chrissy on speakerphone. The lawyers seemed surprised to hear Omar's perfect English. They got the information they needed and outlined a series of steps Omar should take. It seemed that Omar had done every one of them. "Now the papers certifying the adoption," Chrissy said. "Did your daughter and her husband fill them out at the same time they applied for visas? They did? They're not Americans, are they? Right. But you are. Can you see if 'intercountry adoption' is checked on the form?"

Omar had brought a folder of papers out to the garden and now spread them on the low pond wall under the garden light. "Yes. Yes, I see it here."

"But it wasn't an intercountry adoption. You didn't adopt them. Your daughter and her husband did. I've seen this mistake before. I have a feeling if you point out the error, it will help quite a bit."

Chrissy's husband agreed. "How about making that change and getting back to us?"

Roger noticed Amal and Hekmat standing by the garden wall listening. They both ran and bent over the phone, adding their thanks to Omar's and Roger's.

Karim had made tea. They sat around the low table asking Roger about Chrissy and John. Karim decided he wanted to become a lawyer. His father laughed. "Just be sure you always read every word and check the right box."

Several weeks had passed since Hekmat delivered a corrected adoption certification to the American Consulate. Omar had postponed his own return to the States so they could all fly to Baltimore together. Everyone was on edge. They'd just seen a TV news report that the U.S. President planned to drastically cut the number of refugees allowed into the U.S. and deny visas to athletes, students, business visitors, and even people coming for medical reasons from any countries that harbor enemies of the United States.

"I hope he doesn't think *we're* enemies," Amal sighed.

Omar shook his head. "All foreigners are enemies. That's what he tells his crowds."

Hekmat decided to make another enquiry at the consulate. He returned with perspiration stains under the arms of his shirt. Everyone searched his face hopefully, but he muttered something in Dari that didn't sound optimistic. He told Roger, "The visa official said that recent regulations prevented issuing visas except in a few special cases. He asked my occupation. I said I'm a business man. He said they were still giving a few business investment visas but even those were going to be stopped soon."

"How much would you have to invest?" Omar asked. "I've heard it's a lot."

"Half a million dollars, at least, the visa official told me."

"It's all right, Papa." Amal patted Omar's shoulder. "We'll stay here. You'll just have to keep coming to visit us."

Roger didn't want to give up so easily. "Hekmat, what if you could find an American partner and go into business together?"

Omar perked up. "The owner of my restaurant is looking for a partner to open up a second restaurant. He needs about a quarter of a million dollars."

Hekmat stroked his chin. "I might be able to borrow that much using Quick Mart as equity. Would the owner be willing to tell the consulate I was investing twice as much?"

Omar gave Roger an embarrassed glance. "I've heard this is done all the time. I'll contact him."

Amal rolled her eyes. "My husband wants to get rich. And he thinks America is the place to do that." She bounced Laila on her lap. "Me, I'm content right here. Besides …."

Omar finished for her. "Amal thinks it's too dangerous to live in Baltimore. Too many murders. Too many shootings."

"An average of one person is shot to death every day in Baltimore," Amal said. "That's what I heard on the news. And three or four times that many are wounded by guns. And more than two people die every day in Baltimore of opioids. That's what I've read."

"But we don't have bombings and gun battles in America," Roger countered. "Or at least not many. Baltimore's like Kabul. There's lots of killing, but the odds are it won't be you."

"Will we all have to carry guns in America?" Karim asked.

Hekmat laughed. "Yes, and Mama will have to mow the lawn in a bikini."

"*Khodā nakoné*," Amal burst out. "God forbid. You'll just have to go without me."

Omar tried to calm her. "If you don't like it in America, you can come back any time. No more talk about murders, guns, and drugs." He went into the kitchen to prepare some tea.

31

Floating tea leaf

As long as Roger's money held out, he planned to keep teaching Sima and Musa in the mornings and meeting Sophie after her class. He'd been bringing groceries now and then to Omar's house, but after some weeks, his account was almost empty. He was checking it when Sophie texted.

Can you come right away to the training school? Nora wants to see you teach.

He texted *What??* but there was no answer.

When he arrived, Nora told him she and Lexi were going to Belgium with DeWoot to help with recruiting. This was going to be the last day of classes until they returned. "When Sophie told me you were volunteering at Mamtāzi High School, I suggested you come and give my class a math lesson."

"I don't understand."

"They need help with methods of teaching basic arithmetic."

Sophie picked up a notebook. "Here I've written Dari and Pashto for "add, subtract, multiply, divide—words like that."

"It's OK for men to teach women?"

"It is," Sophie explained. "There are women teachers, but doctors, mullahs, even teachers are mostly men."

"So by training you mean—"

"Teaching a model lesson."

The women were already crowding around Roger, trying out their English. Nora signaled for them to go into her classroom. They stood at their desks, waiting for Roger's permission to sit down. "*Befarmāid*," he said, gesturing with his hands. A round of giggles burst out. He took attendance, reading the names from Nora's list.

More giggles at his pronunciation. He let them have their fun for a minute, then put on a serious face.

"I need money," he declared. As expected, they understood that. He stood stiff and unsmiling as a hush blanketed the room.

"I have fifty dollars," he said. "I need Afghan money." And the problem of this foreigner trying to exchange money and buy ten kilos of rice and two dozen eggs immediately became a lesson in using all the terms Sophie had written in her notebook. Roger first acted out the part of a bewildered customer, then of a shopkeeper patiently showing him how to make the calculations. After that he switched to another scenario. "I have twenty-five dollars," he said, and he had one of the women become the shopkeeper. The class seemed to be having fun. Roger definitely was.

Nora checked the time on her phone. "Break time." She, Sophie, and Lexi nodded to each other and led Roger outside. "I have a proposal," Nora announced. "Femmes en Crise wants to recruit more teachers. Well, Roger, we watched you give a lesson, and we think we should hire you."

Roger was confused. "Really? I thought it was, you know, a female thing."

"So far our recruits have all been women, but there's no reason they have to be. The teachers we train, of course, are women."

Sophie nodded vigorously at Roger, encouraging him to accept.

"You would start as soon as classes resume," Nora explained. "Same salary as ours. Housing included. You can have the room next to Sophie's." She handed Roger a contract in French, Dutch, and German. "I'll translate for you."

Roger waved that off. "No need to translate. Where do I sign?"

The three women applauded. Just then DeWoot pulled up in his Suburban.

"A new teacher for Femmes en Crise," Nora announced.

DeWoot shook Roger's hand. "Happy to have you. I've heard good things about your teaching." Then he turned to the girls. "With the new funding—recovered thanks to Sophie and Roger—it's time to go back and recruit even more volunteers. Nora, Lexi, I've arranged our flight to Brussels for tomorrow afternoon. Sophie, there's still time to change your mind and come along."

"Sorry. I've just been back home. I should stay here and make lesson plans." Sophie avoided DeWoot's eyes.

Lexi gave her a quick look. "Yes. And help the new guy make his."

"That's settled, then." DeWoot zipped the contract into his attaché. "Sophie will stay and bring Roger up to date. Nora and Lexi will come with me. Can you ladies be ready by tomorrow afternoon?"

When Roger told Omar and his family the news, they were ecstatic. After dinner, Amal sent Karim out to buy a watermelon and a kilo of cherries to celebrate.

After one more night at Omar's, Roger could stay with Sophie longer than ever before while Lexi and Nora were in Belgium. On his mat in the dark, he texted her. *You awake?*

I can't sleep. Too excited.

Really? What about?

Don't tease. You know.

Together at last!

Until September!

They texted good-night, but Roger lay awake listening to Omar snore and thinking about the days with Sophie that lay ahead. They would be alone in her room, four walls making them free. Now that he had a job in Kabul, everything was going to work out.

When he taught Sima and Musa the next morning, Musa observed, "You smile today," and Sima laughed, "Yes, I see."

"I am happy," Roger enunciated, and they repeated it together.

Grinning at the three of them, Amal brought a tea tray from the kitchen, then sat on her cushion with Laila to listen in on the lesson. When it was over and Sima and Musa went out to play, Amal sat down beside Roger and refilled his tea glass. He told her Sophie was going to be alone for a couple of weeks. "She wants me to stay with her in Green Village." He prepared himself for her disapproval.

She responded with, "Have you seen the beautiful marriage hall in Kabul?"

"I've passed by it. Amal, I guess you know there are difficulties. Sophie and I would like to get married, but that's not possible yet."

"*What is to come will be better for you than what has passed. Soon God will grant what you wish.* It's in the Koran, the Bright Morning Surah, and I'm sure it's true."

"Your confidence encourages me. That's for sure."

Roger had waited for his tea to cool. It was always served far too hot to drink right away, at least for him. He picked up a lump of sugar and put it in his mouth to sip the tea through, Afghan-Russian style. When he looked into the glass, there was a green tea leaf floating on the top.

"What is it?" Amal asked. Then she saw the tea leaf. "Somebody is coming to see you."

32

For or against

Roger walked to the ATM to get some of his remaining cash. While he was out, he bought some rice and tea to bring to Amal before going to meet Sophie in her room.

When he got back to Omar's, a tan car with a smashed door was pulled up haphazardly in front of the house. Inside, Omar, Amal, Hekmat, and Karim stood frozen, scowling at him as if he were a devil or an evil jinn. No one spoke a word. Roger searched one face after another until his eyes hit on a large foreign woman seated in the dim corner on a chair that must have been brought into the room for her.

It was Jill.

Roger tried but couldn't close his gaping mouth. Jill stared menacingly at him. No one spoke a word. They seemed to be waiting for an explanation from Roger. Finally, Omar ventured, "We are surprised, Mr. Roger." Then Amal said, "You told us Ms. Jill was dead. We believed you."

Jill was thinner than when he'd last seen her. Her hair was tangled, and her left hand was wrapped in a soiled, frayed bandage. She gave him a slow, squint-eyed nod as if to say, "I caught you."

More than anything, Roger wondered what Omar's family had already told her. Did Jill's silent glare mean she'd heard about Sophie? He realized it was time for him to break the silence and say something. "Jill," he gulped, "you're alive?"

She rose from the chair. "Looks like it, huh?"

"Your hand—you're hurt?" It was all he could think of to say.

"Scorpion sting. One of the nasty black ones."

Amal burst out, "Black scorpion! Evil jinns often take this form."

She wrung her hands.

Jill held up her bandaged hand. "I killed it after it stung me. I think you're right saying it was an evil jinn."

As if to give the explanation Roger seemed incapable of, Omar told Jill, "A soldier was killed in America. We all thought it was you."

"No," Jill said. "He was another evil jinn." She stepped toward Roger, and he flinched. "I need to talk to my husband in private."

Out in the yard, Roger sensed hidden eyes watching them from the house. Jill walked unsteadily, possibly an effect from the scorpion's venom. She began, "I didn't touch any of the money in our joint account, Babe. I guess you noticed. Only used my own money from a couple of jobs before we met. I came back to Baltimore from North Carolina to make you rich. You weren't there. The Rover was broken into. I didn't know where you were."

"You were in North Carolina?"

"Grayrock's training camp there."

"You were hiding from that Special Forces guy?"

Jill scoffed. "I was in hiding, but not from him. Let's get to the point. My vault key and papers were taken from the Rover."

Roger tried to deflect the blame. "You think that Special Forces guy took them?"

Jill had been calm, but he could see anger rising in her green eyes. "No. I took care of him as soon as I got his note."

"Took care of—"

"Took him out. Whatever you want to call it. After that I figured I'd better go to our training camp until it blew over. You don't seem to want to talk about the missing key, do you? I was sure Lyle broke into the Rover and took it, planning to take all the money for himself. I caught a plane to Kabul as soon as I saw the break-in. But now I'm thinking you have my key." She seized him by the wrist with her good hand.

Roger blurted out the truth. "Lyle threatened to kill me if I didn't get it to him."

"I searched his villa. Had to break in. It was completely empty."

"Even if you find it, you need two keys. Lyle's dead, and he had the other key."

From beneath her khaki shirt Jill pulled up a chain with a key dangling on it. "You mean this one?"

Roger was speechless.

"When I got here, I found out Lyle was on a mission and took care of him."

"You mean—"

"You want the details? All right." She sighed as if this was wasting her time. "IEDs, they call them. Improvised Explosive Devices. If the hajis can make them, so can we. I found out Lyle's route back to the camp. Waited in a dirt ditch. His truck blew to pieces."

"You killed Lyle?"

"He deserved it. Too bad about his driver. I thought Lyle would be alone in the truck."

A chill ran through Roger's body.

"When I crawled out of the ditch, the scorpion stung me. I squashed it with my hand and went and got the key from Lyle's neck."

Jill's knees shook. For a moment, Roger thought she would fall, but she caught herself. "They say you can die from these scorpion stings. I almost did. I pulled my motorbike out of the ditch and rode away from the scene. I guess I passed out. An old haji found me, took me and the bike to his village. He and his wife said lots of prayers. An old lady in the village brought some dirt, said it was from a ziarat, a shrine, I guess. She rubbed that on the hand and some time later—I don't know how many days—I could talk, then walk."

"You were in that village until now?"

"I got back to Kabul this morning. When I saw Lyle's villa was cleaned out, I came here to find out if he hid it somewhere at Omar's. What a surprise. Omar said you were here." She pulled Roger closer with one hand, put her face close to his. "So where's the key?"

"I gave it to Lyle. Like I said."

"You better not be lying. Listen. Lyle must have told you about the money. With him gone, it's just you and me to share two million three hundred thousand dollars. I've never been sorry I married you, Babe. I'd do it again. I know you don't approve of Grayrock or some of the things I've done. But with all that money, I can retire from that line of work, and we can have a happy life together."

"But—"

"No buts. You're either with me or against me."

"Jill, you've killed people." He wasn't sure she heard. Her body went limp. She fell towards him, and he held her up. In a few seconds, she stood steady again. "Thanks, Babe. I'm OK. Still a little dizzy now and then from that scorpion bite. They say it wears off after a few months."

"You want to sit down a minute?"

"No. I'm going back to Camp Rectitude. A guy who works there told me Lyle was shacking up with a foreign girl. If you don't have the key, maybe she does. He was probably going to use her to open the vault, then take all the money for himself. I need to track her down."

With that, Jill walked back through the house waving good-bye to the family. Her car almost hit another as she lurched back onto the road and raced away at a breakneck speed.

Roger went back in to face the family. It seemed they hadn't told Jill about Sophie. But did they think he'd been lying to them about Jill, that he'd been lying to Sophie?

Omar took Roger's arm. "We were listening. From the kitchen window. This woman admitted to two murders." He led Roger inside to a cushion in the corner and sat him there. "You have to calm yourself, Mr. Roger." Omar wouldn't let him get up until his tea had cooled and he finished drinking it.

Roger finally put down the empty glass. "Jill said she was going to track Sophie down. That shouldn't take her long. Meanwhile Sophie's alone in her room. I need to go."

"But if Ms. Jill finds the two of you together, she'll understand everything. She's dangerous, Mr. Roger. You could ask Miss Sophie to come stay with us."

"I've already caused you too much trouble. Besides, if Sophie's not in her room, Jill will come back here."

"You could call that Major Crimes agent, Siavash."

"Maybe later. Right now I'm going to Sophie's."

Seeing Roger in a state of panic, Amal brought more tea to calm him down. Before the tea had a chance to cool, his phone rang. "From Sophie," he told them, and ran to the yard to take the call. Omar and Hekmat followed.

Sophie was crying. "Roger, I'm scared. Your wife is alive. She came here just now. She started to choke me. She thinks I'm Lyle's girlfriend. She said this would be the last day of my life if I didn't give her the vault key. So, Roger, I gave it to her."

Omar and Hekmat could hear Sophie's voice. "*Vāy khodāye man,*" Hekmat exclaimed. Omar echoed in English, "Oh my god!"

"She's going to the vault tomorrow morning," Sophie said. "She thinks the money's still there. I'm terrified, Roger."

"I'm coming to get you. We'll find somewhere to hide."

Hekmat had an idea. "I'll call my friend, tell him to send Ishak here on his motorcycle. You and Ishak can take Miss Sophie to his parents' house in Morad Khani. She can hide there."

"Can Ishak come right away?"

"When he hears Miss Sophie is in trouble, yes. You can be sure."

33

Hidden away

Ishak drove his small motorcycle like a frantic beast fleeing a predator, Roger clinging on behind. They snaked through the early evening traffic using sidewalks and oncoming lanes, squeezing between cars, buses, and trucks. Ishak had a permit to enter Green Village issued to his repair shop. Dust swirled in the setting sun when they slid to a stop in front of Sophie's housing unit.

Roger slung on one shoulder the backpack of food Amal had given him and carried Sophie's pack on the other. He seated her between Ishak and himself, and they sped away past the guards at the compound gate and at the Green Village entrance. A haze hung over the city making it hard to see much more than the red taillights ahead. Sophie held her arms tight around Ishak's waist, and Roger held onto her as the bike leaned and weaved through the city center, then whined louder as they drove faster along the darker roads leading south towards the old section where Ishak's parents lived.

It was almost dark when they reached the narrow dirt lanes of the Morad Khani district. Ishak and Sophie's dark hair was blanched with dust, and Roger's eyes and teeth felt crunchy. Ishak's cycle was the only motorized vehicle on these unlit passages. They slowed to avoid people walking home from work. Roger expected they'd have to get off and walk at any minute, but Ishak wound and skidded all the way to the old wooden gate of his parents' house.

Ishak's mother, father, and the goat in the courtyard cried out in surprise. Roger and Sophie were greeted like family coming back from a long trip. They sat on a kilim carpet in a room lit by a single gasoline lantern. Roger had learned a few greetings in Dari by now, but when those were finished, he sat like a young child listening while Ishak and Sophie did all the talking. A word he'd seen on signs and Googled came up—*khatar*, danger. Ishak and Sophie must have been explaining why they'd come. He recognized the word *motahel*, married, and was sure Sophie was explaining she and Lyle were never husband and wife.

Ishak's parents nodded agreement on something that drew an amused but firm refusal from Sophie. She told him, "They say they'll build two extra rooms for us. So we can live here comfortably."

So it seemed Sophie had told them she and Roger weren't married, either. A shadow of distress dulled her eyes. Roger hadn't had a chance to talk to her on the motorcycle ride. And there still was no time for a private conversation.

Roger checked the reception on his phone, excused himself, and went into the courtyard to call Siavash. "Jill's alive. She threatened to kill Sophie. Sophie had to give her the vault key."

"Slow down," Siavash pled. "So Sophie's somewhere safe now? Thank God. I'll report this to Jackson."

"Another thing. Jill has Lyle's key. She's the one who planted the IED that killed him. She took the key from his body."

"Say that again? Never mind. How long are you staying there? Come back tomorrow if you can. We have work to do."

When Roger went back inside, Ishak and his mother had already brought towels, plastic buckets, and soap into the room along with a chador for Sophie. "We're covered with dust," Sophie explained. They headed for the public bath house. Ishak's mother took Sophie by the arm as they followed the men down the sandy lanes to a large public hamam. Omar had told Roger that when the Taliban ruled the country they had closed down all the bath houses but that many had reopened when their reign ended. Lots of Kabul residents, especially in this old sector, had no running water.

There were separate sections for men and women. Roger and the men stripped to their shorts, left their clothes on a stone shelf, and stepped onto a warm marble floor in a large steamy room. Men sat on stone ledges or stood pouring buckets of water over their soapy heads. The light was dim, and Roger didn't feel the stares he'd anticipated as he gratefully washed the dust from his body. The men were in no hurry to leave the warm water and steam. Roger sat beside Ishak and his father as they chatted with friends. He had no idea what Sophie was experiencing in the women's section. He'd heard from Omar that in large hamams like this there were private stalls for women.

The cool evening air felt good on his clean body as they walked back to the house. Ishak's mother served a late dinner. Roger didn't know how much of it came from the heavy bag of food supplies Amal had sent with them, but he did recognize some sweets she had made—and the goat remained alive. Tea followed, and Roger was glad to see his glass contained no floating green leaf. As soon as Jill found out the money had been taken from the vault, he was sure to be transformed in her mind from a naïve but useful husband into an enemy. He counted on Siavash and the FBI agent catching her and sending her to prison.

He watched as the mats were laid out for the night. There was another room besides the kitchen, but the plan seemed to be for all of them to sleep side by side in the main room—Sophie, the mother, the father, Ishak, and then Roger, in that order.

Roger waited until they all seemed asleep. Then he crawled around and tapped Sophie on the shoulder. "Are you asleep?" Without answering, she got up and went out into the courtyard. Roger waited to see if anybody stirred, then followed.

Sophie stood watching the sleeping goat. Roger said, "I'm sorry Jill hurt you."

She looked down, and he noticed tears on her cheeks.

"Everyone thought she was dead, Sophie."

She pulled away from his hand.

"You'll be safe here until they find her."

Sophie's answer was a loud sniffle.

"I won't let her stand in our way, Sophie. Nothing has to change between us."

She shook her head. "She's your wife. How can you say that?"

"I mean I know she—"

"How could you have loved someone like her? She told me if the money's not in the vault, she'll come for me and she has 'ways to make me turn it over.' Those were her words."

"I never knew how ruthless she was. I was stunned when I heard she stood by and watched as Lyle murdered that Belgian guard. And now, just today, I found out she's even more evil." He didn't know if he should go on.

Sophie finally looked him in the eyes, waiting.

"Jill told me she killed that Special Forces soldier and that she planted the IED that killed Lyle."

Sophie seemed to be gasping for air.

"So I'm going back tomorrow to help Siavash arrest her. She has to be stopped."

Sophie gripped his shirt. "Don't go, Roger. If she finds out we withdrew the money, she might kill you, too."

"I don't know if she would actually—"

"I do. I saw it in her eyes. She wouldn't hesitate a second."

Roger and Ishak left two women crying at the gate as the motorcycle took off for Omar's Shirpur district the next morning. When Ishak dropped Roger off at Omar's, nobody was home. A note on the door said they'd all gone to visit Hekmat's aunt. They wouldn't be back until the next day.

Roger texted Sophie. *I'm back now. Miss you already.*

Everything's changed. This was supposed to be our time alone together.

At least you're safe.

Safely hidden away like an Afghan woman?

Roger didn't know how to reply.

Sorry. I'm so confused. I'll wait for you to come get me.

Roger wanted to tell her that would be soon, but there was no way he could be sure.

He called Siavash. "I'm back at Omar's. No idea where Jill is."

"I still have a guard at Omar's house. How about Sophie? Is she safe in Morad Khani? You sure? Now let's catch Jill. You say she got the second key yesterday afternoon? With both keys, she might not know she needs Lyle's death certificate."

"Yeah. She told Sophie she was going to the Grayrock vault this morning to look for the money. If it wasn't there, she'd go back and kill her."

"So by now she probably knows the vault is empty. And when she doesn't find Sophie, she'll probably come for you. I'd better send another agent to watch the house. If she shows up, they'll arrest her."

Roger paced around the pond Omar-style for a while, then went into the kitchen and heated some water for tea. Now and then he cracked open the front door to see if there was any sign of Jill. He noticed two of Siavash's men in an alley across the street sitting mostly hidden behind a pile of mud bricks. One of them was asleep.

He texted Sophie again.

Good time to talk?

We're eating lunch.

Not goat, I hope.

Very funny. I'll call you later.

Roger found a chicken wing they'd left for him in the refrigerator and some cold rice. Then Dan called.

"Roger? Hey. I'm in Florida with Mom and Dad. Wait, I'll put it on speaker phone."

"Roger? Roger, can you hear me?" His mother tended to shout when she was talking on the phone to someone far away. "I was so sorry to hear about Jill. Danny says she's still missing. That's sad, but I've read that if one partner is terribly unhappy in a marriage, sometimes it's better—"

"Yeah, Mom. Like it says in those magazines, our 'relationship was strained.' So even if Jill turns up—"

"Can you talk louder, Roger? I hear you have a lady friend. Isn't it a little too soon for that? Are we going to meet her? When are you coming home? What are you doing over there?"

"Visiting museums, mosques, parks. There's an old caravanserai they've completely restored. I'll send you some pictures."

"I'm worried they'll hire a replacement for you at Saint Michael's."

"Actually, Mom, I have a job teaching here now. I don't know how long it'll last."

That rendered his mother speechless. His father spoke up. "How much does it pay? I've heard you can make a fortune in one of those NGO jobs."

"I don't know yet. Not a fortune, I'm sure."

His mother recovered enough to say, "Roger. I've read that people make rash decisions when a relationship has gone bad. I read of a case where one man whose wife left him—"

"I can't hear you, Mom," Roger lied. "Dan, I'll send you a check. Would you mind paying the rent on my house until I know for sure what I'm doing?"

"Well at least it's good to hear you still plan to come home," his mother sighed.

"Mom, can you put just Dan on? Something personal. Dan, Mom can't hear, right? Listen, Jill's turned up here in Kabul. She told me she's the one who killed that soldier at Fort Davis."

Dan obviously didn't want to alarm their parents. All he ventured was a throaty "I see."

"Jill's here looking for the money they stole, threatening Sophie. Sophie's in hiding. Before Jill reappeared, I planned to get a work visa and stay in Kabul until Sophie's contract ends in nine months. Now, with Jill on the loose, I don't know if it will be safe for Sophie to stay and finish out her contract."

Dan kept his reaction to "So. I'll keep your rent up to date. We'll talk more later."

That night he called Sophie again. The phone rang quite a few times before she answered. "Hi, Roger. I had to come out to the yard to talk. Ishak's parents are already asleep."

"I'm here alone tonight. Omar's family all went to see an aunt."

"I'll come back. I'll call a taxi."

"You can't do that. Jill threatened you. She could come here any time."

Sophie let out a sigh. "Meanwhile I'll be here playing with the goat and trying to carry on a conversation with Ishak's parents in my basic Dari. One good thing. I get TOLO TV News on my phone. The three of us sit around watching the afternoon broadcast."

"Oh? Sounds like great fun."

Sophie replied with that Dari dog-phrase. "Oh, Roger, I don't know how long I can stay here."

34

No eat dog

The next day Omar got a call from Baltimore. The Khyber restaurant owner wanted to talk to Omar's son-in-law, Hekmat. Omar later told Roger, "The owner got the agreement Hekmat sent him. He'll sign it and have it faxed to the American Consulate here. Hekmat already has the loan commitment, so he'll soon be officially an investor—*allowed* to bring his money to the U.S."

Roger didn't ask if the agreement falsified the amount of money Hekmat was actually bringing. He let that go.

When the consul received the paperwork, he wanted the whole family to come for an interview. They dressed in their Western finest. Even Karim wore a suit. Amal wore a long dark dress with a scarf lightly covering her hair. She'd dressed Sima and Musa up somehow to look like little American kids.

When the taxi returned later that afternoon, the whole family climbed out one after another like happy clowns from a packed circus car. They were shouting, laughing, jumping up and down. Hekmat's grin covered his whole face. "Got the visas!" he shouted. "All of them. We're going to America."

Karim and the little ones chased each other up and down the street. Roger gave Omar a high-five. Hekmat looked puzzled but wanted a high-five, too. Amal took a big breath. "Let's hope for the best."

Roger modified the surah she had encouraged him with before. "*What is to come will be better than you imagine. God will grant what you wish.*" When Amal stared at him in surprise, he said, "It's in the Koran."

Hekmat wanted everybody to eat "American food." He ran to

his Quick Mart.

"Oh, no," Amal said.

Omar tried to stop him. "I don't think—" But it was too late.

They waited at an empty table munching pumpkin seeds and pistachios. Finally Hekmat burst through the door with a large plastic Quick Mart bag. They stared in silence as he took out, first, bottles of Pepsi and then handfuls of items wrapped in white paper. "Hot dogs!" he announced.

Sima screamed, held her mouth, and ran off. Musa watched her, then seemed to understand. "Dog?" he said. "No eat dog." He ran after her.

Hekmat pulled something else from his bag and unwrapped that. It looked like some kind of doughy fritter. "Apple pie," he beamed.

"I'm not going to America," Karim announced. "I'll stay here."

Everybody studied Roger. He gingerly unwrapped a lukewarm reddish hotdog in a stiff, pasty roll and took a bite. It was horrible. "Mmm," he said. "Delicious."

"Let me see." Omar took one, sniffed it, took a little bite, and washed it down with a swallow of tea. "This is not an American hotdog," he declared.

Roger felt obliged to eat all of his, which he managed to get down with three glasses of Pepsi. Hekmat did the same. Amal brought leftover rice and stew from the kitchen. "You can cut the hot dogs up and mix them in," she suggested. Omar tried that, but the others skipped the hot dogs altogether.

This would be Roger's last night with Omar's family. He gave them his address in Baltimore and his brother's and parents' phone numbers. "I feel like you're my second family. I hope we'll stay friends for life."

"Won't you change your mind?" Omar urged. "You and Sophie could come with us. There are still seats available on the plane. I hate to leave you alone here when Ms. Jill is still a threat."

Roger said he needed to stay and help get Jill arrested. "Besides, as you know, I now have a job at the school where Sophie teaches."

Hekmat offered to let him stay in the house after they were gone. He said he'd feel relieved knowing Roger was there to take care of it. He gave Roger the lock code. "If all goes well for us in America, and after you've returned to the States, I'll put the house up for sale. But for now, the house is yours as long as you need it."

"How long will you stay in Kabul?" Amal asked.

"As long as Femmes en Crise wants me to teach for them. The way things are now, anything can happen." He feared what Jill might do, and Amal knew it.

That evening, while everybody was packing, Roger went out to the garden to take a call from Siavash. "Roger, our stakeout guys there at Omar's house report no sign of Jill yet. She might still think Sophie's the only one who knows where the money is."

"Jill's probably staying at Camp Rectitude. Can you go look for her there?"

"Negative. As you know, Afghan police aren't allowed in the Grayrock camp."

"Could you have Sophie's room watched, too? Jill will probably go back looking for her."

"I don't have the manpower."

Roger thought a minute. "I could stay in Sophie's room in case she comes."

"I don't know if I can let you do that. Jill murdered Lyle when she thought he'd cheated her. If she finds you in Sophie's room and realizes you're together—"

"I'll keep the door locked and call you and Jackson when she comes. But I can't go there until tomorrow. This is the last night before Omar's family goes to the States."

"Tell them bon voyage for me."

When Roger went back in, Omar and Hekmat were the only ones still awake. They were discussing the details of their flight. Roger said he'd get his brother to pick them up at the airport. They refused several times before they accepted. Roger texted Dan, and Dan said he'd be there.

On his mat that night, when everyone else was asleep, Roger texted Sophie. *You awake?*

Yes. Thinking of you. My hosts are snoring in the next room.

Mine are snoring here in the same room. They got their visas. They're going to America tomorrow.

And I won't be able to say good-bye? Roger, that's it. I'm coming back. I'm not afraid.

No, Sophie, please don't. We need a little more time to catch Jill.

I want to be with you.

Wait just a little longer. Please.

35
Learn Dari Fast

The main room of Omar's house was littered with suitcases, bags, and piles of clothes, Roger's packed duffel bag among them. At the door, Omar gave Roger a long hug. Then Hekmat, then Karim, then Amal. Sima and Musa stood shyly at a distance. Roger picked them up one after the other for a hug.

He didn't know if the plan was to fit all of them plus Roger into the same airport taxi. It turned out it was. Roger held Musa on his lap. Sima was on Hekmat's lap. The baby Laila was on Amal's. The baggage was in the trunk and tied to the roof.

The airport stirred up memories for Roger—coming to Kabul for the first time, watching Sophie escape from Lyle, flying home alone wondering if he'd ever see Sophie again. Now, with Jill alive and pursuing them, he and Sophie were being forced apart again.

When the time came for Omar and his family to board, Sima and Musa took Roger's hands and pulled towards the gate. Most of the discussion in the house had taken place in English. They seemed to think Roger was going with them. Tears in her eyes, Amal told Karim to take their hands and lead them towards the boarding ramp. For her, Hekmat, and Karim, this was as much a trip into the unknown as it was for the little ones.

Roger stood at the window watching their plane take off. Would Amal be able to adjust to the new life? Would Hekmat really become rich? As for the children, he had no doubts. They would soon become as American as … hot dogs and apple pie.

It was not yet nine in the morning. He hailed a taxi but didn't know where to tell it to take him. Omar's empty house? Sophie's empty room?

"Shahr-e-Naow Park," he told the driver. The park near Karim's school.

Roger shouldered his duffel bag and wandered by a row of little shops crowded together near the park. He'd never taken the time to glance inside them before. He stopped at a book shop and went in. "*Sobh bekheir*," the owner greeted him, which Roger by now knew meant "Good morning." Without Omar or Sophie to translate, he was on his own in Kabul now. Motivated by the challenge, he glanced at the rows of books with titles he couldn't read until the shop owner pointed out a display of textbooks, picked one up, and showed it to him. *Learn Dari Fast.*

Roger found a park bench and immersed himself in study. Combining *Learn Dari Fast* and Google Translate, he memorized a list of useful phrases. He chuckled to find the literal meaning of expressions he'd often heard. *Pedar sag*, for example, something Sophie had called him, meant "father-dog." She was calling him a son of a bitch. The book said it was "a gentle aspersion, often used lovingly or humorously."

He thought over recent comments Sophie had made from her isolation in Morad Khani. Was her insinuation that he was hiding her away like an Afghan wife meant lovingly and humorously? It sounded more mocking and satirical. Roger fought to dismiss the thought of possibly losing Sophie's respect over this separation. Why not take a taxi to Morad Khani right now and bring her back? But until Jill was caught, they'd be living in fear.

The sun was getting hotter. Men sleeping in the park stirred and moved into the shade. Roger took off his suit coat and tie and rolled them into his duffel bag. Indian music blared from a nearby tea shop. He went in and found a seat next to a turbaned old man with white eyebrows. "*Salaam.*" The man's voice was deep. "*Befarmāid,*" he said, pushing a plate of blueberry scones towards Roger. This was a chance for Roger to try out his list of phrases. To the best of his knowledge, the conversation went like this:

"You are lost?" the old man asked as Roger searched for phrases in his book.

"No." Roger wiped some sweat from his forehead.

"Hot outside," the old man said. He signaled the waiter to bring Roger some tea.

"Yes, hot. Thank you."

"Davoud." The man pointed to his chest.

"Roger."

"Raja. Good name." The man studied Roger's face. "You are not lost?"

"No."

Davoud eyed Roger's duffel bag. "You are traveling alone?"

"Yes. For now."

"Do not sleep in the park."

"No, I won't."

"You are welcome to sleep at my house."

"Thank you. I have a place to sleep tonight."

"Alone, I think. I see your face."

"Yes, but I'm waiting for someone."

"Ah, your wife?"

Roger was about to say no but realized he actually was waiting for his wife to appear. "Yes," he said.

"Yet you look sad." The old man lifted his eyes and recited something.

"I don't understand," Roger told him. "Will you repeat it?"

Davoud slowly enunciated it so Roger could write it down in Latin letters:

Chun modati barāyad sāyé namānd aslan
Kaz dur jāyegāhi khorshid dar kaminst.

"From the Koran?" Roger asked.

"No. From a poem by Attar. Not difficult." He pointed to Roger's book. "Find the words later. You will see."

Roger read out his transliteration to make sure he got it right, and all chatter in the tea shop came to a halt. When he finished, he received a loud round of applause.

Now what? Roger didn't want to go to Sophie's room early and sit around. The auto repair shop where Ishak worked was nearby. He could try out his new Dari phrases on him.

The repair shop manager eyed Roger's duffel bag and seemed to think he'd come to sell black market parts. "I have come to see my friend Ishak," Roger enunciated in his best Dari.

The manager dropped a wrench on the floor in surprise. "Yes. I'll get him."

Ishak rewarded Roger's efforts at Dari with a wide grin. "Miss Sophie," he asked, "is she good?"

"Yes. I think so."

"My mother says Miss Sophie is sometimes sad."

"Please thank your mother and father for taking care of her." Roger hoped that came out right.

Ishak's reply came straight out of Roger's textbook. Literally, it was "Please. I beg you."

"She wears your bracelet every day." Roger mimed the word "bracelet."

Ishak's face turned red.

"Let's call her now." Roger dialed but got no answer. Ishak began wringing his hands.

"Don't worry. She'll come to see you when she comes back to Kabul." Roger shook Ishak's hand, then the manager's hand as he left.

He stopped at Hekmat's Quick Mart to get some food to take to Sophie's room. "Hot dog?" the clerk suggested.

"Um, no, I don't think so. He searched the glass case for something that didn't need cooking.

"Pizza?"

Roger looked it over—definitely not something he'd call pizza. But he took two slices anyway.

It was going to be a long lonely night in Sophie's little room.

That evening Roger called her. "Guess where I am now."

"I don't know." She sounded gloomy.

"In your bed."

Her response was not at all what he expected. "Roger, a friend of Ishak's mother heard whisperings about us at the public bath. The neighbors say it's wrong that I'm with you. We're not married. Plus somehow they found out you have a wife."

"Ishak's mother told you this?"

"Yes. It's like she and her husband never thought anything about it until their neighbors started talking."

"How did they find out I have a wife?"

"I don't know. The point is, you do."

"Sophie, you do understand I'm trying to protect you, right?"

"Yes, but don't you want to be with me? You're making jokes about being in my bed."

"I shouldn't have. I'm sorry. I had no idea what you're going through."

"I feel like I can't look the neighbors in the face. I'll never be able to go into that bath house again. I wish I had gone to Belgium with Lexi and Nora."

"What if I come and get you? And we find somewhere else for you to hide?"

"Where?"

"I don't know." He could tell she was crying. "I'll try to think of something. I'll call you tomorrow. Is that OK?"

She sniffled a "'Yes" and "Good-bye."

36

Grieving husband

After a sleepless night, Roger called Siavash, hoping he could suggest another place for Sophie to stay. Siavash told him the police didn't have a budget to put her up in a hotel, but he'd see if Jackson knew of a place. "So, there's no sign of Jill yet? You were there all day yesterday, right?"

"Well, a good bit of the day."

"I'm not happy about trying to arrest her in Green Village, anyway. As long as Sophie's not there, Jill has no other choice but to come to you." Siavash paused for a moment. "You say Omar and his family have left for America? Any chance you could go to his house and wait for Jill to show up?"

"Well, they said I could stay there and gave me the lock code, so—"

"All right. Give me a call when you're in."

Before Roger could punch in the lock code at Omar's house, a car rumbled down the street towards the house with a loud scraping sound. He recognized it as Jill's, which now had a bent fender rubbing against the front tire. Across the street, Siavash's men were busy eating breakfast. Roger was sure he knew what Jill would want. He texted Siavash. *To the bank. Now.*

The car screeched to a stop, and Jill jumped out, her face red with rage. "I went to the vault with my two keys, and that fussy jerk told me an American guy and a woman already came and emptied the vault. He followed all the procedures. That's all he would tell me." She clenched her jaw. "I'd hate to think that guy was you. Is it possible you and Lyle's Belgian mistress decided to take the money for yourselves and run? Don't you understand? I was never going to cut you out, Babe."

"That wasn't me," he lied. "I gave the key to Lyle. Maybe he took the money from the vault before he was killed."

"Using his Belgian bitch to stand in for me? I can't wait to get my hands on her."

"He probably put the money into the fake company bank account."

"So you know about that account? The papers were taken from the Rover along with the key. I've been trying to remember the name of the bank. I guess you have the papers. So tell me."

"I don't have the papers, but Lyle told me it's the Pulshui Bank, not far from his villa."

She grabbed Roger's arm. "Come on. You're going with me. If this is a wild goose chase, there's going to be hell to pay."

Driving the stick shift car with one hand, Jill maneuvered into a space in front of the Pulshui Bank. Roger noticed Siavash's truck already parked across the street. Jill pulled open the bank door with her good hand and nudged him inside with a knee. The guard's eyes widened at Jill's curt demand to see the "honcho." He said, "*Telefon–e-hamrā*," pointing to a basket of cell phones. Jill brushed past him, but he caught her around the waist. "I lost my damned phone in the desert," she yelled. Roger dropped his in. The guard searched Roger and called the woman behind the barred counter to give Jill a pat down.

At the disturbance, Daghal came in from his office in the back. "Americans making trouble? Well, well. What else is new?"

Jill stood at least a head taller than Daghal. "Don't tell me you're the bank president, little guy. OK, we have some private business."

As Daghal led them into his office, his glance showed he recognized Roger, but he said nothing. The money launderer was nothing if not discreet. He let Jill speak first.

"My partner Lyle White opened an account here with me as co-owner."

"With you as co-owner?" Daghal glanced wide-eyed at Roger.

He'd been led to assume Sophie was to be the co-owner. But he only frowned, waiting for an explanation.

Jill rubbed her temple with her good hand. She still seemed to be in a fog from the aftereffects of the scorpion sting. "Not under his own name, dummy. I can't ... my husband will remember the name. Something like—"

"Bebsi," Roger said.

Daghal slid his chair back, both hands on his desk. "This is your wife?" he asked Roger suspiciously.

"Forget that," Jill growled. "We're talking about Lyle White and an account he set up here."

"Calm down, please. I had discussions with Lyle White about setting up an account. But it was never set up. And now I understand he's dead."

Jill leaned over his desk, seized him by the shirt. "Before he died, idiot. An account he set up before he died."

Daghal reached under his desk. Roger heard a faint buzz outside his office door. The guard rushed in, locked Jill's arms behind her back. Another guard came and held Roger. They looked to Daghal for instructions. "You're never to set foot in this bank again," he shouted at Jill and Roger. He said something in Dari, and the two found themselves out on the street.

Siavash and Jackson ran up while the guards still held them. They showed their identification. "Jill Williams, you're under arrest for murder, grand larceny, and attempted money laundering." Jackson reached to handcuff her, but she twisted away from the guard, kneed Jackson in the groin, and gave Siavash a flying kick in the knee that sent him to the ground.

Jill ran to her car, started the engine with a roar, and squealed out into the street in front of a speeding Toyota land cruiser. The crash was deafening. Smoke burst from Jill's overturned car.

Roger ran to the driver's door that had swung open. Blood covered Jill's face. He managed to pull her out onto the street. Holding her head in his lap, he bent to see if she was breathing. "Jill?" he cried. "Jill?" He held her head in his hands. The green was fading from her eyes. Roger wasn't sure if she was conscious. But then, with a wheezing rattle that came from deep in her chest, she breathed out, "Roger? Roger, listen. Find that money. It's all for you now, Babe. I fought hard for it. Don't let our enemies take it." Her body was limp and heavy.

"Jill," he said again, leaning closer. But she was dead.

A crowd started to form, and a TOLO TV News van pulled up behind the wrecked land cruiser. A TV photographer snapped a picture of Roger holding Jill and began filming. A woman reporter fired questions at Siavash and Jackson, blocking them as they tried to make their way towards the crash. Then she ran to ask Roger, "Your name, please?"

Roger didn't answer. Siavash and Jackson showed their badges and tried to move the crowd back. In seconds, police and ambulance sirens blared out, and policemen in riot gear forced even Siavash and Jackson away with the crowd.

Roger was still on one knee, holding Jill's head in his lap.

"Passport," a cop said when he saw Roger was a foreigner. "You are Roger Williams?"

The reporter heard his name, and Roger saw her write it down. The cop took Jill's wallet with her passport from her pocket and read her name. "Jill Williams." He turned to Roger. "Is this your wife?"

"Yes."

The reporter wrote that down. More videos were filmed and pictures snapped, by the news truck and by the onlookers. Two medics from the ambulance rolled a stretcher next to Jill and lifted her body onto it. One had a badge on his white coat saying *Emergency Medical Technician* in English. "Please," the EMT said to Roger, indicating he should get into the ambulance. The policeman drove behind with Jill's passport and papers.

In the ambulance, the EMT felt in vain for a pulse. "Sorry," he told Roger. The ambulance stopped at a building signed in English, *Kabul Emergency Hospital*. Inside, the EMT shook his head at two men in white gowns. The stretcher was rolled through swinging doors, and Roger wasn't allowed to follow. At a desk in the waiting room, a clerk laboriously copied Jill's information into a log book, then gave the wallet to the policeman standing by.

"Grayrock?" the cop asked Roger. "Then we will send the papers to them."

Siavash and Jackson were waiting outside. Siavash put his hand on Roger's back. "She was your wife. As bad as she was, this must be hard for you. We'll give you a ride to Omar's."

"Not yet," Jackson insisted. "We'll need to debrief first."

Roger and Jackson sat across from Siavash at his desk. Siavash buzzed somebody to bring tea. "It might help calm you down," he told Roger. "Always works for me."

Siavash recorded Roger's description of what went on in the bank. There wasn't much to report. "Coming in with Jill rather than Sophie made Daghal suspicious," Roger told them. "Jill got rough. Daghal had the two of us thrown out."

Jackson was clearly disappointed they hadn't taken Jill alive. "We could have learned a lot by questioning her. What did she say to you after the crash? When you were holding her. I'm sure I heard the word 'money.'"

"Money?"

Jackson gave him a suspicious look that Roger found insulting.

"Oh," he replied, "Jill told me if we found the money to give it to charity."

"Bullshit," Jackson scoffed.

Siavash gripped his desk, leaned towards Jackson. "The money has already been returned to Belgian foreign aid. You know that."

"Just being thorough. There could be more that Jill and Lyle stole." Jackson shrugged. "Anyway, I already have enough to convict Senator Steinherz. That's the most important thing."

Siavash shook his head. "As for Daghal, there's nothing new we learned today. I still need to get something on him that our corrupt officials couldn't manage to explain away. Otherwise, I might have to drop the case."

While Siavash and Jackson went on talking, Roger sipped his tea, lost in his own thoughts. He'd previously adjusted to the idea that Jill was dead. But seeing her die in front of him was a new shock.

Siavash closed his notebook. "Good enough, for now. Roger, my driver will take you back. You can get some rest."

Jackson held up a finger. "But don't leave Kabul without letting me know. I might have more questions. And I might have to bring you back to the States eventually as a witness when the case against Steinherz swings into full gear."

As the Major Crimes truck wound away from snow capped mountains glistening against a deep blue sky, the memory of standing with Sophie to admire a similar scene tore Roger out of what now seemed a terrible nightmare. He'd left Sophie hiding away in a place where she now felt the people's disapproval. She needed him. He reached into his pocket. His phone wasn't there.

"Drop me off at the Pulshui Bank," Roger told the driver, remembering he'd left his phone in the basket by the guard station. "I'll walk from there."

But the bank was closed for the day. On the way to Omar's house, he passed the Nike store and a few other shops, then saw a cluster of people watching a television broadcast through the window of an electronics store. The TOLO TV afternoon news was reporting Jill's spectacular car crash. A close-up flashed on the screen—Roger, kneeling, with Jill's head in his lap. "Mr. Roger Williams, an American, holding his wife after the accident," the description said in English. "She was taken to the Emergency Hospital." Roger heard sympathetic tsk-tsks in the crowd.

The sun was setting as Roger made his way towards Omar's, but waves of heat still shimmered up from the sidewalk and radiated from the sides of the buildings. His face felt hot. He was thirsty, hadn't drunk anything that day except one glass of tea. As he stepped into Omar's house, the room started spinning, and he slumped to the floor. He didn't know how long he was out, but when he awoke, it was dark.

Nobody seemed to have land lines in Kabul, and almost everybody had a cell phone. Except Roger. He needed to call Sophie but couldn't. He turned on Omar's television to see what time it was. The late news was already on. There it was again. The news media seemed fascinated with the picture of the American holding his wife's head in his lap, an open mouthed look of pain on his face.

The Green Zone curfew was in effect. He couldn't phone for a taxi, and it was too late to go out looking for one to go and pick up Sophie at Morad Khani. He still felt weak and realized he hadn't eaten anything that day except a cold piece of pizza. He searched in his bag and ate the other one. But his stomach revolted. He curled up on the carpet in pain until he fell asleep again.

When he awoke the next morning, he felt better but still weak. He found some hard boiled eggs Amal had left in the refrigerator for him and made some tea, then went out and sat on the edge of the pond to eat. A shrill *ak-ak-ak* made him jump. The magpie landed on the top of the garden wall.

Roger jumped up and rushed to the bank to retrieve his phone. The street wasn't as crowded as usual. He realized it was Friday. The bank was closed.

He took a taxi to the Morad Khani district and made his way through the dusty lanes to where Sophie was staying. Ishak's mother opened the gate and stood in the entrance, a chador pulled over everything but one eye. "Not here," she said loudly so he could understand her Dari.

"Where is she?"

"We saw the news yesterday." Luckily the Dari word for news was news. "She went to Green Village." Ishak's mother made a hand gesture to mimic crying.

Sophie's bed was neatly made. Roger had left her room in a hurry the day before without bothering with it. He held her pillow to his face, breathing in the fresh scent of Sophie's hair. She must have slept here the previous night when he was at Omar's. He collapsed into her chair, trying to catch his breath. There was a note on the desk.

Roger, I stayed awake all night hoping you'd come. I've gone to look for you at Omar's this morning. If you're not there, I don't know what to do. Please call me.

But Sophie wasn't waiting at Omar's locked house when Roger got there. Where could she be? The only place he could think of was the Ariana Café.

The old waiter dried his hands on his white apron. "We saw your face on the news yesterday. They said that was your wife."

Roger nodded, and the waiter glared at him. "Your girlfriends will be surprised."

Roger ignored the implication. "Have you seen them?"

The waiter clicked his tongue, raising his eyebrows to indicate *No.* He turned back to the counter without taking Roger's order. A few customers were staring at Roger as if they recognized him from the news. Roger left in a hurry.

There was no new note for him when he checked back in Sophie's room. And she wasn't waiting at Omar's when he went back there. He walked by the bank again just in case they opened Friday afternoons. Of course, it was closed. He'd have to wait until the next day before he could call her.

Sophie's note had sounded desperate. "I don't know what to do," she'd written. Roger didn't either. Unable to sit still, he began to pace up and down the streets for hours. When a police car passed by, he slowed down, trying not to look suspicious. When he finally realized he was hungry, he went to the Quick Mart. A newspaper lay atop the counter. On the front page was a picture from yesterday's news video. Beside Roger's head was a caption in Dari and under it in English "Grieving husband!"

"Mister," the clerk said. "Your wife. I am so sorry." He wrapped some grilled chicken and flat bread in paper. "Please take this. I am so sorry."

Roger bowed his thanks and left at once. All he wanted was to get out of public view. He closed Omar's door behind him and dropped to a cushion on the floor. The room was shadowy with a single beam of light streaking in from the open walkway to the garden. American houses should have courtyards like this, he thought. A place to be outside yet unseen. He took his chicken and bread to the pool edge with a sigh of relief.

But even here he was being observed. The magpie croaked at him from the top of the wall. *Ak-ak-ak. Ak-ak-ak.* Roger imagined a sense of urgency in its call. He tore off a piece of bread and tossed it towards the wall. But the bird ignored it and went on *ak-ak-ak*-ing.

Tired from all his walking that day, Roger fell asleep shortly after dark. He either dreamed of the magpie calling or actually heard it in his sleep. He couldn't tell which.

When Roger awoke, it was still dark. He had no idea what time it was, but then he heard a rooster crow. It must be close to morning. What time did banks open in Kabul?

Finishing the grilled chicken took only a few minutes. A shower took only a little longer. By then the dim hint of sunlight from the garden had broadened in the shadowy main room. He sat watching the light on the carpet, waiting for it to spread, but he could detect its movement no better than watching the hands of a clock. Time seemed to be standing still. He fell asleep again, dreaming that Sophie was lost in a dark forest and his only hope of finding her was to wait for the sun to come up.

Roger was the first customer at the Pulshui Bank. As the guard began to search him, the woman behind the barred counter window looked up. "Ah. Mister Roger Williams. I saw the news. Your wife's accident. What a tragedy."

The guard stopped his search. Roger pointed to the basket by the wall. "I forgot to take my phone when I left." The guard gave him a sardonic smile suggesting he hadn't forgotten Roger's forceful eviction from the bank.

Five messages. Roger leaned against the adobe wall outside the bank and read them in order.

Thursday.

Message 1: Roger, we saw the online TV news report. You look devastated. Did Jill survive? Call me.

Message 2: I'm coming back to Green Village now. Please call me.

Message 3: You're not in my room. Where are you? Why don't you call me?

Friday.

Message 4: Roger, you weren't at Omar's either when I checked. That picture of you with Jill is heart breaking. Maybe I can understand. But please call me.

Today.

Message 5: Still no word from you. I called my mother. She begged me to come home. So I'm getting on a plane for Belgium now. You can call me if you want.

The Turkish Airline agent confirmed that the only plane that day had left Kabul an hour ago. He checked other airlines. "No, nothing else until tomorrow."

Roger sank to a squat and called Sophie. No answer. She was probably still on the plane.

37

Disposition instructions

In the shady edge of the park, a drug addict and a homeless old man were stretched out on sheets of cardboard. In the States, Roger thought, they'd be told to move along. But as he watched, a passerby gave each one a coin or two. *"Lutf-e-shomā ziāt,"* they responded. "Your kindness is great." It pleased Roger that he now understood this common phrase.

He checked the time. Four more hours and he might be able to reach Sophie in the Istanbul airport. He needed to understand how she could leave so suddenly, without saying good-bye. *That picture of you with Jill is heartbreaking,* she'd texted him. That was pretty much her explanation. True, it was shocking to have his wife die in his arms. Even though Jill had threatened, "You're either with me or against me," he knew she naively assumed he'd be with her, no matter what she'd done. He found that pitiful. Perhaps absurdly touching.

Is that what Sophie saw in the picture? He'd looked devastated, she'd texted. But that's not how he'd felt. It was more a sense that he might have helped Jill if he'd stood up against her. "Heartbreaking," Sophie had written. But what he'd actually felt should not have broken Sophie's heart.

Sophie was gone. Omar and his family were gone. The Femmes en Crise school where he was scheduled to teach was closed until September. What was there to keep him in Kabul, any longer? Yet he was determined not to move from the park bench until he heard from Sophie.

His phone rang and his heart jumped. It was only Siavash.

"You doing OK, Roger? And Sophie? Now that she's out of

danger?"

"Sophie went back to Belgium."

"You mean permanently?"

A lump formed in Roger's throat, and he couldn't answer.

"I hope not. We need more people like her here. I'll miss her if she doesn't come back."

Roger cleared his throat. "Yeah."

"Something else. Jackson was trying to get in touch with you. Mind giving him a call?"

Roger didn't feel like talking to Jackson but called anyway.

Jackson sounded annoyed. "You never answer your phone? I'm going to need you to come to the embassy to give evidence against Senator Steinherz."

"You mean now? I can't—"

"It's all set up. Come to the legal attaché office in the embassy. We'll be waiting for you."

Roger sat at the table trying to smooth the wrinkles out of his suit coat. He swore to tell the truth, and Jackson asked the first set of questions. A gray-haired woman with thick glasses recorded the deposition on a stenotype. A young man in a turtleneck shirt operated a rack of audio and video equipment. When Jackson got around to asking Roger to describe in his own words his meeting with Daghal, the senator, and Sophie, the memory of Sophie sparring with the senator choked him up.

"And when that meeting was over, Mr. Williams, I understand you saw the video of the senator making unwanted sexual advances towards Miss Martens. Did she also describe this harassment to you?"

"Yes."

"We haven't been able to locate Miss Martens. Do you know where she is?"

"She went home to Belgium." His voice was shaky.

Jackson leaned towards the microphone. "The existence of the video along with other allegations by women against the senator, I would suggest, allow us to go forward with charges of sexual harassment and bribery without calling Miss Martens to depose at this time."

Jackson walked out with Roger. "That's all we need to bring the senator to trial. You'll need to be in the States when it comes up."

"When do you think that will be?"

"Hard to say. These things take time."

While he waited for a taxi, Roger dialed Sophie's number. No answer. She should be in the Istanbul airport. Maybe her phone was still in airplane mode. He left a voice message. "Sophie, I love you. I really need to talk to you. Please call."

At Omar's there was nothing for Roger to do but wait. In another three or four hours, Sophie should have landed in Belgium. Maybe he'd try to go find her there.

A thumping on the front door roused him from his thoughts. Roger recognized the armed man in a black Grayrock T-shirt as Chopstick, who had come to help empty out Lyle's villa.

"Sir, you are Roger Williams?" Chopstick handed Roger Jill's leather shoulder portfolio. "The deceased's effects. Sorry for your loss. Grayrock has followed your wife's disposition instructions to send her remains to Veterans Cremation Service in Baltimore. Her burial wishes are on record at that location."

It was the first Roger had thought about Jill's "disposition" and burial wishes. Maybe he assumed Grayrock would take care of it. He sat on the edge of the pond and opened the portfolio that had served as Jill's private, off-limits office. There it was. The Rover key. And his Civic key, too. And both vault keys, one still on a chain. The wallet they'd used to identify her at the hospital still held some U.S. and Afghan money and her passport. He laid these out on the pond ledge and flipped through the papers.

The contents of the portfolio had been kept secret from him so long he felt guilty looking at them. Grayrock orders, directions to various places in two countries, hand-drawn and printed-out maps, business cards, and even a copy of their marriage certificate. An envelope was labeled "Medical Evacuation/Return of Remains/Insurance."

She wanted to be buried in the Baltimore National Cemetery, which only accepted cremated veterans, its brochure said. A page torn out of the crematorium pamphlet had a circled notation: "Remains can be preserved no longer than seventy-two hours."

With a throbbing head, Roger realized there was no one but him to take care of all this. Jill had no living relatives. It seemed she had married him not only to serve as a naïve straw man to facilitate her money laundering. She also needed a husband to manage things if she died.

Roger didn't know how long he'd been staring at the single goldfish swimming in circles when his phone rang. It was Sophie.

"Roger, I got your message. You said we needed to talk. Whatever it is, I understand. You must be going through a lot."

"My phone was in the bank. I didn't get your messages until after you left."

"It's OK. You don't have to explain."

"I feel lost without you, Sophie."

She was sniffling. "But?"

"What do you mean?"

"I know there's something you need to tell me."

"I wish I could fly there to be with you."

More sniffling.

"I can't, though. I have to go back to the States. I'm the only one to take care of Jill's—"

"It's all right, Roger." She was crying. "I'm sorry. I can't talk any more now." She clicked off.

Roger looked at the reflection of the setting sun in the pool. What if he just didn't go back? He paced around the pool a few times and realized he needed to call Dan.

"What?" Dan shouted. "First you tell me she's probably dead, then not dead after all. Now you tell me she is?"

"It's definite this time, Dan. The body's been shipped to Baltimore."

Dan was atypically silent.

"I know this sounds crazy. She died in a car crash. Now I don't know what to do."

"Come home. That's what you need to do. You're on record as her husband. You're obliged to take care of this."

"Obliged meaning?"

"It's the god damned law."

Roger sighed.

"You can't just let this go, Roger."

Dan had offered to pick him up at Dulles. Roger bought his ticket and wanted to spend his last night in Sophie's room. Bad idea, it turned out. Everything brought back memories—the paper-covered window Sophie had peeped out of, the bathroom door he'd hid behind, the Grayrock disguise she'd worn to the vault, and then the memory of Sophie's mischievous eyes when she announced, "You notice Lexi's not here?"

Sophie's good luck jacket, the one Amal had sewn the Koran talisman into, still hung on the arm of a chair. She'd left without it. Roger dropped onto Sophie's bed. What chance was there he'd be able to fall asleep without her here with him? It was his fault for asking her to stay in Morad Khani even after Ishak's parents realized he had a wife. He'd asked her to put aside her humiliation. "You idiot," he cursed himself, punching the mattress with his fist.

He brought Sophie's number up on his phone but hesitated to press Call. She'd been crying and said she couldn't talk any more. She almost sounded like she was giving up on him. It wouldn't help to remind her he was going back to the States the next day.

III

38

Double burial

The transfer in Istanbul was painful. His time there with Sophie had been like a dream. Now he sat alone on a plastic airport chair looking at his phone. It was only an hour earlier in Belgium. Lunch time. But what could he say? I'm in Istanbul where we were first together? That wouldn't be likely to dry her tears. He decided to wait until he had something more upbeat to tell her.

The rest of the trip home was a blur. A surge of musty air greeted him when he opened his old house door on Shadow Cove Avenue. Dan followed him in, eager to look through Jill's papers. Roger made him a cup of coffee and, thinking of Omar and Amal, dropped a tea bag in some hot water for himself. He told Dan he wanted to call their parents and Omar and let them know he was back in the States.

"Mm. Hold on. Look at this." It was the card of an attorney on Charles Street. "I wonder if Jill left a will." Dan tapped the card on the table. "She has no living relatives, right?"

"That's what she told me."

"Here. Call the number on this card. I'd like to know what business she had with the guy."

"Not now, Dan. The first thing I need to do is call the Veterans Cremation Service. I don't know what they do with the body after the seventy-two hours is up."

The raspy-voiced woman who answered called him "Hon." He needed to come in and choose an urn. "You understand," she cautioned, "the VA pays a minimum amount. Survivors are responsible for what's not covered."

Dan came along with him. Roger declined but Dan, perhaps understandably, wanted to see the body. He came out of the "holding room" pocketing a copy of the death certificate.

The woman put her hand on Roger's arm. "We'll contact the cemetery for you, Hon. Will there be a memorial beforehand? That would be extra, of course."

Roger wasn't inclined to draw this out, but he had a thought. He'd told people Jill was dead, then had to tell them she wasn't. Would his parents, Omar, Amal—even Sophie!—ever believe him? "Sure," he said. "No problem. Let's have a memorial."

"Now the urn." The woman led them to a shelf to choose from. The prices gave Roger a shock. He was running low on money. But one of the urns featured an embossed eagle with raised talons that reminded him of the Grayrock logo. "If I get that one," he asked Dan, "could you—"

Dan flashed his credit card. "I got it. It's perfect."

The National Cemetery lay at the Baltimore city line on a busy street across from a line of brick row houses. Roger had driven along Frederick Avenue many times without noticing the wrought iron fence or endless identical white grave markers strung out in waving lines across the rolling lawn.

Roger's parents had insisted on coming up for the funeral. His mother had put on a little weight since they'd moved to Florida, and her hair was now a combination silver-blonde. His father's long, wavy white hair looked exactly as it had the last time he'd seen him. Roger telephoned Omar, and Omar came with his family, too. They gathered under the towering pointed roof of an open pavilion supported by fieldstone columns. Sitting on black iron benches cemented into a concrete slab floor, they faced a gray wall hung with plaques of the military services. Jill's urn had been placed on a bare, waist-high slab reminiscent of an altar, its gilded eagle gleaming in the sun.

A uniformed man from the National Cemetery approached stiffly and said something about valor, sacrifice, and duty to country. Roger's mother, who'd been kept in the dark about Jill's crimes, wiped tears from her eyes, while Dan shook his head and Omar gritted his teeth. Roger was glad Sophie didn't have to be here. He'd decided to put off contacting her until the funeral was over.

As they left the cemetery, Roger's mother took him aside. "I didn't mention this before. You seemed too upset. It's usual to invite your friends to a gathering afterwards. That's why I cleaned up your house. And cooked those casseroles. You know, in case you want to."

Roger's mother served tuna fish casserole as well as ham sandwiches—which Omar and his family passed on—while his father handed out bottles of beer—which Omar and Hekmat gratefully accepted. "It's an American custom," Omar told his daughter. "We need to fit in." Hekmat agreed, yet he seemed puzzled by something. "No Pepsi?" he asked Roger.

Omar's family didn't talk about Jill. They were excited to be living in Omar's "American" house. They had gone about the process of fitting in with lightning speed. Karim was already enrolled in school and a star on the soccer team. Sima and Musa were in a special language program and already speaking without any trace of an accent. Hekmat was making plans to open an exclusive restaurant, and Amal had joined a babysitting group so she could take a quilting class at the community college. Omar urged Roger and his family to come visit when they could.

Roger's father asked about the dust covered Land Rover with the broken window in the driveway. "Was it Jill's? Looks like it was vandalized. Those babies cost a fortune. What are you going to do with it?"

Roger shrugged, but an idea was forming in the back of his mind.

"And didn't you have a Civic? What, you traded up to that Camry?"

"The Camry's a lease."

His father shook his head. "Young people these days."

Roger's mother heaped more tuna casserole on Roger's plate. "I've been following the news about Afghanistan. Those negotiations in Doha? It looks like the United States is going to withdraw its troops. They say the Taliban already have control of large parts of the country. Promise me you won't go back."

"I do wonder what's going to happen if we suddenly pull up and leave, Mom. But if you could see the enthusiasm of the women Sophie teaches, the women I'm going to teach, you'd understand why it's worth it. I'll go back for about nine months. Then I'm thinking of returning for a month or so every summer after that. *Enshallah.*"

"What?"

"God willing."

"Yes. Here, Roger." She took something from her purse. "Wear this Saint Christopher medal to protect you in your travels."

"Sure, Mom."

Roger's father checked his watch. "We'd love to stay a few days, Son, but we have to fly back right away for a crucial condo meeting."

Omar's family, ever on the alert for the "American way," took that as their signal to leave, too.

Roger's mother hugged him. "I know you're sad, but maybe it's for the best, Dear."

After everybody left, Roger sat at his kitchen table staring at his phone. The funeral was over and there were only a few more details to take care of. That's what Sophie needed to know. He rang her, but got no answer, so he left a text. *I miss you. Please call me.*

She'd been crying the last time he heard her voice. "I can't talk any more now," she'd told him. Maybe she still felt like that. Roger's throat tightened. He typed another text. *I love you, Sophie.* He thought of adding that he'd be back in Kabul soon. But when he thought of her cramped spartan room, he realized that if Sophie wasn't going to be there, he might as well wait until September when the Femmes en Crise school reopened. He simply clicked Send.

The mail Dan had picked up while Roger was gone still lay piled on the table. Roger sifted through it. Nothing but junk mail. Some was addressed to Jill. She had three different "final notices" that she needed to act fast before the warranty on the Land Rover ran out. Somehow the memory of Jill leaving him with that locked, useless car made him grip his hands all over again into sweaty fists. It was still parked there, a mocking Grayrock monument to his gullible bond to Jill.

He dumped Jill's portfolio out onto the table and picked up the key. The car's battery had to be re-attached, then a spot cleared on the grimy windshield. He brought a trash bag to cover the rain-sogged seat. With a few groans, the engine started. He drove to Dan's.

"Want to take a ride to the Patapsco State Park?" He figured there was still just enough gas.

"It's getting late, Roger. The park closes at sundown."

Roger insisted Dan follow him anyway. He drove the Rover along the river until the paved road came to an end at a turn-around. It was late on a week day, and as he expected there were no other cars. The leaves lining the high bank were a blend of gold, red, and rust. Roger and Dan both got out to take in the late summer view.

"Nice," Dan said. "I remember coming here when we were kids. But you want to tell me what's going on?"

Roger kicked the Rover's fender. "I guess you don't hate this car as much as I do."

"Actually, I think I do."

"OK, then." Roger drove the Rover across the leafy dirt to the edge of the high river bank at the deepest part of the river where he and Dan used to fish. Leaving the door open, Roger shifted the car into four-wheel drive, released the parking brake, put it into drive, and rolled out onto the ground. They watched as the car slowly edged towards the cliff, then tumbled down, flipping once, and landing nose-down with just the broken tailgate window above the water line. In a minute, a line of bubbles streamed up from the window and the Rover sank below the surface.

"That's two items buried since you've been back," Dan commented.

"Think Grayrock will miss it?"

"I doubt it. Even if they do, they rake in so much money from the government they can easily write anything off."

"Yeah. Even human life."

39

Blood money

Back at the kitchen table where he did his serious thinking, Roger decided he'd go to Brussels. It was almost September, and he hadn't heard from Sophie. He needed to see her now. Something was wrong. With no idea how he'd pay, he was Googling airline flights when Inez Gonzalez phoned.

"Hello, Roger can you hear me? Are you still in Afghanistan? I wonder if you've found Jill yet."

"Sad news, Inez. I found her, but soon after that she was killed in a traffic accident."

"Oh my God! That's awful. So are you coming home?"

"I'm actually back home."

"That's wonderful. But, Roger, I need to tell you that Father Joy has hired somebody to replace you."

"Sure, fall classes start in another week. He didn't have a choice."

Inez chuckled. "He could have made a better choice, I'll tell you that."

"You know the person?"

"My niece knows him from college. His name's Bucky. She introduced us at the shopping mall."

"I take it you weren't impressed."

"My niece was surprised when he told us he'd got the job. She told Bucky, 'I didn't think you knew much about math.' You know what he answered? He took out a little green pocket Bible and tapped it. 'Everything the boys need to know is in there.'"

"I'm getting the picture."

Inez chuckled again. "He married young. My niece also knew his wife at college. She wears long, loose dresses—like a prairie pioneer, my niece says."

Inez seemed to be blossoming in her retirement. She'd never ventured into anything remotely like mockery when she was working at Saint Michael's.

"He's a captain in the Soldiers of Christ, my niece tells me. He tried to get her to join the Handmaidens of Christ, like his wife. My niece told him she didn't look good in baggy clothes."

Roger had a vision of Afghan women in burqas.

"Father Joy had doubts about hiring him, but a major donor to the school recommended him, so—"

"Uh-huh."

"I've been talking too much, Roger. Sorry. I miss our times together at the school." She paused. "I think you would like my niece. She's funny. And very pretty."

"Yes, she sounds interesting. But I don't—"

"Of course. What am I thinking? You're still getting over your wife's passing."

Roger wasn't ready to bring up Sophie. He let it go.

"Another thing." Inez sounded excited. "They're advertising for English as a second language teachers and basic math teachers at the community college. It seems there are lots of Syrian refugees. I just thought you might want to look into it."

The refugees Inez mentioned had probably arrived before the current President was elected.

"Here I am telling you what to do. Sorry, Roger."

"No, Inez. I appreciate it. I came back for the funeral, but I have a similar job lined up in Kabul. So I'm planning to go back there for nine months or so."

"Oh my. Well, that does sound interesting. Be careful."

When he hung up, Roger went back to the online airline schedule. Whether he flew to Belgium to meet Sophie or waited and flew to Afghanistan, his credit card was almost maxed out already. At first he'd tried not to use money in the joint husband-wife account attributable to Jill's salary, but that was nearly gone now, too. He checked his account online and noticed the last payment from Saint Michael's had never been deposited.

Father Joy was pacing in front of the Saint Michael statue muttering prayers from his breviary. He looked up. "Well, Roger Williams. Welcome back to civilization. I hope you haven't come to—"

"Not to ask for a job, Father. I know it's too late. It's about my last paycheck."

The old priest's face blanched. "I prayed over my decision to put a hold on that deposit. I thought you would get in touch right away and I could convince you to extend your contract. Now I'm afraid I've had to hire ... anyway, God's will be done."

Or a wealthy donor's will, Roger thought.

Father Joy frowned. Something else was obviously bothering him. "If you did come back, there was a problem I needed to warn you about. Just after you left, Kirk told me he saw you and Inez Gonzalez leave in the same car together."

"I remember. My car was out of gas. She gave me a ride home."

"Still, our boys are extremely curious about their teachers' private lives. The last thing we want is a scandal. A man and a woman not his wife leaving in a car together?" Father Joy slowly shook his head from side to side. "I was never in favor of hiring female teachers. The distraction—if nothing else, the distraction works against the goal of keeping these young men godly."

Inez was of an age more likely to distract Father Joy than any of the students, Roger thought.

"So you've been to the home of the Taliban, Roger. I'm sure you must have found it very different from our world here at Saint Michael's."

"I did. For example, they only pray five times a day, not seven. And the Taliban think women shouldn't even go to school, much less become teachers."

The priest gave him a blank stare.

"Anyway," Roger said, "about the paycheck."

"Yes. I'll tell the bursar to release it right away."

"Thanks, Father."

Father Joy turned back to his breviary with a frown.

Roger sat calculating how much money he'd need to fly to Belgium and realized that even after Father Joy deposited his last paycheck, he wouldn't have enough. He must have dozed off because he woke up, head on the kitchen table, with a piercing headache. The shrill bark of a neighbor's dog shot like a knife through his brain. The dog always barked at the mailman. It must be at least three in the afternoon.

Roger looked at the figures he'd drawn on a scrap of paper, then tossed it away. At the clank of the mailbox by the porch, he went out to breathe in some fresh air and get the mail. One large envelope seemed to be an actual letter. "Reginald Blunt, Attorney at Law." With an address on Charles Street. He must be the lawyer whose card Dan found in Jill's portfolio. But the letter was addressed to Roger.

Jill, it seemed, had made a will, and Reginald Blunt was the executor. Roger was the only beneficiary. He was asked to come into the attorney's office with a witness and his marriage certificate for a reading of the will. Roger feared there might be some funeral requests he hadn't been aware of and didn't carry out. As far as he knew, Jill owned nothing but the few things she'd left here in his house. Even the Land Rover hadn't belonged to her. He threw the rest of the mail on the table and called Dan.

Reginald Blunt's office was in the basement of a stone building not far from Baltimore's Washington monument. On the wall behind his desk hung photographs of fighter jets, some flying in formation and some landing on an aircraft carrier. An American flag stood on a post in the corner. Blunt had intense bloodshot eyes and a graying crew cut. "I work with vets from all the services," he told Roger and Dan. He put on thick-framed reading glasses to make out the will, enunciating each phrase emphatically as if conveying a military command.

It turned out that Jill had a life insurance policy naming Roger as the beneficiary. Her active duty insurance had been converted to Veterans' Group Life Insurance, into which she had continued to pay. "Value of said insurance," Blunt recited, "currently amounting to four hundred thousand dollars, U.S."

Roger thought he hadn't heard right. Blunt went on. "I also leave to my beloved husband any funds remaining in my Veterans Federal Savings and Loan Association bank account, to which I have added his name."

Roger was speechless. That must be the account Jill said she'd been living on after she left in pursuit of the witness she killed—the account holding money from "other jobs." At the time, Roger had let that go. But now the money was coming to him. His hands shook as he wondered what those other jobs might have been.

Luckily, Dan was alert and focused. Because the insurance policy was from a veterans group, Reginal Blunt had a claim form Roger could fill out immediately. When they left, Blunt saluted. "I am indeed sorry for your loss, Sir."

"Celebratory beer?" Dan asked in the car.

"I'm sorry. I just want to go home."

"All right. So at least it looks like you're going to be able to pay me back for this month's rent." Dan grinned. "Where is Veterans Federal Savings and Loan, anyway?"

"Never heard of it."

"I'm thinking. Jill was your age. She couldn't have salted away too much."

Roger asked Dan to come in for some ramen. When he shoved the mail aside to clear room on the table, an envelope he hadn't noticed caught his attention. From Veterans Federal. With a hitch in his stomach, Roger tore it open. It was a monthly statement. There was his name next to Jill's. Amount: three hundred twenty-two thousand dollars and some change.

Blood money. It had to be. Who had Jill killed to get this? And now Roger was holding it in his hands.

"What the hell? Bad news?" Dan whistled through his teeth when Roger handed him the statement. "Not a bad nest egg for a twenty-nine-year-old. Of course, it's not the two-point-something million she missed out on."

Roger gasped for breath.

"What did she do to get this, Roger? Did she tell you?"

"No. She never told me she had it until shortly before she was killed."

"All this money, yet I never heard her talk about money." Dan looked around Roger's kitchen. "She never urged you to fix this place up? Or move to a nicer place?"

"No. She wasn't, I don't know, materialistic."

"Never seemed to be."

"She did tell me she'd soon have enough to buy me a house on North Charles Street."

"Buy *you* a house?"

"Yeah, that's the way she put it sometimes. I'm sure she was OK with living here indefinitely herself."

"So if she didn't care about money—"

"I think what she liked was getting it. Taking it. It was like a game." Roger shuddered. "A zero-sum game."

"A game that leaves the losers in their graves."

"Yeah. Like war."

40

A clean slate

Dan had given Roger articles he'd torn from the newspaper dealing with the murder of Special Forces sergeant Randy Bowles. Roger thought he should give Jill's money from "other jobs" to the wife of the man she'd killed. But Bowles didn't have a wife, just a "former girlfriend." He'd been arrested for assaulting her, and she'd fled to Texas.

Bowles was killed by a large caliber bullet, but the gun was never found. His girlfriend was at first a "person of interest," but she'd been in Texas at the time of his murder. Roger also read that before Bowles was killed, he was under investigation "in connection with the murder of innocent civilians during his tour in Iraq." There was a theory that he might have been killed by a U.S. relative of one of the Iraqis he'd shot, but so far no suspect had been found. Investigators considered it "cold case." Roger decided to leave it at that. Jill's "blood money" weighed on his conscience, but it would have to go to a better cause.

Most of the articles about the murder of Sergeant Bowles were written by a reporter from Anne Arundel County and reprinted in the Baltimore paper, which was running a number of reports on Senator Steinherz. Despite FBI agent Jackson's attempt to keep the investigation under wraps, charges against Steinherz of sexual harassment by one staff member, then by two others had come to light. With media attention on him, reporters uncovered evidence of donations by Grayrock to Steinherz's campaign fund. Soon rumors of direct payments to Steinherz himself appeared on Facebook and Twitter.

Agent Jackson woke Roger up with a call at five in the morning. He sounded angry. "Where is Sophie Martens? Minister DeWoot told me she left Belgium after getting a letter from somebody in Baltimore. I need to contact her, get her agreement to testify at the Steinherz and Corelli trial."

Roger, too, was desperate to contact her. Now that he had money, he'd already decided to go meet her in Belgium before returning to Kabul. But he'd taken his passport to the Afghan Consulate to apply for a work visa. He had to wait for that. He told Jackson he was surprised to hear she'd left Belgium. He'd let him know if he heard from her.

Sophie getting a letter from Baltimore was odd. Dan wouldn't have sent her a letter. Omar? He called him.

"No, Roger. I'd let you know if I did. Besides, I don't know her address."

Roger realized he didn't, either.

"Does she have any relatives in Baltimore?" Omar asked.

"No. She has an aunt in New York."

"I wish I could help you, Roger. I've been thinking about Sophie's Femmes en Crise. An aid group like Sophie's that works towards educating women would be the Taliban's first target when the Americans leave."

"Maybe that's why all the women quit except Sophie and two others. They had to go back to Belgium to recruit."

"I'll tell you, Roger. If my daughter wanted to go train Afghan women to be teachers now, I wouldn't let her."

Roger let this sink in. In Kabul, the U.S. and Afghan guards and police had been the forces restricting his life, not the Taliban. In Kabul the Taliban bombed certain targets now and then, but those targets were somewhat predictable—and guarded. Of course, in large swaths of the country outside of Kabul, the Taliban were in control of people's everyday lives. Roger had no experience of that.

Omar's daughter Amal took the phone. "Roger, I think you

should convince Sophie to come to the Sates and marry you."

"That's what I want, Amal. I'm planning to teach with her in Kabul for the last nine months of her contract, then ask her to come with me to the States."

"And get married?"

"Yes."

The conversation ended with Amal's "*Alhamdulillah!*"

Without putting down the phone, Roger punched in Sophie's number. "The number you dialed is not in service at this time." Was she keeping her phone turned off? Something was definitely wrong. She hadn't answered his calls or messages for days. Roger had DeWoot's number and called him.

"Lexi got one text from Sophie saying she'd gone home," DeWoot told him, "and she was coming to Brussels to help us recruit. Then she texted Lexi that she'd received a letter from Baltimore. After that, Sophie's phone went dead. She never came to Brussels. None of us know her parents' number or address. If she doesn't contact us in another day, we'll check her records in the Femmes en Crise office."

"You haven't done that yet?"

"Well, Lexi thought it was something personal and we shouldn't interfere."

Personal? Maybe Lexi thought Sophie had come to see Roger. But he hadn't written that letter. It didn't make sense.

"We had no luck recruiting," DeWoot went on. "The women we talked to thought it was too dangerous if NATO and the U.S. forces were planning to pull out. But Lexi and Nora are going back to finish their contract. They hope you and Sophie will join them."

"I'll come as soon as I get my work visa. I might be late for the start of classes."

Before he hung up, Roger made DeWoot promise to let him know if he heard from Sophie.

He lay in his bed rubbing his temples. Sophie lived in a small village in the southwest of Belgium. She'd told him the name, but it was difficult to pronounce and he couldn't remember it. Martens

was one of the most common names in the country. He tried searching for her on the internet anyway but came up with nothing.

He turned on the Washington TV channel to watch the morning news. The reporter was describing Grayrock lobbyist Ignacio
Corelli as a possible accomplice of Senator Steinherz in the case they
were calling "Bribegate." A picture of Iggy and Steinherz standing
together flashed onto the screen. "The FBI will not comment on the
ongoing investigation," the reporter said. "But a lawmaker familiar
with Grayrock operations suggests this may be only the tip of the
iceberg."

Roger's satisfaction at seeing these criminals exposed was cloud-
ed by worry about Sophie. He shut off the TV and went back to
staring at the ceiling until he fell back asleep.

Roger dreamed of the old white-eyebrowed man in a turban
he'd met in a teahouse in Kabul. In the dream, the man was trying
to tell him something, but Roger couldn't understand. He didn't
even know what language he was speaking. He woke up to the
barking of the neighbor's dog. Mailman.

Mixed in with the junk mail was an official-looking letter.
Dulles, Virginia Traffic Authority. It was a notice that his Civic had
been towed from the airport hourly parking facility to the Dunder
Garage for exceeding the maximum allowable parking time. He
could pick up his car at Dunder's. The notice gave the phone number.

"Dunder," a gruff voice boomed.

"I'm calling about my—"

"Plate number?"

"Just a minute."

"Call back when you got it."

Roger called Dan instead. Dan found it hilarious. "Who parks
their car in the hourly rate lot when they're flying to a foreign country? No need to answer that. I'll take you."

Instead of a door, the Dunder Garage had a bullet proof window at eye level. Roger rang a buzzer, and waited. A narrow panel

eventually slid open, and Roger gave his plate number.

"A thousand four hundred," the bearded man growled through the slot. "Cash only."

Roger gawked. "I don't have that much cash on me. I have a credit—"

"ATM in the airport." The slot slammed shut.

The airport was at least ten miles away.

Dan chuckled. "I can't imagine what this would have been like if Jill had been with us."

"There would have been gunfire for sure."

When they got back and were finally let through the iron gate to the lot, Roger couldn't spot his car. He beeped his key, and a tan Civic's lights flashed. Roger wiped it with a finger. It was black underneath.

"Oh, God. What's that smell?" Dan stepped back from the open door. A half-eaten fish sandwich lay on the passenger seat.

"Don't throw that shit in this yard," Dunder shouted. His beard was so thick you couldn't see his mouth move when he talked. Roger had to turn on the wipers to see through the windshield. He scraped the sandwich and an armful of chip bags, wrappers, and paper napkins into a heap and threw it out into the yard just before they passed through the gate.

As soon as he parked the Civic in his driveway, he checked the mail once again. Still no passport with his work visa from the Afghan Consulate. He caught himself pacing back and forth on the porch.

To calm down, he decided to wash and clean out his car. Maybe it was crazy, but it felt like he was washing away traces of the mess Jill had made of his life. The sanitizing took a couple of hours, but the car finally smelled much better and gleamed like new. He sat on the porch step finally feeling like he could start over with a clean slate.

41

Enemy invaders

Roger had deposited part of the insurance check into his savings account and bought certificates of deposit with the rest. It was just money, but it boosted his confidence that he could go and find Sophie—wherever she was. He kept trying to call and text her while he waited for his visa to come and always got her not-in-service message. Finally DeWoot called him.

"We found her home number and address. Her mother told me Sophie was depressed. Then she got a letter from Baltimore and told her mother she had to fly to Kabul. Did you send her that letter?"

"No. You're saying she's alone in Kabul now?"

"That's right. Her work permit had already been renewed, but Lexi and Nora are waiting for theirs. If they don't get them soon, Sophie might have to start up the fall session by herself."

Roger was determined not to let that happen. He got Sophie's home phone and address from DeWoot before he hung up, shuddering at the thought of Sophie back in her little room alone. He wondered if her parents spoke English. He'd taken a French course in high school, but that was useless. Maybe they spoke Flemish or German, not even French. The thought of calling to introduce himself and ask about Sophie was terrifying. He opened his laptop, went to Google Translate, and typed in some phrases, opening one tab for French, one for Flemish, one for German. His hands were slippery on the keys.

"*Allo.*" It was a woman's voice. Her mother.

"Uh, *je suis* Roger Williams."

"Mr. Williams? I am surprise you call." She spoke English. Roger's blood pressure dropped a little.

"I'm worried about Sophie, Mrs. Martens. I've been trying to call her."

"I have told her not to answer. We argue. It is about you. It is no good she take man from *épouse blessée*."

Roger quickly typed that in. Wounded wife. "No. What do you mean?"

"I have seen the picture. You holding your wife. So sad."

"It's true I was sad. Even though my wife had left me, I was sad when she died."

"Excuse me? Please repeat. Did you say she died?"

"Yes."

"I am sorry. Sophie has seen the news in Kabul. The report did not say she died."

"Grayrock doesn't report deaths to the news. They consider it bad publicity."

"No report of death? Bad publicity? It is terrible. Sophie has not understood your wife died. I have told her she must let you be with your wife. The wife you were holding in your arms."

"Mrs. Martens, when Sophie and I fell in love, we thought my wife was gone forever. Now Sophie doesn't answer my calls."

"I am sorry. I have convinced her to block your number."

"Can you call her and explain?" Roger realized he was asking Mrs. Martens to tell Sophie, once again, that Jill was dead.

Sophie's mother sounded doubtful. "I will have to think about this."

So Sophie assumed Jill was still alive. She probably thought the accident made Roger feel he needed to take care of her. Sophie was bowing out. The only way for Roger to get in touch with her was to fly to Kabul. He had the money. He knew the flight schedules. His bag was packed. He was ready to leave as soon as his passport with the visa arrived from the Afghan Consulate.

Lately the newspapers were saying that the U.S. had reached a deal with the Taliban to withdraw five thousand troops from

Afghanistan as soon as the U.S. President approved, which he was expected to do. Some writers warned of the danger for NGO volunteers once the Taliban were no longer held in check by U.S. forces. They seriously doubted the Afghan government would be able to protect them.

With the Femmes en Crise classes due to begin in a week, Roger was glued to the news. The Taliban had agreed to a cease-fire, but there still were sporadic attacks on Afghan government troops. Nevertheless, the U.S. President held to his plan to withdraw U.S. troops. NATO countries announced they would withdraw their troops as well.

Roger called the Afghan Consulate and spoke to an official who sounded annoyed. "You must understand that work visas take longer to process. You should receive your passport with visa soon."

"Soon" told Roger nothing. He called Omar, who answered in the restaurant and urged him to come in. When Roger got there, Omar was in the kitchen training some new cooks he'd hired. Pans clattered, shouts in Dari, Pashto, Spanish, and English rang out in the steamy room. On a shelf in the corner, a TV was tuned to BBC News. Roger had to raise his voice to ask Omar to call Sophie for him.

"You want me to call her?" Omar was distracted by a huge pot of rice starting to boil over.

"It's a long story, but would you just call?"

Omar dialed the number Roger gave him, then held out the phone for him to hear. "Your call cannot be completed at this time."

The kitchen suddenly became silent. The cooks and busboys gathered in front of the TV. In emotionless tones, the announcer read, "A tractor bomb exploded near Green Village in Kabul, a compound housing international aid organizations. The blast was felt at a distance of several kilometers. A Taliban spokesman said many rooms and offices of the 'enemy invaders' had been destroyed."

Roger grabbed Omar's arm for support.

"At least sixteen persons are reported dead," the BBC continued, "and many more are injured."

When Roger got home, his passport was in the mailbox. Before even sitting down, he bought a ticket online for that night, called his parents, and asked Dan to drive him to the airport.

42

The shadows

The flight to Kabul was torture. The ground below, then the clouds, ocean, and finally the desert inched by in slow motion. When he arrived, early on the morning after the bombing, Roger had hardly slept for twenty-four hours. He must have looked weak. The taxi driver asked if he was sick.

The main gate to Green Village was barricaded, but the driver knew another way in. He and Roger both had to get out of the taxi and be searched by an American guard while another went through the taxi and its trunk, then lay on the ground to look underneath. At the Femmes en Crise quarters there was no guard. Some of the windows were shattered, but the buildings were still standing. Roger climbed the stairs with shaky knees.

He fumbled with the lock code, trying several times before it opened. In the dark, dusty room he reached for the light switch. The light didn't come on. "Sophie," he called. "Sophie." The only answer was a siren in the distance.

He opened the door to let in some light and made his way farther into the room. The sheets on Sophie's bed were tossed aside. A dirty cup and dish sat in the sink. And the jacket she'd left behind with the talisman sewn in had been taken from the arm of the chair. She'd been here, but she'd left all of a sudden. "Sixteen dead and many more injured," the BBC report had said. Roger dropped trembling onto her bed.

When he got stiffly up, he made his way out through debris-strewn roadways to the temporary headquarters of the Belgian Ministry of Foreign Affairs hoping Sophie might be there or they would know where she was.

No guard stood at the door. The ministry windows were shattered and dark. Most of Green Village seemed to have lost electricity. Without hope, Roger pounded on the door. A dog barked inside. Roger tried the latch and the door swung open. The dog came running out with a whimper. The shadowy hallway inside was strewn with shredded paper. The building was vacant.

Roger sank onto the doorstep, head in hands. Car and truck engines roared not far away, but the area around the ministry was eerily silent. He wondered if the Belgian forces had already pulled out of the country. He called Minister DeWoot.

"No, I haven't heard from Sophie since the bombing." DeWoot's voice was hoarse, as if he'd been on the phone for hours. "I don't have much time to talk. We're reevaluating our mission. I don't want to alarm you, but I think you should check for her at the hospitals."

Men beating their breasts and women moaning behind the masks of their burqas stood and squatted in lines outside of the Kabul Emergency Hospital, the only place Roger knew to look. He stood at the end of the line behind a man and woman who sat on the pavement eating bread and wondered how long it had been since the line moved. Most of the victims of the bombing had been Afghans who lived just outside of Green Village, some shot indiscriminately by Green Village guards. Their lives had been lost simply because the "enemy invaders" had carved out a fortified compound in their neighborhood. Near Green Village there were protests against the occupation by the Coalition Forces, but here at the hospital, Roger, obviously an American, felt no hostility. Maybe common tragedy created some kind of a bond.

Roger had eaten nothing but an apple since he left the States. He might have been staring at the couple on the sidewalk. In any case, the man offered him some bread, which he gratefully accepted.

"*Vahshatnāk*," the man said, shaking his head. His wife tisked. Roger had heard this word often since he'd returned this time and had looked it up. Dreadful.

The line into the hospital swayed and bulged but never moved forward. These people probably knew their relatives were inside, but Roger was waiting in line only to ask if Sophie was there. And there were other hospitals. It seemed hopeless. Until now, Omar, and also Sophie, had always been there to help him find his way in this city. He bowed his thanks to the couple who had fed him and wandered off aimlessly.

Turning a corner, he found himself walking past Lyle's villa. It seemed still empty. His throat swelled painfully at the memory of first meeting Sophie in that house. She had brought new life into him.

He was tired, and he'd left his duffel bag in Sophie's room, but he didn't want to stop walking. He passed Omar's house, remembering how Sophie kissed him on the cheek in front of everybody the night she'd been given a heavy dose of Xanax. And how Omar had teased him with a Hafez quote about the secret of his love being out.

He walked on towards Karim's school as if keeping on the move would stop him from thinking. He reached the park but didn't want to sit on the bench. The bread hadn't been enough. He was still hungry and went to the tea shop he'd been in once before.

The old man with thick white eyebrows and white turban who had quoted a poem for him was sitting there in the same place. Roger remembered his name, Davoud. He greeted Roger like a friend.

Davoud had thought Roger looked like somebody with no place to go on that day. Roger probably had the same look now. "Still lost?" the old man asked. "Here, sit beside me." He ordered some kabobs and rice.

Roger took out his Dari phrase notebook. "This time I'll pay," he managed in Dari. The old man grinned, clearly taking the offer as no more than polite ta'ārof. The food came fast, and Roger wolfed down more than half of it. Davoud ate more slowly. He seemed to be thinking. Finally, he took a piece of paper from his waistband. "Attar's poem. Did you find the meaning?"

Roger was pleased to have understood this but felt his face flush. "A few words. But not all."

Davoud spread the paper on the rough wooden table. "I found the English. Here." He turned the soiled, limp paper to face Roger.

For the time will come when nothing remains of the shadows,
Since the sun lies in ambush from afar.

As on the first time they'd met, the old man offered Roger a place to sleep at his house. Again Roger refused, saying he was going to meet a friend.

"Your wife. Yes, I remember." As Davoud said this, the wrinkle on his old forehead suggested he didn't believe it this time either.

Sophie's dust-filled room had no cooler or lights, so Roger went to Omar's house to stay there instead. Staying in either place without Sophie was going to be hard. He dragged a mat onto the floor. It was still early, but he needed to take a nap. Yet his mind wouldn't sleep. The memory of covertly texting Sophie in the next room brought a lump to his throat. They'd been in separate rooms then but their hearts were together. He never thought one day he'd be wondering if she was alive.

43

The sun's ambush

After a restless night, Roger went out into the garden. The sun was rising over the eastern wall, sending thin shafts of light onto the surface of the pool. The single goldfish hung motionless in the water as if it had given up its fruitless circling. Roger sat on the ledge watching it, as motionless as the fish.

A strident *ak-ak-ak* brought him out of his trance. Roger jerked up, and the sun, higher now, flashed in his eyes. From the top of the wall, the magpie fixed Roger in its gaze. A splash in the pond announced the goldfish setting off into motion again. Just then Roger's phone beeped. Sophie. He couldn't believe it.

Omar said you're in Kabul. Is it true?

Roger's hands were shaking. *Yes. Where are you? Are you OK?*

I'm with Ishak at the repair shop.

Are you OK?

Yes. I'm fine. Roger, I love you. I made a big mistake.

In no time, Sophie was standing at Omar's front door, the sun sparkling in her blue eyes and shimmering in her long dark hair. She threw her arms around Roger.

"Sophie, you're not hurt? Were you at Green Village when it was attacked?"

"I went to my room, picked up some things, and went to see Ishak. I was in his room over the auto repair shop when the compound was bombed. Last night I stayed there with him."

"I went to your room. I tried to check at the emergency hospital. I thought I might never see you again."

"Roger, forgive me. I thought I was doing the right thing to break off with you. I thought Jill was still alive and she needed you."

At the soft touch of her lips, all the anguish of their separation vanished like shadows dissolving in the sun. Without speaking, they lay in each other's arms kissing with an intensity born of desperate longing.

Sleep must have finally overcome them. Roger awoke when Sophie snuggled up against him, shivering slightly in the broad, cool room. He pulled a quilt over her. "You awake?"

"Yes." She kissed his cheek and looked up, blinking.

"We're alone at last, Sophie. Free inside these four thick mud walls." Roger stretched, and his hand fell on Sophie's amulet jacket. "You left this in your room when you went home to Belgium."

"I was in such a hurry. That picture of you holding Jill broke my heart. I felt so bad. I wanted to let you be with her and take care of her for the rest of your life." She pulled Roger's hand to her breast. "Feel my heart. It still pounds when I think about it."

"Jill was already dead when that picture was taken."

"Omar told me. I'm sorry, Roger." Her breast was heaving. "I'm happy now, but I still feel guilty."

"Are you forgetting she threatened to kill you? And me, too?"

"It could have been jealous bravado."

"No. She meant it. It wasn't jealousy. She wanted that money."

Sophie sighed. "Omar reminded me she'd murdered two people. Still, what I saw in your face wasn't fear. It was grief."

Roger remembered Jill in her last breath telling him to find the money and keep it if she died. It was like her dying wish to win the game through him. He said, "Jill never felt guilt in committing crimes that outraged normal people. She had no moral compass. It wasn't so much that she meant to be evil. It was almost as if she didn't know any better."

"I understand. And you felt sorry for her."

"Maybe a little."

They made love again. Drifted off to sleep again. When Roger awoke, Sophie's head was resting on his chest. He lifted a strand of her hair to his face. Four walls. Sealed in privacy. Whatever city, whatever country they were in didn't matter.

Sophie stirred, wiped her lip, met Roger's eyes, giggled. "Where are we?"

"Alone in—"

"Just kidding. I know. What time is it?"

"Don't know. You hungry? No eggs. Hekmat and Amal gave the chickens away."

"Over there. In my backpack. I brought Kabuli pulao from Ishak. His mother made it for him but he gave it to me." She hopped up and slipped on the jacket with the Koran quote amulet. It was just barely long enough to cover her torso. "As soon as I got back to Kabul, I put this on, and that's when Omar called me. Just saying. I never should have left without it."

"You believe Amal's superstitions?"

"More like I feel protected when I think about her sewing the quote into my jacket."

Remembering the Saint Christopher medal his mother gave him, which he kept in his pocket rather than wear around his neck, Roger understood what she meant.

They ate cold pulao on the low table. Roger didn't know whether it was a late lunch or early dinner. He finally remembered to ask Sophie about the letter from Baltimore. "DeWoot thought I sent it," he said.

"It was from the executor of Lyle's will. I didn't know this, but people in somebody's will don't have to be named. If you don't know who you'll be married to when you die, you can just say you're leaving it to 'my wife.' If you don't know how many children you'll have, you can say 'my children.' Lyle made his will that way. But I guess he realized he might never have a wife or children." Sophie's face reddened.

"I don't—"

"He wrote if there were no wife and children, his savings and life insurance goes to 'my live-in partner.' Reginald Blunt, the executor, said people 'with Lyle's propensities' usually put it that way."

"How did Blunt get your name?"

"He called Grayrock, and they found somebody who came up with it. My home address was on those papers the Grayrock doctor had us fill out."

"So Lyle left his money to you?"

Sophie stared at him with delicately raised eyebrows. "Do you think he really meant me?"

Roger frowned.

"Ishak. That's who he meant. You saw Lyle's bed and clothes in Ishak's room."

"But did he know Ishak when he made the will?"

"No. I guess he just knew there would be an Ishak."

Roger closed his eyes.

"I told the executor Lyle would want the money to go to Ishak. But he said proving that would be 'problematical.' He said it was already documented on the papers we signed that I lived with Lyle. Besides, maybe Ishak's family wouldn't want him designated Lyle's 'live-in partner.' So I took the money and insurance, came back to Kabul, and put it into a bank account for Ishak and his parents."

"*Barik-e-allah.*"

"Well done? You think? You're not disappointed I didn't keep it? You wouldn't believe how much it was."

"How much?"

"Well, Ishak will be able to start his own auto repair shop."

Roger hated to bring up Jill again. But now was the time to tell Sophie she'd left her life insurance and savings to him. "It's also a lot of money. The money in her savings, though, is from 'other jobs,' according to Jill. I hate to think of what that means."

A shadow crossed Sophie's face, but Roger went on. "I want to give the 'other jobs' money to the families of Jill and Lyle's victims."

Sophie nodded.

"But the Special Forces soldier Jill killed has no family. Do you know anything about the Belgian guard Lyle shot?"

"I do. He wasn't married, DeWoot told me. His life insurance and a large compensation from the Belgian Embassy went to his parents."

Roger thought for a second. "So no need to give it to them. But I don't want to keep that money."

"You'll find a good cause, Roger. Don't worry."

They fired up the water heater, washed the dishes, showered, then stood wrapped in Amal's white bath towels as if ready for bed with the sun still bright in the sky.

Sophie smiled. "Omar said we could stay here."

"Yeah. Your room in Green Village isn't very livable just now."

"I should call DeWoot and tell him we'll be able start classes again when the school opens in a few more days."

"Right." He put his arms around her waist. "Do you have to call him now?"

"No, it can wait."

All that late afternoon, evening, and night Roger and Sophie made up for the time they'd been apart. They clung to each other as if afraid to let go. While the city around them still resounded with horns, squealing brakes, and occasional sirens, Roger and Sophie lay oblivious in a world populated only by themselves.

44

Martyrs

According to reports Roger read on his phone, the Taliban said the Green Village bombing was meant to drive "foreign enemies" from the enclave. Eight foreigners were killed and twenty-five were wounded, and about four hundred foreigners were evacuated. Yet now, two days after the attack, just as it had done after the mosque bombing and the Defense Ministry bombing that Roger had witnessed, the city of Kabul returned to normal.

He and Sophie walked to Hekmat's Quick Mart for some groceries. On the way back, Sophie's phone rang. DeWoot. When the call ended, she told Roger the temporary headquarters of the Belgian Ministry of Foreign Affairs in Green Village had been abandoned after the bombing. "They'll handle everything from Islamabad in Pakistan from now on. But DeWoot still hopes we can continue the Femmes en Crise classes."

"Should we go back to your room in Green Village to get my duffel bag and your books and things?"

"Can't we have one more day before we go to work? I want to cook something good in Amal's kitchen."

Having a whole house to themselves was a new thrill, especially this walled house with its traditional design stressing privacy. He helped shuck peas, cut carrots, and slice meat which Sophie turned into a dark Belgian stew using beer which the Quick Mart clerk fetched from below the meat counter when they asked for it.

Roger turned on Hekmat's radio.

"No news," Sophie pleaded. "Music. The Taliban can't hear us in here." She tuned in a program of traditional Afghan songs. "Take my hand. Can you dance?"

"I'll fake it."

"That's all I'm doing."

The whole great central room was theirs, with no furniture to restrict their circling and swinging. And eventually their clinging and kissing. A bead of sweat ran down Sophie's temple. Roger kissed it off and began to unbutton her blouse. "The Taliban can't see us in here, either." His voice was throaty. Sophie put her arms around his neck, waiting for him to finish. Then she helped him with his shirt. Roger felt her warm skin against his. Stepping from their clothes, they held each other and continued their dance.

In the taxi to Green Village the next day, Roger got a call from Agent Jackson. "I ran a check on airline passengers. Found out you and Sophie are both in Kabul."

"Yes, she's here with me."

"Come to the legal attaché office at the embassy. There's a statement for Sophie to sign."

Sophie nodded agreement, and Roger told the driver to head for the U.S. Embassy instead. They walked across the embassy compound to the office the FBI was using. Roger was surprised to find Agent Siavash of the Major Crimes Task Force there with Jackson.

Siavash beamed when he shook their hands. "I was very, very worried about you two. I drove by Omar's house. It was empty. So was Sophie's room at Green Village. And then, two days ago, the Green Village attack."

Siavash and Sophie had come to sign an agreement to testify against Senator Steinherz if he was brought to trial in the States. Roger recognized the gray-haired woman with thick glasses who had recorded his deposition. This time, she was only a witness to the signing. Roger's previous deposition had been enough to set the investigation in motion.

Jackson slipped the papers into a thin black briefcase. "We might not need any of you to testify at a trial if the case goes as planned. The evidence against both Grayrock lobbyist Ignacio Corelli and

Senator Steinherz is overwhelming. We think we might get both of them to admit guilt to some of the charges in return for not recommending a jail sentence. But anything can happen."

Siavash sucked in a breath and let out a long sigh. Everyone searched his face. "Sorry," he apologized. "I'm happy with the results for Steinherz and Iggy. It's just that the legal system is tougher to navigate in Afghanistan. I found out the banker Daghal has friends in our Justice Department. Anything less than catching him red-handed won't be enough to charge him."

Roger sympathized with Siavash. He saw him as an advocate for honesty and justice in a government plagued by corruption—and more importantly a caring human being. When they left the legal attaché office, he surprised Siavash with an Afghan-style hug. Sophie said something to him in Dari that made him smile and blush.

It was still mid-morning when Roger and Sophie stood at the busy Massoud Circle trying to flag a taxi. As they moved closer to the road, a gray minivan weaving recklessly almost ran them over. Nearby pedestrians tisked and cursed as the speeding van turned squealing down Shash Darak Road. Roger and Sophie were still waiting for a cab when the explosion shook the ground under them.

Dark gray smoke rose over the air just a little south of them. Traffic stopped. In minutes, the whine of sirens began. Sophie clutched Roger's arm. "Not again. Today it's down near the NATO headquarters."

"It sounds like they hit the same checkpoint they bombed when I was last here, when I was going to the USAID office to look for a job."

With no chance of getting a taxi, and Green Village too far away, they walked back towards Omar's house along Wazir Ali Khan Road, north of the embassy compound and the NATO headquarters. Sophie coughed from the smoke and pulled her blue hejab over her mouth. An ambulance squeezed past cars by driving partly on the sidewalk, pushing the crowd up against the buildings. "Stop a minute," Sophie cried. "I need to catch my breath." She clung to his arm, breathing hard.

With panic in the streets, men calling out, women holding children's hands, Sophie drew no attention clinging to Roger all the way back to Omar's. On the way, Roger got a call from Siavash asking if they were OK.

They collapsed side by side onto Omar's mat. For some time neither spoke. The Taliban considered people who killed themselves in bombing attacks like this "martyrs" sacrificing their lives to keep "enemies" from destroying their religion. Roger tried to get into the mind of these "martyrs." In the religion classes at Saint Michael's, Father Joy praised martyrs, too. He led the boys in prayers to them. The difference was that Father Joy's religion was in no imminent danger of being overwhelmed by invading foreigners. The age of the martyrs whose lives Father Joy regaled the boys with was long past, having receded into the realm of legend.

Sophie was asleep. Roger softly brushed some dust from her cheek, remembering their happy intimacy of the night before. With Sophie's devotion to educating the women of this country, it was hard to imagine anyone thinking of her as an enemy. Yet her work was exactly what the Taliban considered enemy activity. Roger couldn't help wondering if Omar was right. Sophie and the Femmes en Crise were an inevitable Taliban target.

TOLOnews reported on the bombing almost continuously that evening. Roger and Sophie watched the English version on Omar's television. Video showed cars and small shops blown to pieces. At least ten Afghan civilians were killed, along with an American paratrooper and a Romanian diplomat. Over forty-two others were injured. Only hours after that attack, the Taliban car-bombed an Afghan military base south of Kabul where foreign forces were said to be stationed.

Most of the news commentary focused on the peace agreement in Doha that had been practically completed and was said to be ready to be signed by the U.S. President. The Americans had agreed on a troop withdrawal in exchange for a guarantee of security by the Taliban. But TOLOnews quoted Afghan President Ashraf Ghani saying, "Peace with a group that is still killing innocent people is meaningless."

Sophie stared silently at the TV, her eyes glassy. She'd said almost nothing since they got back to Omar's. This was the second bombing she'd experienced in just a few days. Roger sat beside her. She took his hand in both of hers, keeping her eyes on the screen.

They turned off the TV and, without eating or undressing, curled up together on the mat. They dozed off, but the phone calls to see if they were hurt woke them up. The first wave was from Belgium. Lexi and Nora called. They were still waiting for their work permits but planning to return to Kabul as soon as they got them. They'd still had no luck with recruiting, though. News of Taliban attacks didn't help.

Then the next wave of calls. Sophie's mother talked for a long time, Sophie mostly listening. In Baltimore it was still morning when they heard of the attack. Omar called Roger, and then Dan called on the line together with their parents. There was agreement among all callers in this second wave that Roger and Sophie should give it up and come home.

"I just don't want to," Sophie told Roger. "I can't help thinking of those women waiting for me to start up the classes again."

Roger remembered the one lesson he'd given the women at Sophie's school. He'd been eager to teach regularly there, working alongside of Sophie. If she wanted to keep teaching there, he did, too. "I'm with you," he told her.

"My mother wanted me to come home after the Green Village attack two days ago. I told her then that these kinds of attacks are rare."

"Yeah. That's what I thought."

45

Jumping in

The city was calm the next morning. Sonorous calls to Friday prayer reverberated electronically across the rooftops. Roger found Sophie sitting on the ledge of the pond, listlessly stirring the water with a finger. She looked up, smiling.

Roger said, "I've often wanted to jump in that pond. On hot days."

"The original purpose of these ponds—*hoz*, they call them—was to store water for washing. Clothes, dishes, your body."

"Yeah? Hekmat cleaned it out and filled it with fresh water just before they left." The morning sun was hot. Roger felt the urge to wash away the discouragement of the previous day. He slipped out of his clothes and splashed in.

"Hey, you're crazy. You're getting me wet."

He flicked a handful of water on her.

"How is it?"

"Nice and cool."

"I'm coming in."

Roger watched with bated breath as she dropped off her clothes and jumped. The goldfish darted to the far side of the pool. The water was up to their waists, and they sank down, ducking their heads. Roger kissed her under water.

After only a few minutes, Sophie stood and said, "Look at that goldfish. We're intruding in its world." Roger got out, extending a hand to Sophie, and they both stood facing each other, dripping on the pond ledge.

The deep rumble of a large motorcycle out in the street stopped at the house. There was a knock at the door. With wide, chastened eyes, Sophie clasped her hand over her mouth. A chill ran over

Roger's skin as they froze in place.

Sophie ran for a towel, Roger following. As they dressed sound-lessly, they listened. There was no second knock. Then the motor-cycle thundered away.

Roger cracked open the door. No one was there. The street was quiet.

Sophie peeped from behind him. "Look." She picked up a bou-quet of roses, carnations, and narcissus. There was no note. She held the flowers to her breast.

"Who do you think they're from?"

"I'm guessing Ishak. This is like him."

"He must be riding a bigger motorcycle now."

Sophie's lips widened into a happy smile.

The roads were pleasantly clear of traffic except near mosques. The taxi quickly brought Sophie and Roger to the Femmes en Crise housing gate, which hung open, unguarded. "The guards might have been evacuated after the Green Village attack," Sophie guessed. "Let's check Nora's room first."

Nora's window was blown open. Glass and fine sand covered everything. The light wouldn't come on. Sophie and Roger picked up books, papers, clothes, everything that looked worth saving, and loaded them into one of the black plastic trash bags they'd brought. Sophie retrieved a photo of Nora's parents from the wall over her desk that reminded Roger of Grant Wood's painting of that rural couple standing stiffly in front of their house.

Sophie's room wasn't in as bad shape, but neither room was liv-able now. They gathered up Sophie's things, too, along with Lexi's. Roger could tell Sophie was holding back tears as she gave a last look at the empty room. They dragged three enormous trash bags down the stairs to the waiting taxi.

At Omar's house Roger gave the driver a large tip. Lots of things became easier in Kabul now that he no longer had to worry about money. "I think I'll pay Hekmat rent for his house," he told Sophie.

"Good idea. And can Lexi and Nora stay here when they come back?"

"Of course. We have plenty of room. And it's closer to your school."

Sophie's school was scheduled to reopen the next day. Sophie called DeWoot and told him she and Roger would be there.

Roger asked her for help in planning a lesson.

"Just do what you did that one time. It was perfect. Maybe stick with basic arithmetic for a while."

"Can we handle the classes ourselves until Lexi and Nora get back?"

"We'll have to. We'll just jump in and see."

Roger fidgeted on the way to the school. The women stood waiting in hejabs for Sophie to unlock the building. Sophie gave every one of them a hug. As soon as they went inside, the women dropped their hejabs onto their shoulders. Roger noticed there were fewer women than before.

"Is it because of the bombings?" he asked Sophie in a low voice.

"Maybe. But in Afghanistan, how can I put this, there's less emphasis on regular attendance."

"Same thing in the Baltimore schools. And some of them worry about mass shootings, too."

The first activity on the agenda seemed to be gathering in one classroom and chatting in Dari, Pashto, and English. The women giggled when Roger tried out the little Dari he knew. As far as he could tell, they were more interested in what each of them had done during the break than in the two bombings that week. Roger relaxed, watching them talk, mostly keeping quiet himself. Sophie seemed more like one of them than a teacher. It was a reunion of friends.

Only enough women had showed up to fill one classroom. Roger watched Sophie teach a lesson on molecular structure. It was amazing how quickly adults assumed the role of children, actually became children, when that's how they were taught. When it came time for Roger's lesson on fractions, he was tickled to find the same thing happening.

And then it was time for lunch. Everyone, including Sophie, had brought something to eat at their desk. A woman with a touch of gray in her hair scrolled on her phone while she ate kofta kabob wrapped in thin bread. "Your president has tweet," she said to Roger. "I have cancelled the meeting," he says. "What meeting is this?"

Roger had no idea.

"I called off peace negotiations," the woman read from the President's tweet.

Roger, like all of his countrymen, had grown used to impulsive tweets from his president that were irrational and dangerous. "He's probably angry that an American soldier was killed in the latest bombing. Let's hope his aides talk some sense into him and he pretends he never said it. That happens a lot."

But the meeting that was called off? Roger wondered about that for the rest of the day. It wasn't until he and Sophie got back to Omar's and turned on the TV that they learned of the international stir the President's tweets had caused.

Apparently, no one else knew about the meeting, either. It was a meeting with the Taliban that the President had secretly planned to hold at Camp David in the U.S. When he found out a U.S. soldier had been killed in the latest bombing, in his fury at the insult he publicly called off this meeting that no one had been told about. Everyone in the U.S. Congress and news media, when they heard about the meeting, considered it had been an atrocious idea, especially since it was to be held just three days before the anniversary of the September 11, 2001, attack that had brought the U.S. into Afghanistan to defeat the Taliban. In Afghanistan as well as the States, no one knew if the President really meant it, or would stick to it, when he said he'd called off the peace negotiations with the Taliban in Doha.

"It will be more dangerous here, if they're called off," Sophie observed. But despite the threat of danger, she and Roger found a way to block it from their minds that night.

The next few days of Femmes en Crise classes were a thrill for Roger. In the States he'd taught only high school boys. Now he was teaching only adult women. He missed the high school pranks and jokes, but the admiration and appreciation shown by these women brought him to a new level of excitement. They hung on every word—partly, of course, because he was speaking in English—but their faces reflected sincere interest.

When he and Sophie came home to Omar's, they talked about their classes. They planned lessons together, cooked together, washed clothes together, and sometimes even showered together. They lived the life of a newly wedded couple on their honeymoon, a working honeymoon off the beaten honeymoon path but a honeymoon nevertheless.

One evening Roger asked Sophie when Lexi and Nora were coming, and her eyes blanked as if she'd forgotten about them. With only the two of them, they were able to leave the low folding table set up in the big room. Ishak's flowers filled a vase in the middle of it. They began sleeping in Karim's room, where Sophie had slept before, because it was cozier.

By the fourth day of classes, more women had begun to attend. They didn't seem to mind crowding into two classrooms. Roger spent some time learning how to pronounce their names without causing giggles. He asked if it was proper to call them by their first names. They giggled at that. "Most of us only have one name," the graying woman who spoke the best English told him. "Please call me Farzaneh."

When they got home that day, Ishak was waiting by the door. Sophie took his hand and insisted he come in and stay for dinner. Roger went to make tea while the boy sat talking with Sophie. When Roger brought in the tray, it looked like Sophie had been crying a bit. "He came to apologize for his mother and father," Sophie said. "He told them you and I were married. I didn't understand the explanation he gave his parents, but he assures me he convinced them we were married ever since I left the villa. Actually, I think he believes that."

Ishak seemed to like the stew Sophie served with rice. They didn't mention it had beer in it. He told them he'd given some of Sophie's money to his parents to buy chickens and sheep. He was still working at the repair shop with Hekmat's friend. After he learned the business, he planned to set out on his own. With the help of his notebook and Google Translate, Roger understood most of this. *Chickens* and *sheep* he knew. Sophie had to translate *savings account.*

When Ishak left, he took a small card from his pocket with a picture of Imam Ali, whom Shia Muslims like his parents regard as the true successor of Mohammad. It looked like a Catholic holy card. In front of a gold mosque, the bearded Ali in a green turban beamed a kindly look, a gold light radiating from his head. "To keep with you," Ishak said in English that he must have practiced. Roger thanked him and put it into his wallet.

That night in bed Roger and Sophie talked about getting married for real. "We couldn't do it here," Sophie said. "We'd have to become Muslims. That's what I've heard."

"There might be some official at the U.S. Embassy or Consulate who could do it."

"My mother would die. I'm her only child. She's been talking about my wedding since I was born."

"I spoke to her on the phone."

"I know. Until then, she thought of us the way Ishak's mother did." Sophie chuckled. "After you called, she said you sounded nice but I had to be careful."

"A mother's advice. My mother and brother say they need to interview and approve the next person I marry."

Sophie clutched his arm.

"They're just joking, Sophie." Although he knew they weren't.

"Anyway, here we are together now."

46

Happy anniversary

Late into the night they listened on the radio to Afghan music, then Indian music, while talking, making love, and talking again until they fell asleep. Roger dreamed they were getting married in a mosque with Ishak officiating. Then, before the ceremony began, a bomb exploded.

The ground shook under their mat. It was a real explosion. Roger sat up. A loud siren wailed in the distance. Sophie gasped and rose to her knees. "Another bomb?"

"Even louder than that. It might have been a rocket."

"What time is it?" She reached for her phone. "Just after midnight. I can't believe it. Three attacks in the ten days since I've come back. How is this going to end?"

"It sounded like it hit near the American Embassy." Roger ran into the yard. In the eastern sky, brightened by the distant lights of the embassy compound, a huge cloud of smoke ballooned into the air. Abruptly the siren stopped, and the city was choked in an eerie hush.

Sophie followed him out. They could smell the smoke in the night air. They gripped hands, prepared for another explosion, but time passed with no follow-up to the initial thundering blast. They were both shivering in the cool night air and went inside to wrap themselves in a quilt. Sophie's hands were cold in his.

Roger had a feeling this was different from the two earlier bombings the week before. Although one American soldier had been killed then, strictly speaking the attacks were not targeting the U.S. military, something the Taliban had agreed not to do. But a couple of days ago the U.S. President had tweeted that the agreement was "dead." The attack tonight seemed to be aimed directly at the U.S. Embassy.

"Wait a minute." Roger checked his phone. "It's after midnight, so it's September 11, the anniversary of the World Trade Center attack."

Sophie bit her lip. "The Taliban are sending a message."

Still tired from getting very little sleep the night before, Roger and Sophie found the Femmes en Crise women talking excitedly in front of the school building. Farzaneh was reading a report on her phone. She gave them the Taliban version of the attack. They claimed they fired missiles at the U.S. Embassy and that the enemy invaders had suffered casualties in that attack and also in another one that night on the Bagram air base.

"But the American press tells a different story," Farzaneh said. "They say no one was hurt at the embassy. Only one rocket was fired, and it hit a wall at the Defense Ministry, which is near the embassy. No mention of the Bagram attack."

Farzaneh had the best English. But Roger found it sad that every one of the women knew the words *bomb, missile, rocket, attack,* and *enemy.* They chattered restlessly today. A few nervously bit the corner of their hejabs. "Will our school be attack?" one asked Sophie. "No, no," she answered firmly. "But let's go inside now."

It was hard for Roger to keep the focus on multiplying fractions. The women themselves knew how to do this, and Roger's job was to show them interesting ways to teach it.

"Nine over eleven," a woman with rosy cheeks asked. "Why they write it this way?"

"Ah, that's not actually a fraction," Roger explained. "It's—"

His answer was interrupted by nervous laughter and tsks.

"Question," another woman called out. "They say 'megaton.' How many is *mega*?"

The world these women lived in was rife with large-scale tragedies which they'd learned to discuss as dispassionately as the weather. Roger hadn't reached that point yet. He was glad to get back home after class.

News of the 9/11 anniversary attack on the U.S. Embassy reached Sophie's mother late that afternoon. Sophie talked to her a long time, her face ranging from near tears to joy. "Interesting news," she told Roger when the call ended. "Remember when you told me you went to Towson University? I applied for admission to graduate school there, just in case. I forgot about it, but my mother said I got an acceptance letter." Sophie pursed her lips. "She had it when I was home but didn't show it to me."

Roger frowned.

"Because, you know, she thought you were married and I should stay away from you."

"Now what does she think?"

"She'd rather me go to school in America than stay here."

"Safer?"

"Yes. Then I told her about mass school shootings in America and how it seems almost everybody there has a gun."

"Only about a third of them. What did your mother say to that?"

"She wants me to come back to Belgium and raise cows."

Roger's mother and Dan got the news a few hours later. His mother wanted him to move to Florida and get a job she saw advertised in the Medicare office.

"Or we could just stay here," Sophie chuckled, "and take another dip in the pond."

After splashing in the pond, eating a warm meal, and sipping glasses of tea, Roger and Sophie, like most of Kabul's citizens, forgot about missiles and bombs. Roger yawned, thinking of bed. His yawn produced one in Sophie. Her eyes caught his, and his pulse quickened.

Unfortunately, they were interrupted by Sophie's phone. Roger saw the call was from DeWoot. "*Oh, non! Non,*" Sophie sighed. It wasn't good news. Roger put his hand on her shoulder. The call went on for some time with DeWoot doing all of the talking. Sophie took quick breaths, and Roger heard "*Quel dommage*" several times.

When the call was over, Sophie turned away from Roger and stared at the wall without speaking. She was breathing hard.

"What is it, Sophie? Tell me."

"The Femmes en Crise program is canceled."

47

Planting seeds

Sophie cried that night. Roger held her in his arms but couldn't comfort her. The Belgian Ministry of Foreign Affairs had considered the 9/11 attack on the U.S. Embassy the last straw. Their own embassy had already been moved to Pakistan. DeWoot said Lexi and Nora were willing to go back to Kabul and continue the program, but the ministry considered it too dangerous. Sophie should pack up and come home.

She wasn't herself when they went the next morning to tell the women the program had been canceled. In the taxi she sighed quietly with closed eyes. The sight of the women waiting in front of the school made her burst into tears. Somehow they knew what she'd come to tell them. They hugged her with tears in their own eyes before she got a word out.

They went inside and crowded into one room. Sophie dried her eyes on the sleeve of her talisman jacket. "I can only say I'm sorry," she told them. "Miss Lexi, Miss Nora, Mr. Roger, and me—we all wanted to continue the lessons, but my government wouldn't agree."

Farzaneh took her hand. "You have already helped us more than you know. Please don't be sad."

"Thank for help us," the rosy cheeked woman said. "We know you not stay forever. Now beginning our work."

"Yes," Farzaneh agreed. "You have planted a seed. Your garden will grow."

Roger had been choked up himself, and this comment lifted his spirits. Sophie was smiling now through teary eyes. One woman started to sing and the others immediately joined in. Roger heard the Dari word for *rain* and later found out it was a folksong about crops springing to life after a rain.

"We haven't talked about what we'll do now." Sophie avoided Roger's eyes. "I'm guessing you don't want to raise cows."

"I could do that. But you said you'd been accepted into graduate school in Baltimore."

"Should I go? I mean, your family's interview ...."

"Don't worry. You'll pass."

"The semester starts next week. I'd need to get a student visa. I could go to the U.S. Consulate here, but my mother has the acceptance letter."

"Hmm. I think DeWoot owes you a favor. Ask him to get it and expedite it to the consulate."

"I don't know how much the tuition is."

"If you saw my bank account these days, you wouldn't worry about that."

"So ... don't students have to live in a dorm?"

"Absolutely not." Roger pulled her close. "You'll live with me, Sophie. We're going to live together the rest of our lives."

"I'll call my mother and DeWoot right now."

DeWoot said he'd have Sophie's acceptance letter flown to the U.S. Consulate in Kabul as soon as possible. Sophie sent Lexi and Nora's things back to them. Then she and Roger walked to the Turkish Airlines office to check on flights to Baltimore. They passed the Nike shoe shop, the Pulshui Bank, and the casket company on the way. A flatbed truck was stopped in front of the casket maker. Roger pulled Sophie to a stop.

He smacked the side of his head. "I'm so dense. Why didn't I think of this before? Step into this side street with me, will you? I need to call Siavash."

Luckily, Siavash answered right away. "Roger," he said, "I was going to call you after the embassy attack, but then they said no one was hurt. Are you and Sophie all right?"

"Yes. Thanks. Listen, I have an idea how Daghal is shipping money abroad. I'm here at his bank now. Can you get here right away?"

"Well, I have a meeting, so—"

"Before, when I went into the windowless office in the back of the bank where Daghal works, I noticed the safe and a steel door on the side next to the casket maker's shop. It never occurred to me to wonder why that door is there. I suspect he takes the cash into that shop and has the owner secretly put it into a casket. I've seen these caskets being trucked to the airport."

"Interesting. But why the hurry?"

"A truck is outside the casket maker right now."

"Bodies are often taken to the airport to be flown abroad. Are there mourners standing around?"

"No. Oh, here comes the casket now."

"Roger, I can't get to the bank in time. The airport's closer. I'll head there. Can you get a taxi and follow the casket in case they're not going to the airport? If not, find out where they *are* going." Siavash clicked off.

"Taxi," Roger yelled.

He asked the driver in broken Dari to follow the truck. Sophie had heard what he said to Siavash and in much better Dari lied to the driver that their grandmother was in the casket. She held a tissue to her face.

"*Khodā shomarā hefz konad*," the driver said. Roger had heard this often. May God keep you safe.

The coffin indeed was heading for the airport. It rounded Massoud Circle and turned onto Airport Road. The old truck moved slowly, other trucks and cars beeping and swerving around it on both sides like it was a rock in a stream. Roger gripped Sophie's hand. He didn't know what he'd do if they started loading the coffin onto a plane before Siavash got there.

At a guard post, the truck was stopped. An Afghan soldier questioned the truck driver, then looked back at the taxi that had pulled up behind it. He came up to the taxi driver, who apparently gave him a sad story about Roger's grandmother. Both vehicles were waved into the cargo loading area. There was still no sign of Siavash.

The truck and casket headed towards a large plane far from the passenger terminal. Roger kept looking back to see if Siavash was behind them. There was still no sign of him when the coffin reached the wide hatch at the rear of the plane.

Taking a deep breath, Roger leapt from the taxi and threw himself on the coffin. "*Māmāni, Māmāni,*" he moaned, using the familiar word he'd just learned for grandmother.

The plane ramp operator, truck driver, and taxi driver stood aside, giving him a moment. Sophie came up, patting Roger on the shoulder. The three men seemed intrigued by the sight of this pretty foreign woman consoling her brother. The truck driver, possibly used to scenes like this, came and put his hand on Roger, too. Finally the taxi driver led Roger and Sophie away, murmuring either solace or prayers, Roger couldn't tell which.

The coffin was loaded onto the ramp. Then, just as the operator yanked a lever to raise the ramp into the plane, a siren sounded from behind a green and white fuel tanker. Siavash's white Ranger sped towards them and skidded to a stop.

Siavash and his assistant jumped out, his assistant holding a rifle and Siavash aiming a camera. Siavash started taking pictures of the truck and the coffin on the plane's ramp. He signaled to the truck driver to open the casket.

The possibility that somebody's grandmother was really in there made Roger's skin crawl. He couldn't look while the boards were creaked open.

Shouts rang out in Dari and Pashto. Roger turned. Siavash had slit open a burlap bag and was pulling out what Roger recognized by the mustard-color wrapper as a ten-thousand-dollar pack of U.S. dollars. The coffin was stuffed with these packs.

Siavash smiled at Roger.

"Uh-huh," Roger said. "A whole big bathtub full."

Another Major Crimes truck pulled up. The taxi driver was

released, but the ramp operator and truck driver would be taken in for questioning. The agents counted the packs of money, photographed them, wrote down the amounts, got each other to sign various papers, and loaded the coffin into the bed of Siavash's truck.

"Got the evidence we need at last." Siavash shook the other agents' hands and gave Roger and Sophie high-fives. "Now to arrest Daghal. If we're lucky, this is just the start and it will grow into a whole new crop of money laundering arrests."

Roger said he'd been worried Siavash wouldn't get there in time.

Siavash laughed. "We were here before you, parked behind that fuel truck, waiting for them to actually start loading the money onto the plane, which is illegal. We enjoyed the little show you and Sophie put on for us, though. Even though it delayed making the arrest."

48

Scary

Sophie's father had driven her university acceptance letter to Brussels so DeWoot could expedite it to the U.S. Consulate in Kabul. She now had her student visa, and they had their tickets to Baltimore. She and Roger went to the auto repair shop to say good-bye to Ishak. Then, on the morning of the flight, they ate a final breakfast at Omar's table before leaving Kabul together.

Out on Sher Ali Khan Street the low sun cast a pink glow on the adobe walls, and shop keepers called out to people on the busy sidewalk. Several of them wished good morning to Roger and Sophie as they went to catch a taxi. A lump rose in Roger's throat. He heard Sophie sigh. It was hard to leave the place they'd recently begun to think of as home.

Sophie's mother had wanted her to come back to Belgium first, but that wasn't possible because time was running out to register for the fall semester at Towson University. On the ride to the airport Sophie was quiet. From the plane window she and Roger gazed down at the city as it gradually faded into mountains and desert. Sophie leaned on Roger's shoulder and pursed her lips.

"Leaving here, going to America," she murmured. "It's scary."

"Scary going to America?"

"It is."

"I don't think—well, you might have to do active shooter lockdown drills at the university, but—"

"Not that kind of scary."

"You mean you don't know what it's going to be like?"

She nodded.

"And you'll miss people. And miss Kabul."

"Yes."

"You know, Omar and his whole family live near my house. I'm sure they'll be coming over all the time."

"What's your house like?"

"It's old. Actually I'm only renting it. But it's near Omar and near the university. Dan says the owner would like to sell it. If you like it, I could buy it."

She looked at him as if to check if he was joking.

"There are plenty of rooms for your parents and friends to come visit. By the way, do you have a driver's license?"

"Yes, but—"

"I have a car you can use. A lease."

"It sounds like you have this all thought out."

"Just some things I've had in the back of my mind."

"You mean ... since when?"

"Since I first met you."

In the Istanbul layover, Roger and Sophie resisted the urge to break up their flight and stay another night at the hotel where they'd first been together. "But we'll come back some time," Roger promised. Sophie slept with her head on his shoulder most of the remaining trip. When they approached Washington, D.C., he woke her.

"That's the Washington monument. That's the Capitol building."

Sophie's melancholy mood gave way to excitement. She took pictures through the window. As soon as they were off the plane, she stopped on the exit ramp to call her mother, her animated French attracting looks from passengers as they brushed past her.

Dan couldn't take his eyes off Sophie when they met. He was uncommonly speechless. Sophie chattered about herself and her work in Kabul as if she was actually being interviewed. "And I'm looking forward to meeting your mother and father."

"You will soon," Dan said. "They've moved into one of Roger's empty bedrooms while our mother sanitized the house."

"Sanitized," Sophie mumbled under her breath.

"He's just kidding, Sophie."

"Disinfected, then. Decontaminated." Dan was returning to his normal self.

Roger's parents came to the door and broke into smiles the moment they saw Sophie. Considering Roger's previous history, they might have been expecting someone more, so to speak, imposing. Roger's mother trilled, "Come in, Dear." His father took her backpack. "*Enchanté*, is that what they say?"

The house was truly spotless, orderly. Roger's mother whispered in his ear, "I picked up all those, you know, things left behind and I gave them to Goodwill."

His father grinned. "We hear Belgians like beer. Would you like one, Sophie?"

"I would love one."

"Roger? Dan? It's Belgian beer."

The couch had a new cover, and there were new armchairs in the living room, where they gathered to drink beer. Sophie quickly finished hers and accepted another. Her eyes sparkled mirthfully as Roger's father tried to speak French with her. After a couple of beers, Dan asked her if she had a sister.

Roger's mother had prepared one of her standby casseroles for dinner. She carried it to the large dining room, which had always been completely empty but now, to Roger's surprise, held a large table and chairs his parents had found on Craigslist. "Dan's been eating with us while we're here," she said. "Hope that's OK."

Sophie seemed to like the casserole, or at least pretended she did. Dan went home after dinner but said he'd be back the next evening. Roger's parents began yawning and looking at their watches at about 9:30 and soon went up to bed.

Roger was nervous taking Sophie into his bedroom to sleep in the same bed that .... He turned on the light and it was a new bed. Maybe the old one was one of those "things left behind" that his mother had given to Goodwill.

"Alone at last," Roger said. "Sort of."

"I love your family."

"And I want to meet yours."

In bed Roger held her close. "Still scared?"

"No. Not any more."

"Tomorrow we'll go get you registered at the university."

"OK, now I'm a little scared again."

49

Sticking it to the man

Roger took Sophie to register and buy biology textbooks for her classes. His mother had turned one of the bedrooms into a study with two desks. With Roger looking over her shoulder, Sophie paged through one of her books to a chapter on the human reproductive system.

"Interested in reproducing?" Roger quipped.

Sophie took his hand. "Actually, yes."

"Oh."

Her cheeks were flushed. "I mean, maybe get officially married first."

"Right. Would your parents come here for the wedding?"

"Oh! I haven't mentioned anything about that yet."

"We have plenty of extra rooms. Tell them I'll send the tickets."

"Um, when?"

"It's up to you."

Roger was sure her parents would ask about his job. He left Sophie at her desk and called his friend Inez Gonzales.

"I'm glad you're back safe again, Roger. I've been reading the news about Afghanistan. It's terrible."

"Yeah, the job in Kabul didn't work out."

"The community college is still advertising for part-time teachers."

"I wanted to ask you, which branch is that?"

"The Harbor Center."

"Great. I'll give it a try. And guess what, Inez. I met a wonderful woman in Kabul. Her name's Sophie. She's here with me in Baltimore."

It took Inez a moment to come up with her response. Roger

knew she hadn't held a very high opinion of Jill. "Well, good," Inez ventured. "I hope this Sophie is good to you."

"She is. I want you to meet her. I'll call you soon. My parents are here, too."

The community college's English as a second language program was only a short ride from his house, located between the Central Police District building and the Baltimore harbor. After a very brief interview, Roger was hired on the spot to begin teaching English to refugees and basic mathematics to Americans. Part-time teachers were paid very little, but it sounded like a job he'd like.

Sophie high-fived Roger when he got home. "I know you'll be great at it." His mother seemed pleased but wondered if working in the "inner city" was safe. His father asked if the college paid more than high school.

Inviting people to dinner was possible now that there was a table in the dining room. Roger wanted to invite Inez. His mother and Sophie flew into a state of nervous excitement saying they'd need at least a day to get ready.

Roger called Inez again. She wanted to come, but her niece was staying with her. "Bring her along," Roger insisted.

A dining room chandelier that Roger had never bothered to turn on until now sparkled on the new dishes he'd just bought. When the guests took their seats, Sophie filled their newly purchased wine glasses. She and Roger's mother had made Kabuli pulao. Roger's father glanced uneasily at the heaping platter, his preferred sustenance being roast beef and potatoes. "Don't worry, Dad," Dan told him. "We won't make you sit on the floor to eat it."

Inez's niece Camila smothered a laugh. She was truly striking— dark eyebrows, long lashes, and a cute smile that might even be called mischievous. Dan had made sure to sit next to her. She said she'd just been admitted to the Maryland School of Law. "I had to promise my mom and dad I wouldn't end up 'working for the man.'"

Dan raised his glass. "Here's to sticking it to the man."

"Salud!" Camila sang out, the others joining in more demurely, and Sophie clearly not sure what she was toasting.

While they ate, Dan told Camila outrageous stories about his professors in law school. "Just hope you don't get The Cobra for torts. When he gives the examples, he glares at people like he knows something sinister about them."

"Like this?" Eyes ablaze, Camila fixed Dan in an aghast look that could have come from Kurtz crying out, "The horror! The horror!" in *Heart of Darkness*.

Dan choked on his wine, dribbling some onto his shirt.

"Camila was in all her high school plays," Inez bragged. "She won some awards."

"She'll be great in the courtroom," Dan said, dabbing a napkin on his mouth. When the others moved to the living room and kitchen, Dan and Camila stayed at the table drinking wine and talking.

Inez took Roger aside. "By the way, I have some news. You remember that your student Kirk's father was campaigning for election as state legislator? He spoke at rallies outside family planning clinics, vowing to shut them down. Well, he was elected."

"I didn't think he had a chance running on that."

"You missed all the gruesome television ads paid for by I don't know who." Inez seemed to hesitate but went on. "And his son Kirk has been charged with something they're calling 'date rape,' whatever that is." Inez closed her eyes as if to banish the term from her mind. "The papers say the defense will play up Kirk's recent induction as Squire in the Soldiers of Christ."

"Sounds crazy, but that might help him."

"Anyway, people say his father can get the charge dropped."

"I believe it. Who knows? With Kirk's connections, he could end up President or Chief Justice of the Supreme Court some day."

Roger had forgotten about Senator Steinherz and Iggy Corelli until FBI agent Jackson called him. Jackson was in Washington and asked Roger and Sophie to meet him there. The prosecution needed to show the senator and the Grayrock lobbyist that the government had witnesses standing by.

Dan and Camila came with them and went into the Natural History Museum while Sophie and Roger went to find Jackson waiting by a guard booth at the Department of Justice. He led them into a conference room on the second floor filled with men in dark suits and stern faces. Jackson introduced the prosecutors and the lawyers for Steinherz and Iggy. He put two documents on the shiny table. "Is this your signature," he asked Roger. "And are you willing to testify in court to the veracity of this deposition?" He asked Sophie the same questions about a statement she'd just made. "Thank you." Jackson pressed a buzzer. "Miss Brown will see you out."

They found Dan and Camila posing by the tyrannosaurus rex skeleton while someone took their picture. They took a photo of Roger and Sophie for her to send to her mother. "I want to see the White House," Sophie begged. "I want to see everything, but can we go there first?"

Jackson called just as they got there. Roger put him on speaker phone. "They caved sooner than I expected," Jackson said. "The Bureau chief got the defense for both Steinherz and Corelli to recommend their clients plead guilty to some key charges if we don't recommend jail time. I would have preferred to have a trial and put them in jail, but at least they'll both be convicted criminals. Iggy Corelli will lose his job and pay restitution. Steinherz will be expelled from the senate and ineligible to run for office again."

Sophie said she'd dreaded the thought of going to court. She closed her eyes and sighed her relief. Dan gave Roger and Sophie a pat on the back. "You guys did it. Justice prevails."

Camila shook their hands. "Dan told me all about it. Congratulations. Let me get a picture of you two in front of the White House." She held up the phone. "I have to wonder, though. Those two white-collar criminals seem to be prime candidates for a Presidential pardon, considering his penchant for using that power to reward political allies and campaign contributors."

"They'll be pardoned convicts, then," Roger said. "That's still something."

50

Three weddings and an *Enshallah*

"**M**om and Dad say they can come any time before Christmas." Sophie blushed at bringing up marriage again.

"So we have plenty of time to plan the wedding."

Sophie pursed her lips. "Except there's a chance, I mean I could possibly be …."

"What?"

She put her hands on her stomach.

"Pregnant?" Roger pulled her close, kissed her. "That's wonderful, Sophie. So how about next week?"

"I don't know. My friend Lexi got engaged to her boyfriend in Brussels. She says it takes forever to arrange a wedding."

"Oh."

"They're going to get married by a civil registrar first. They'll have a wedding ceremony later. I wonder if we could do that."

Roger had a bad feeling about going to the courthouse. It hadn't worked out well before. This time he wanted friends and relatives to be with him.

"I can see you don't like the idea."

"I do want us to be married as soon as possible." Roger had a thought. "Can your parents come next week? I could get somebody to marry us right here. We could go to Belgium later and have whatever ceremony you want."

"Really? Then maybe Lexi could be my bridesmaid there."

Roger's mother wanted them to get married in a church. "How about getting Father Joy from your school to do the ceremony?"

"I don't think so, Mom. Here's my idea. We get married by a

justice of the peace on the back porch here. Invite everybody. Put chairs in the yard. Have a barbecue."

His mother, probably because the plan was so much better than Roger and Sophie going off to the courthouse, agreed.

A few days later, Roger and Sophie picked up her parents at Dulles airport. Except for Mrs. Marten's flowered dress and Mr. Marten's moustache, they looked like somewhat smaller versions of Roger's own parents. Sophie's mother shook Roger's hand and turned to mutter something that made Sophie smile. Her father greeted Roger at length in English riddled with an assortment of German words. Roger immediately relaxed.

Everything was moving so fast Roger had no time to be nervous. Before he knew it, he was standing beside the justice of the peace and Sophie's father, watching out the back window as the guests began to gather in the yard. Roger's mother was setting up lawn chairs with the help of Amal and Sophie's aunt, who'd come from New York. His father and Hekmat were lighting the grill and drinking Belgian beer.

Roger had also invited Chrissy and her husband John. He wanted them to see little Musa and Sima, the children they'd helped get visas to immigrate. He knew Karim would like to meet the couple, too, since he'd declared he wanted to become a lawyer like them. As soon as the ACLU couple came into the yard, the children ran up to them. Chrissy knelt, taking the little ones' hands.

Under a red leafed maple tree in a corner of the yard, Omar and Inez were laughing together. But Dan and Camila weren't there.

Sophie and her mother came downstairs, Sophie wearing the Afghan dress she'd tried on for Roger in Istanbul. "Magnificent," the justice of the peace commented. "Would the bride and her father like to remain inside while her mother, the groom and I take our positions on the porch?"

"I'm waiting for my brother," Roger objected.

"They're here," Sophie trilled. "From the upstairs window I saw the car arrive." An impish spark lit up her eyes. "That was some time ago."

A car door slammed in the driveway, and Dan and Camila rushed into the yard in what Roger's mother would term "disarray," their hair messed up and Dan buttoning his shirt. Inez looked on, her hand over her mouth.

The justice of the peace coughed. "So. Everybody here? Can we commence?"

Roger's mother joined Sophie's father and Roger on the porch signaling the guests to move to the lawn chairs. Exclamations burst out when Sophie appeared in her stunning dress. Roger tried to concentrate on the justice of the peace's words so he'd know when to say, "I do." When he kissed Sophie, cheers and applause rang out. Roger closed his eyes, thankful for their approval.

Several weeks later, Roger, his parents, and Sophie flew to Belgium to do it all over again in a more traditional ceremony with Lexi as bridesmaid. After that wedding, they all stayed on for Lexi's wedding, with Sophie now Lexi's bridesmaid. Nora and DeWoot attended both weddings. Lexi had accepted DeWoot's offer to serve as an aide in the Foreign Affairs Ministry. Nora had declined. She was starting a new organization to send aid to Afghan children in need.

Roger took Nora aside to learn more. "As soon as our President tweeted that the negotiations with the Taliban were off," he pointed out, "the attacks increased. The Belgian ministry closed down Femmes en Crise. Will you be safe there?"

"I guess you haven't been following the news. The talks in Doha weren't really called off. That was just one of your President's impulsive tweets that he later acted as if he'd never sent. Anyway, I'll be working mainly from Brussels. The new aid group, Enfants en Crise, is partnering with the Afghan Ministry of Public Health. My job will be to keep the ministry honest."

Flying everybody to Belgium and paying for Sophie's wedding there had cost less than a drop in the bucket of Roger's insurance payment. He wouldn't have to worry about money for a long time.

But the money Jill told him came from "other jobs" still weighed heavily on his mind. "I'd like to make a donation to Enfants en Crise," he told Nora. "Maybe when Sophie gets her Master's degree we'll come and join you."

Nora thanked him and smiled. *"Enshallah."*

CPSIA information can be obtained
at www.ICGtesting.com
Printed in the USA
LVHW111348020622
720240LV00018B/430/J